P9-DZN-985

Tracie Howard

NEVER KISS
AND TELL

NEW AMERICAN LIBRARY

New American Library
Published by New American Library, a division of Penguin Group (USA) Inc.,
375 Hudson Street, New York, New York 10014, USA.
Penguin Group (Canada), 10 Alcorn Avenue, Toronto,
Ontario M4V 3B2, Canada (a division of Pearson Penguin Canada Inc.)
Penguin Books Ltd., 80 Strand, London WC2R 0RL, England
Penguin Ireland, 25 St. Stephen's Green, Dublin 2,
Ireland (a division of Penguin Books Ltd.)
Penguin Group (Australia), 250 Camberwell Road, Camberwell, Victoria 3124,
Australia (a division of Pearson Australia Group Pty. Ltd.)
Penguin Books India Pvt. Ltd., 11 Community Centre, Panchsheel Park,
New Delhi - 110 017, India
Penguin Group (NZ), Cnr Airborne and Rosedale Roads, Albany,
Auckland 1310, New Zealand (a division of Pearson New Zealand Ltd.)
Penguin Books (South Africa) (Pty.) Ltd., 24 Sturdee Avenue,
Rosebank, Johannesburg 2196, South Africa

Penguin Books Ltd, Registered Offices: 80 Strand, London WC2R 0RL, England

First published by New American Library, a division of Penguin Group (USA) Inc.

*I dedicate this book to the newest addition to our family,
my beautiful cousin Olivia Imari Phillips,
born May 24, 2004 (so she's a Gemini!), weighing 6 lbs. and 5 oz.*

ACKNOWLEDGMENTS

I recently heard a very wise person respond, "In a hundred years it won't matter," when asked about an issue of marginal importance. So often we become consumed with events, things and people that, in the overall scheme of life, don't warrant the angst and anxiety that we allow them. As a part of my continuing spiritual grown, I'm committed to weeding out such distractions and really focusing on the people, events and things in my life that really *do* matter. Without question, that list starts with my family, who have always given me unconditional love and support, which enables me to fulfill my dreams: my husband and best friend, Scott; mother and driving inspiration, Gloria Freeman; loving sisters, Alison Howard-Smith and Jennifer Freeman; adorable and brilliant nieces, Korian Young and Chelsae Smith; kind and caring mother-in-law, Margaret Mroz; wonderful cousins Ted, April, Saxton and Olivia Phillips; aunts Maryland Cantrell and Opal Chamlee; in addition to many other supportive cousins and family members.

I've also been blessed to have a large extended family of friends who've individually and collectively added so much depth and breadth to my life. They include: Vikki Palmer, Anne Simmons, Vanessa and Bill Johnson, Imara Canady, Pam Frederick and Monroe Bodden, Sharon Bowen and Larry Morse, Antonio and Erica Reid, Denise Brown, Julie Borders, Judith and Juan Montier, Judia and Danny Black, Alicia and Danny Bythewood, Colin Cowie, Stuart Bronstein, Mike and Diane Frierson, Karen, Oswald and Zoë Morgan, Rose Salem, Lorrie King and Edbert Morales, Eula Smith, Selma Strauss, and Dr. William Young. Thank you all! I also want to thank Dr. Erin Holvey, for being a great friend and supporter, and for helping me shape the character, Brooke Parrish.

Most important, I thank God for surrounding me with such incredible people and blessing me continually—in a hundred million years all that He does will still matter.

1

THE EARLY BIRD GETS THE BLAHNIKS

When the bedside phone rang at six o'clock a.m. Brooke didn't need a psychic or caller ID to know who held the other end of the line. "Hello," she muttered, not bothering to clear the gravel from her voice. There was only one person she knew who'd have the nerve to call her at this ungodly hour.

"Rise and shine!" The chipper tone was even more annoying than the telephone's shrill ring had been, especially for Brooke, who was not a morning person.

"You must be kidding," she grumbled, clearly annoyed, as she rolled her eyes without even bothering to open them. What sane person would dare call anybody at this ungodly hour? But there was the problem. Joie was anything but sane, and as a psychotherapist, Brooke was certainly qualified to know.

Joie Blanchard was a free-spirited fashion photographer who lived her life on her own terms with little regard for what others thought of her actions. She wore a shock of long sun-bleached dreadlocks, and lots of attitude. She was the most uninhibited person Brooke knew, and her polar opposite. "Wake up, sleepyhead! The early bird gets the worm," she chirped, completely unfazed by the moans and groans of discontent coming from the other end of the phone line.

Brooke dragged the covers way up over her head. "Which is

exactly why I'm still in bed. I can do without worms, thank you. Good-bye." She was ready to reach outside of her warm, down-feathered cocoon and replace the phone on its cradle. Maybe if she lay still in the dark she could race back to dreamland before its doors were shut tight.

"Wait," Joie urged, raising her voice, knowing she was seconds away from a dial tone. "This is important; don't hang up!"

Brooke rolled onto her back in symbolic defeat. "Okay, Joie, but I can't imagine what could be worth an hour of my sleep." Her alarm clock wasn't due to go off until seven thirty. She'd have just enough time to have her requisite cup of Illy coffee, skim the *New York Times* headlines, shower, and dress before dashing out of her East Sixty-first Street apartment in time to make it to her office on Fifty-seventh Street by nine o'clock.

"What if I told you there's a Manolo Blahnik sample sale, and the doors open at eight?" Joie said smugly. She knew how to get Brooke's attention.

Images of half-price designer shoes quickly cleared away Brooke's cobwebs. Few things were more tempting to her than sleep, but a Blahnik shoe sale was definitely one of them. Suddenly propping herself up on one elbow, she asked, "Is this the first day?" Like every other savvy New York shopper, she knew the second day of a Blahnik shoe sale would yield nothing but an assortment of size-six and -ten leftovers.

"Not only is this the first day, but it hasn't even been announced to the public yet," Joie one-upped. "But I found out last night from one of my shoe-obsessed model friends." She could hear the stirring of Brooke's bed linen in the background. She smiled slyly at Brooke's predictability.

"Where is it?" By now she was sitting on the side of her bed, searching in the dark for her pink bunny house slippers. If she could make it there by eight o'clock, she could do a quick round of power shopping and still make it to her office in time for her nine o'clock appointment.

Joie told her an address on Broadway, between Forty-first

and Forty-second. "I'll meet you in the lobby at eight," Joie said and hung up the phone.

Brooke yawned away the remnants of her night's sleep and stretched her lithe five-eight frame before shuffling into the slippers that sat parked at the foot of her bed. As she reached for her cashmere bathrobe she was wide-awake, with visions of sexy slingbacks prancing around in her head. She headed down the hall into the kitchen, where she filled up her Italian stove-top coffee brewer with a healthy dose of Italian espresso. While the aroma from the hot brew filled the air, she wandered to the front door of her ground-floor apartment to retrieve the newspaper from the stoop. It bore the usual slew of depressing headlines: "Instability in the Middle East Causes Global Concerns," "Charges of Bribery Smear City Election," "Crime Stats Reach a Ten-year High." No wonder there was no shortage of neurotic patients for her thriving practice. Deciding not to taint what was starting out to be a promising Friday, she tossed the paper onto the antique rolltop desk that sat in her foyer and headed back to the kitchen for a hit of java.

After her caffeine fix, Brooke quickly showered and fell into her morning routine: She dressed in one of her understated designer suits, brushed her thick, dark hair back into a ball at the nape of her neck, and applied a hint of makeup to her buttery-caramel complexion. Her look was classy, but casually elegant. She was a head turner, but she was completely oblivious to her stunning good looks. This blind spot was one of the less visible scars from a disastrous and abusive marriage, followed by a string of Mr. Wrongs. Though therapy had healed many of her emotional wounds, others seemed destined to remain raw. She found it cruelly ironic that she could so aptly analyze other people's problems, but was totally incapable of doing anything about her own. What she wouldn't do to be able to trust a man enough to fall in love, or in lust, for that matter.

She grabbed her briefcase and headed west on Sixty-first, grabbing a taxi the minute she hit Park Avenue, which she took as a good omen for the rest of the day. Ten minutes later she was hurrying into the building, where Joie stood waving to get her attention.

"We don't have much time," Joie said. She consulted her watch like a drill sergeant prepping for a strategic battle.

"I know, I've got to be at the office before nine," Brooke agreed, feeling like a fellow commander preparing for the battle-field.

Joie had her dreads piled high on top of her head, and long crystal chandelier earrings dangled from her ears. She was in perpetual motion, with her hands gesturing and eyelashes bat-ting. "We need a game plan," she surmised once they stepped off the elevator onto the showroom floor. "Why don't you start at one end of the floor, and I'll take the other. If you see any size nines with potential, you grab them, and I'll do the same for eights. Once we meet in the middle we'll go through the bounty and divvy it up. That way we'll see everything in half the time." This was serious business for Joie, an admitted shoe whore.

Brooke was more of an equal opportunity spender, although shoes definitely ranked high on her list of material indulgences. Being a therapist, she was able to easily diagnose her shopping neurosis. Her obsession, she deduced, was driven by the need to fill a void in her life, namely the absence of a husband, boyfriend, companion, or even a good fuck buddy. She had definitely been in a serious drought over the last two years, and the forecast didn't appear to call for even a hint of rain. She hadn't met one guy who was the least bit interesting or appealing, only duds and dogs, and she had sworn off kissing them both. So for the time being, shopping would have to do in lieu of sex.

With their battle plan ready, the two women scoured the rows of shoes like farmers picking corn, eventually meeting in the middle carrying stacks of shoe boxes, barely able to see over their tops. After sorting through their potential suitors, Brooke hurried to the register with four pairs to add to her impressive collection, while Joie remained seated, pondering the eight lonely soles that begged to go home with her.

"Listen, I've gotta run. I'll call you later." It was eight forty. If she rushed, she could grab a cab and make it uptown and across in less than fifteen minutes, but every second would count.

"Call me later," Joie said absently, still fondling the tip of a black snakeskin mule with a four-inch heel and pinpointy toe, wondering whether it would literally be a one-night stand, something she didn't mind in a man, but wouldn't tolerate in a mule.

Weighted down by her briefcase and two full shopping bags, Brooke darted to the elevator, barely catching it before the doors closed shut. She was feeling good about herself as she entered, watching a gaggle of women who'd just exited, undoubtedly looking for the size eights that she'd made out with. A minute late and a Blahnik short, she silently mused as she smugly pressed the elevator's button for the lobby floor. As the small lift began its decent with her and one other passenger in tow, she was busy calculating the best street on which to commandeer a taxi when it suddenly lurched to a grinding halt, causing her to teeter precariously on her three-inch pumps. Reacting quickly, the other passenger instinctively reached out to steady her fall.

"Thank you," she said, flustered. For the first time she noticed that the only other person in the elevator was a handsome black guy. The man was dressed to kill, and he smelled of Jo Malone and an enticing citrus aftershave. She stood there looking up into his warm, dark eyes, inhaling everything about him.

He flashed a smile, as though he could read her thoughts. "Anytime."

She suddenly felt embarrassed; her guard had accidentally fallen down, leaving her vulnerable and exposed. Before she could regain her composure, every floor number on the panel of the old elevator car lit up and began blinking erratically like a winning Vegas slot machine. Then came complete darkness as the car jerked again. So much for good omens.

"Whoa! I think we have a problem," the handsome stranger said, setting his briefcase down.

Beads of sweat peppered her brow as her temperature began to climb. "Wh-what do you mean, a problem?" she asked anxiously. Her breath now came in short, shallow gasps.

He saw the traces of fear descend on her smooth, even features and decided he'd best make light of the situation. After all, a stuck elevator and a hysterical woman—no matter how beautiful—were too much for him to handle before nine o'clock. "I'm sure it's nothing," he reassured her.

"No, b-b-but there is a problem, and w-we can't . . . we can't get out of here." Her eyes darted furtively around the tight enclosed space, as her chest rose and fell visibly with each short intake of breath.

"Here, let's put these down, and you relax." He set Brooke's packages aside and turned to face her. In slow, deliberate tones he said, "Many of these older models aren't as automated as the newer ones; sometimes they just need a little manual intervention. That's all." He shook his head slowly from side to side, as though he were explaining the roundness of the earth to a naive five-year-old.

Aside from chronic shopping syndrome and some heavy baggage from a bad marriage, claustrophobia was another of Brooke's issues, one she'd faced since the second grade, when an older neighborhood kid locked her in the doghouse in his backyard and left to go have dinner. It was hours before anyone found her, so being stuck in an elevator was a waking nightmare.

Seeing the panicked expression on Brooke's face, he held her shoulders to calm her down. "Everything is going to be fine," he said, looking fixedly into her eyes to be sure that she was really hearing him. "Listen to me. I'm going to pick up the phone and call the operator. I'm sure they'll be here in no time at all."

Her breathing continued to come in choppy gasps, while a clamminess coated her skin, and she was dizzy and felt really nauseous. Holding her shoulder gently with one hand, he reached for the red phone with the other. Without taking his eyes from her he said, "This is Taylor Hudson. I'm in one of your elevators, and it's stuck." Though his tone was insistent, he kept any trace of fear or urgency out of it. After listening to the receiver, he nodded. "How long will it take? Okay. Yes, we're okay." He looked at her, nodding his head as though to confirm his words.

He hung up the phone and turned to Brooke. "We'll be out of here in no time. They are working on it now." This seemed to ease her anxiety somewhat. "Just an electrical problem, nothing serious."

She took a deep breath, willing herself to calm down, embarrassed at her loss of control. Thank God her patients couldn't see her now. "I'm okay," she said, slowly nodding her head, while taking deep calming breaths and praying that she wouldn't throw up.

After her breathing returned to normal, he said, "You look a lot better. You know, I was a little worried about you."

When he smiled she noticed again just how handsome her knight in Armani armor was. He was six-two, solidly built, and the color of chestnuts, dark and smooth. He wore his hair cut shadow short, with a mustache and goatee that framed a full, sexy mouth.

"My name is Taylor, Taylor Hudson," he said, extending his hand.

She summoned her composure. "I'm Brooke Parrish."

"It's nice to meet you, Brooke."

She could feel him appraising her and was glad that she'd worn a silk pencil skirt, rather than the gabardine pleated slacks she'd considered. "Same here." She blushed. "I just wish it were under other circumstances." Why did she have to have a full-fledged panic attack in front of the handsomest and nicest guy that she'd meet in years? She chided herself. They were all nice on the surface; it was the layers beneath that hid the dirt.

He was still holding on to her hand. "If it weren't for the

circumstances, we probably *wouldn't* have met. You would've dashed off with your bags, headed . . . ?" He gave her a questioning look.

For the first time she remembered the shoes, and had literally forgotten about her appointment. Recalling it made her anxious. She hated being late for her patients. They had enough problems to deal with without being kept in a waiting room. "To work, actually." She checked her watch nervously.

Taylor noticed. "It shouldn't be too long."

"I hope not. I have an appointment waiting."

"Lucky appointment." He flashed a killer smile. "Do you work in the area?"

"No, I work on the East Side. Fifty-seventh Street. What about you?"

"Downtown. On Wall Street," he answered, visibly charmed by her. "What brings you to the West Side so early in the day?" He looked down at her packages for a clue.

She smiled and bowed her head. "A little shopping."

"Here?" He looked puzzled, since they were in an office building.

She shrugged her shoulders. "A Manolo Blahnik shoe sale on the twenty-third floor," she whispered, as though it were top-secret information.

"Oh," he said, like that explained everything.

At that moment the elevator jolted slightly, and once again he held on to her, but this time it wasn't panic he saw in her eyes.

Her heart did beat faster, and her temperature did rise, but not for the same reasons as before. When the doors opened seconds later, they were still holding each other. "Well, um, thank you, Taylor," she said, awkwardly reaching down for her bags.

Thinking fast, he said, "Why don't you thank me over a cup of coffee?" When he smiled, his eyes twinkled in the most appealing way.

She looked at her watch. "I really can't. I do have an appointment waiting."

He shoved his hands into his pants pockets, as if to say, I'm staying put until I know I'll see you again. "Well, can I get a rain check?"

"Sure." She was a bundle of nerves, having forgotten how to flirt. Though it had been a long time, she did manage to casually reach into the side pocket of her briefcase and hand him her business card. After saying their good-byes, Brooke headed through the lobby door and out onto Broadway, silently thanking Joie for being an annoying early bird, and hoped that Taylor wouldn't prove to be a worm. A second later, a cab drifted to a stop right in front of her. Yet another good omen, she thought, smiling.

2

DESIGNING WOMEN

"No, honey. That chintz pattern is all wrong," Kiernan barked into her cell phone as she cut a path through the lunch-hour crowd across Nineteenth Street leaving ABC Carpet & Home. In exasperation she shrieked, "I don't know why people waste money hiring me when their bad taste always prevails." Kiernan was once one of the city's rising stars on the interior-design scene. Though her reputation still carried weight, due to the hard-hit New York economy, her business had suffered terribly.

After half listening for just a few seconds, she abruptly cut the person on the other end off. "I don't care what her husband says. If I wanted his opinion, I'd have asked him for it. The only thing he needs to contribute to this project is his checkbook." She stabbed her finger into the air as she made her point. "You got that?" She flattened the end button on the T-Mobile cell phone and stuffed it back into her purse, never skipping a beat. She was brilliant with design concepts, but her people skills often fell short. She could be as charming as a cobra's trainer, or as ornery as the snake itself.

"Who was that?" her assistant, LaTeesha, asked. The poor girl was nearly out of breath, trying to keep up with Kiernan's long strides while burdened down by an armload of purchases the decorating diva had just made. Like an eager puppy, she was happy to traipse alongside Kiernan, the first adult who'd given her any positive attention in her whole life. Her father had been MIA since before her birth, and her mother was too busy trying to keep her head above water and raise seven children to pay much attention to any of them.

"It was that idiot Henri, the curtain designer." Kiernan rolled her eyes. "Said Claire Brooks called him directly to change the fabric I selected. Said her husband didn't like it." She sniffed. "What the hell does he know?"

Once the twosome reached Park Avenue South, they crossed over and headed into Triage, a cavernous candle-strewn restaurant that was a favorite among the artsy crowd. "A table for two," Keirnan said, barely making eye contact with the waifish hostess.

"Do you have a reservation?" the young woman asked in the haughty manner that New York bar and restaurant employees had patented.

Annoyed, Kiernan huffed and glared at the girl absently. "From what I see I don't really need one, now, do I?" It pissed her off when peons—white and model thin or not—who were paid by the hour tried to give her a dose of attitude.

LaTeesha stood behind her, wishing she could disappear into one of the large bags that she was forced to haul around while Kiernan carried only a small LV clutch. LaTeesha Ingram was a struggling twenty-year-old who'd had her share of hard knocks in her short life, so she was thankful when her mentor from the Big Sisters organization helped get her the job with the highly respected interior designer. They hoped it could be the start of a real opportunity for her to see how those outside of the projects worked and lived. At the very least it would keep LaTeesha's probation officer off of her back. She'd been arrested with a group of kids who were on a shoplifting rampage through Macy's at Herald Square. Though LaTeesha didn't steal anything herself, she refused to tell on her friends who had, so they were all hauled away and booked on theft charges. As a first-time offender, she was sentenced to probation.

As much as she loved her job and admired her boss, she didn't like her drastic mood swings. Just hours ago Kiernan was giving money to a panhandler and offering to buy the man a hot meal, and now she seemed to be rude and angry at the world. LaTeesha never knew how she'd be treated by Kiernan. One day she'd be taking her to a fancy restaurant and showing her which fork to use, and the next day she'd treat her like an indentured servant.

Peeved at Kiernan's snide remark, the young hostess snatched two menus from under her stand and snapped her head as she turned to leave, nearly slapping Kiernan's face with her long blond hair. "Follow me," she fumed as she led them through the restaurant to a table that sat near the kitchen.

"This is unacceptable," Kiernan pronounced, with a hand planted on her hip. "If I had wanted to work here, I'd have asked for an application, not a table." She stared at the agitated young lady with her cheeks sucked in, daring her to make a verbal comeback. By now she was spoiling for a good fight.

The hostess replied with a tart smirk of her own, as sour as if she'd sucked hard on a spoiled lemon. "Take your pick," she finally said.

Keirnan led the trio just inside the elevated section of the restaurant to a table that sat dead center. Her belief was that half of the fun of going out to eat in New York was being seen doing it. Once she plopped herself down in the seat that faced the entrance, she barked out an order to the annoyed hostess. "Send over our waitress, will you?" she demanded while unfolding the white cloth napkin across her lap.

The hostess stormed off in search of the unlucky person who was assigned to the difficult woman's table.

Before LaTeesha could set aside the avalanche of bags she'd hauled in, Kiernan turned on her next. "Did those tile samples come in from England yet?"

"Not yet, but I'll check as soon as we get back to the office."

"See to it that I have those by the end of the week," Kiernan snipped, expelling a burst of air as though LaTeesha were personally responsible for the shipment's delay.

Kiernan didn't have a chance to find another target for her insatiable ire before she spotted a tall, thin blond woman sauntering into the restaurant. "That's Pia Renwick, one of the editors at *Architectural Digest*," she whispered loudly as she briskly ran her fingers through her shoulder-length weave and pulled a silver compact from her handbag along with a tube of brick red lipstick. She quickly lacquered her lips and pursed them together to blot the color evenly. As the rail-thin woman passed their table Kiernan made an amazing personality transformation. "Pia, darling! Hi, how are you?" she purred in a most solicitous tone. LaTeesha was amazed at the way Kiernan made it from zero to a hundred in ten seconds flat. In her two months with her, one lesson that LaTeesha had learned well was that in the "real world" people were essentially big, fat phonies. They made a show of kissing each other's cheeks, while angling to place sharp knives in the other's back. Though the ghetto was certainly not Park Avenue, at least she always knew where people were coming from; after all, when you were trying to survive, who had time or energy to craft elaborate pretenses?

"Oh, hi, Kiernan. It's good to see you, darling. How are you?" Pia was dressed all in black, and wore an oversize pair of black sunglasses to hide her eyes.

Kiernan was full of smiles and oozed charm. Not one trace of the bitter nag that she'd been only minutes before was left behind. "Oh, I'm busy as ever. I'm finishing up a couple of East Side brownstones, and have a couple of loft spaces down in SoHo that I'm just starting, but nothing really splashy. You know, I'm always looking for the next really special project." Kiernan was a trained liar. The truth was that at this moment she was looking for *any* project. Her entire life depended upon maintaining a fabricated image of herself she would do anything to sustain. On the outside, Kiernan was like an elegant swan gliding along a pristine lake, while underwater, where you couldn't see, its legs paddled furiously to stay afloat.

Pia looked thoughtful as she removed the monstrous spectacles from her face and dangled one end between her bleached white teeth. "You should come by the cocktail party the magazine's giving to honor Eva Rupert tonight. She's one of the board members at the Guggenheim," the woman said, flipping her wrist. "Anywho, she just bought a fabulous town house in the East Sixties—a real showplace—and I hear she's in the market for a decorator," she whispered, raising her thinly arched eyebrows suggestively.

"Oh, really?" Kiernan asked, leaning into her and smiling, looking for more information. With Wall Street in the toilet, the economy sucking wind, and an never-ending war, no one was spending the kind of frivolous money they had in the good old days, which for her were the mid-nineties. Boy, did she miss the five-thousand-dollar bathroom sinks and the imported Italian marble. Now everybody was shopping at Gracious Home, ABC Carpet & Home, or for those whose pockets were really hit hard, the dreaded Home Depot. But a fancy writeup in *Architectural Digest* and a good referral in the right social circles could make all the difference to stabilize her plummeting bottom line.

"I'll tell you what. If you drop by," Pia leaned in confidentially to say, "I'll be sure to introduce you two." Just then she spied another blonde who'd just walked in, and waved, signaling that she'd be right over. "The Guggenheim from seven until nine," she said, as she made her way over to greet her friend. "I'll make sure your name is on the list."

"Count me in." Kiernan blew a kiss good-bye, still wearing the too-tight fake smile, but the minute Pia was out of eyesight, the mask dropped away as though a light had suddenly been switched off.

When the waitress appeared with pen in hand, Kiernan

ordered a dirty martini with Grey Goose, thinking it was a fitting way to start the weekend. She loved being a part of the New York social scene and was a born-to-the-manor socialite, if only in her own mind. But what others didn't know couldn't hurt her. If nothing else, she'd learned the social ropes in this town and could dazzle on the trapeze with the best of them, though lately the act was becoming much more difficult to pull off, with her marriage falling apart at the seams and her money drying up faster than an imagined oasis in the middle of a dry desert.

Kiernan turned to face LaTeesha. "Now that's class," she said, tilting her head in Pia's direction. "The woman knows everybody, and is on the board of every important charity in the city." She looked thoughtful. "You know, I really should get involved in charity too. But then I again, I do have you," she said, patting LaTeesha's hand, as though her comment were a compliment. LaTeesha was too infatuated with Kiernan's ritzy life to be insulted.

After the drinks arrived and lunch orders had been given, LaTeesha dared to say, "What lofts in SoHo?" As far as she knew, the project they were finishing now was the only one on the schedule.

"Were you eavesdropping on my conversation?" Kiernan nearly slammed her martini glass down, causing the drink to run over its edge onto her hand.

LaTeesha shrank back into her chair. "I wasn't eavesdropping. I was just sitting here."

Kiernan flung the liquid from her hand, nearly flinging it into the girl's face. "Well, mind your own business," she hissed, never bothering to answer the question posed. She operated under the assumption that the best offense was usually a good defense.

"I'm sorry." LaTeesha dropped her head. She was learning that Kiernan was about as unpredictable as the Bermuda Triangle, and just as volatile.

After stopping by the office to return a few phone calls after lunch, Kiernan hightailed it home to do a quick change for the cocktail party. The Calvin Klein pantsuit she'd worn all day was fine for lunch, but cocktails with New York high society called for a touch of glamour. She strolled into her Central Park West apartment building, sailing arrogantly past Frank, the doorman, without a nod, but carefully listening for his customary greeting. She loved his British accent and the way he addressed her with a respectful, "Good evening, Madam Malloy." It made her feel as if she'd really made it. Only during quiet moments alone was she haunted by her insecurities.

The elevator ascended to the thirty-ninth floor, where she got out and walked into her spacious three-bedroom apartment, with its enviable view of Central Park in its fall regalia. This view was her coup de grace, never failing to impress clients, friends, or foes. Her husband, whom she had met initially as a client, bought the twenty-five-hundred-square-foot apartment four years ago as an investment. Since he'd hired and then married Kiernan, the place had been redecorated twice. On each occasion she insisted that they keep up appearances—it was good for business, hers as well as his, she argued. The end result was a picture-perfect showroom with about as much warmth as the Antarctic in the winter, much like their marriage at this point.

"Honey, I'm home," she sang out as she breezed through the living room, past the office, and into the bedroom. She'd tried to call him earlier, but he wasn't at the office; nor was he answering his cell phone. She planned to catch him at home and twist his arm so he'd go to the gala with her. A handsome man on her arm was always a good accessory, she thought.

"Honey, I'm home," she repeated. There was still no answer, only silence. When she reached the bedroom, instead of her husband there was a note on her vanity that read:

Have a client dinner tonight, so don't wait up. See you in the morning.

Her chest rose and fell sharply as her angst built. She tore the note into little pieces, then fell face-first onto the silk duvet. She pounded the down filling fiercely with both fists while kicking her legs up and down like a spoiled-rotten two-year-old. When she realized that her tears might stain the beautiful russet fabric, she just as quickly composed herself and sat on the side of the bed, wiping the salty tears from her eyes with the back of her hands, swiftly shifting gears. She'd deal with him later. Right now she had an important event to go to.

She hopped up from the bed and moseyed over to the art-deco vanity that sat catty-corner in the spacious French Victorian bedroom suite, and sat on the damask-covered seat, studying her face the way one might appraise an overripe melon at the market. She had her mother's smooth, tawny brown complexion, which she considered her best asset, even though wrinkles had begun to betray her, popping up around her mouth and creeping out from the corners of her eyes. They were her father's eyes, she'd always been told, light brown pear-shaped orbs, as deep as an abyss. Sometimes looking into the mirror it scared her to see him looking back. On closer inspection, she saw her gray roots peeking out from her scalp, a stark contrast to the black dye her stylist used to cover the rest of her hair. It had been two weeks too long since she'd paid a visit to Joseph's Salon. She reminded herself to make an appointment first thing in the morning. For now mascara would have to do, so she ransacked her cosmetic bag for a tube of Yves Saint Laurent's and began stroking the wand over the telltale signs of her forty-plus years.

After donning a beautifully cut, deep navy Donna Karan cocktail dress and draping on a three-carat diamond necklace, matching channel-set bracelet, and two-carat earrings, she decided that she looked sophisticated enough to hold her own with the tea-and-crumpet set. When she sauntered out from the canopied entry to her swanky building, a car and driver sat waiting. She'd had LaTeesha schedule one, figuring that it wouldn't do to be seen hopping out of a lowly taxi by anyone in that illustrious crowd. One of her biggest regrets was that she didn't have her own personal car and driver. Not that they couldn't afford it; her husband was just too simplistic to understand the importance of it. There was yet another reason she had to figure out how to get her hands on his money.

As the car eased up Central Park west to the Eighties, they passed a tattered old woman panhandling on the street corner, stooped over by the heavy burdens of life, begging for anything that a stranger could spare. Seeing a woman in such dire straits hit a little too close to home. As the car drifted past her, Kiernan turned her head away, repulsed and frightened by the tragic sight. She pulled her ivory pashmina tighter around her shoulders, as if the expensive garment could magically ward off doom and despair. By the time the car made the turn onto Fifth Avenue and cruised to a stop in front of the Guggenheim, Kiernan was composed. While the driver held open her door, she stepped out of the Town Car and strolled haughtily into the museum as though she owned the place.

If there had been a blackout that night on the island of Manhattan, the main room of the Guggenheim would have shone brightly in any regard, lit up as it was by the sheer volume of brilliantly cut jewels that bedecked the fingers, throats, and earlobes of those present. Kiernan waded right into the pool of social sharks, armed with her revived ego as an effective repellent.

She sauntered through the expansive room, relieving a waiter of a flute of champagne along the way. "Agatha, darling, how are you?" she crooned to a silver-haired matron with skin so thin and so tight that her veins were a virtual road map traveling across her face.

"Kiernan, it's good to see you. You look fabulous, darling." The two shared a showy, if fake, air kiss.

"As do you," Kiernan said, discreetly scanning the room for Pia or any other specimen with a higher perch on the precarious New York social ladder.

Agatha gestured to the woman next to her, who wore a pile of red hair elaborately coiffed atop her head, and had so many face-lifts that the corners of her eyes could have met in the back of her head. "Have you met Angelique Myers? She's one of the curators here."

"Howwww do you do . . . ?" the woman asked in the nasal affectation of an upper-crust dialect.

"I'm fine, thank you. I'm Kiernan, Kiernan Malloy." She extended her hand, careful to avoid squeezing the five-carat pear-shaped diamond boulder on the woman's bony ring finger.

"Kiernan is a renowned interior designer," Agatha added as she nodded her head.

"Oh, reeeaaally?" the woman declared, raising her finely arched brow. "You know, the name does sound familiar." She carefully appraised the attractive, well-dressed black woman.

"As well it should," Agatha insisted. "She's been written up by the *Times, House and Garden*, as well as *Vanity Fair*."

"How do you two know each other?" the woman asked, curious as to how a black woman could possibly have penetrated these rarified social environs.

Before Kiernan could answer, Agatha said, "My husband's firm hired Kiernan to redecorate their Madison Avenue offices. And it turned out beautifully, I might add." She smiled like a proud den mother who'd been astute enough to pick the one prized student from the barrel of otherwise bad apples.

But Angelique wasn't as easily impressed. "What school did you attend?" she quizzed.

"Vassar," Kiernan said with a perfectly straight face. It was easy to tell that bald-faced lie to a white woman, but she would never dare do so to a black person. She had learned early on that there were only two degrees of separation between any two

black people from a certain station in life—one to which she re-
grettably hadn't been born.

"Oh, really?" Red Top cleared her throat. "Where are you
from?" she continued probing, the way many white people felt
entitled to.

"Boston. And you?" Kiernan was accustomed to the inquisi-
tion, the need to justify her existence as a top interior designer in
the lily-white world of moneyed New York.

"The Upper East Side," the woman replied, as though that
said it all. The identification of the city, state, or country was inconsequential. The look of entitlement and privilege was worn
brashly. "And what part of Boston?"

"Excuse me," Kiernan said, as if she hadn't heard the question. At that perfectly timed moment she saw Pia in a cluster of
men and women holding court admirably alongside a statuesque
blonde who wore a daring Versace that clung in just the right
places while draping in others. She seeped sex in a Marilyn
Monroe sort of way, oblivious to all but that which concerned
her. She possessed that rare mixture of self-assuredness and
nonchalance that it had taken Kiernan years to badly emulate.

"Pardon me." Kiernan smiled, giving Agatha a hug and dis-
entangling herself from Angelique's clutches.

"Pia, darling, how are you?" She hugged the editor as
though she hadn't seen her in many moons, as opposed to just
that very afternoon.

"Hi, sweetie! I'm so glad you could make it. You look fabulous!"

"So do you," she lied. Pia wore an emerald green ball gown
that was much too overwhelming for her sallow complexion.

"Let me introduce you to Eva," she said, turning to face the
Marilyn Monroe blonde. "Eva, this is the interior designer ex-
traordinaire, Kiernan Malloy."

The two women appraised each other like two hungry felines
circling a bowl of warm milk. Eva wore her wealth like a second
skin, a casual grace that Kiernan both admired and envied.

"It's good to meet you, Eva. Beautiful dress you're wearing—whose is that, Versace?" Kiernan was proud of her knowledge of high fashion.

"No, actually, it's mine," Eva said, as she threw her head back and released a throaty chuckle.

"Touché." The two women clinked glasses, just as Pia was off to conquer the next social rung.

"So I hear that you are an amazing decorator."

Kiernan decided to go for the direct approach. "Yes, and I hear that you just purchased a fabulous town house."

"That would be correct."

"We should meet to discuss the possibilities." Kiernan slid open her crystal-encrusted Judith Lieber evening bag and pulled out a business card. "Here's my information."

"I'll give you a call."

"I look forward to it." Kiernan smiled. If nothing else, Kiernan Malloy knew a good opportunity when she saw one, and she didn't need a lit marquee to spot this one. She left happily a half hour later, strolling back through the grand building and into the comfy confines of her chauffeur-driven car. This time when she passed the destitute woman, she didn't even notice her.

3

THE HANDSOME STRANGER

A run through Central Park was almost as good as mental therapy for Brooke, not to mention quite a bit cheaper. She ran five miles religiously every Saturday and Sunday morning to help chase away the stress that gathered after a fifty-hour week of seeing one troubled patient after another. Their list of problems ran the gamut from simple boredom and narcissism to full clinical depression and extreme paranoia. As a result, in one-hour chunks of time they unleashed their most deviant demons for her to tame. She was convinced that Sarah, one of her long-term patients, came twice a week just to have someone to talk to. Brooke had half jokingly suggested that she join a social club instead and save herself the one hundred and fifty bucks an hour. But if all her patients followed suit, or discovered the joys of shopping and jogging, what would she do with her life?

Brooke downed the last drop of coffee and laced up her well-worn cross-trainers, anxious to feel the adrenaline rush and the warm burn in her hamstrings as she sliced through the crisp autumn air. She was nearly out the door when the phone rang. Her heart skipped a beat, just as it had yesterday in the office whenever she'd seen her phone line light up. Though she attempted to ignore it, she knew the cause was about six-two and dark chocolate. She chided herself. She knew it could not possibly be him calling; only her office number was printed on her business card. Besides, he might never call. She was certain that a man as handsome and charming as Taylor must collect women's phone numbers for casual sport. In that respect, it would be best if he didn't call at all. The last thing she needed was to go ga-ga over a bona fide Casanova.

Snatching the phone off the hook, she said, "Hello?"

"Hey, girl." It was Joie. "What's going on?"

"I was just on the way out the door for a run." She suddenly remembered their shoe-shopping excursion. "By the way, how did you make out yesterday?"

"Seven new pairs of friends, I'm ashamed to say." Though she didn't sound the least bit contrite. There were few, if any, indulgences that Joie denied herself.

"At those prices you had no choice." And Brooke was the wrong person to come to for a dose of shopper's guilt.

"Hey, I saw you walk out with a pretty full bag yourself. Did you make it to your appointment on time?"

Brooke heard a muffled voice in the background. "No, in fact, I was twenty minutes late. I got stuck in the elevator. Can you believe that?"

"You, stuck in an elevator? I'm surprised I didn't hear ambulance sirens from the twenty-third floor." Over the years Joie had witnessed Brooke's phobia up close and personal. In fact, on one occasion they were on a flight from London when Brooke got stuck in the closet-sized restroom because the door was jammed, and it took the rest of the flight for Joie to calm her down.

Brooke laughed. "Believe me, you would have if it weren't for this guy who happened to be stuck with me." She blushed just thinking about their close encounter. She could vividly imagine the teasing scent of his cologne and the easy flirtation that lurked behind his smile.

"He must have been a medic," Joie joked.

Brooke smiled and slid down the foyer wall onto the hardwood floor, crossing her legs beneath her Indian-style. "No, but he did have an exquisite bedside manner. You should have seen him, the way he took charge and made sure I was okay. He was"—she fumbled for a word to adequately describe him—"amazing. He was so caring and gentle. And did I say he was drop-dead gorgeous?" Her skin warmed at the mere memory of him.

"Brooke?"

She was snatched from the elevator back to reality. "What?"

"Do I hear what I think I hear?"

"What are you talking about?"

"It sounds like someone's got the hots." This development was music to Joie's ears. For years she'd been trying in vain to get Brooke to give a guy half a chance, or at least get herself laid, but she found fatal flaws in everyone who'd shown any interest in her, and most girls would have drooled over her leftovers.

"No. He was just a really nice guy, that's all," Brooke said unconvincingly.

Joie cut to the chase. "But I did hear gorgeous, didn't I?"

Brooke blushed again. "An Adonis," she finally confessed. Forget the burn of stretched hamstrings; she was enjoying the burn that came from a case of lust. It had been far too long, she thought, fanning herself.

"So . . . ?"

Again Brooke heard a muffled voice in the background. "So what?"

"So when are you seeing him again?"

"I don't really know." She stood up and stretched, ready to get on with her workout, especially now that she felt a lecture coming on.

"Don't tell me you blew him off." Given Brooke's history, Joie would not have been surprised if Brooke had. She had no idea how her friend managed to live the celibate life that she did, especially since Joie was having enough sex for both of them, and couldn't understand any woman who deprived herself of something that felt so damn good.

"Believe it or not, I did give him my card."

"Either he *was* an Adonis, or you were delirious with phobia. I can't remember the last time you even gave a guy your phone number. This, missy, calls for a celebration." There was rustling in the background and the sound of a stifled giggle—Joie's.

"Not yet. Remember, he hasn't called."

"But he will."

Above the tussle of bed linen, Brooke heard a man's voice and Joie's laughter. "It sounds like someone's doing a little celebrating of her own." It was undoubtedly Brent in the background, intent on some carnal attention in lieu of breakfast. Brent had been Joie's live-in lover for the past nine months. Brooke wasn't sure if theirs was a relationship or a matter of sexual convenience—primarily Joie's. Brent was handsome, if a bit too polished. Nice, but without the taste of grit that Joie usually found appetizing. But he needed a roommate at a time when Joie needed an apartment, and as a bonus he was sexually handy. And above all else he adored her, so he never questioned her freedom, which, of course, appealed to her.

"One of us has to—" Before she finished the sentence the phone was pulled away and Brooke heard the sound of muffled laughter, followed by assorted deep moans.

She pulled the phone from her ear and smirked. "I guess I'll talk to you later," Brooke said, and hung up, shaking her head slowly. Though sometimes she envied Joie's easygoing attitude toward sex and life in general, at other times she worried that perhaps her friend was a little too easygoing. But who was she to talk? She who hadn't had sex with a warm body in almost two years. Certainly vibrators—however efficient—didn't count.

Joie fumbled to put the phone back onto the receiver to save Brooke the live and raunchy audio track that accompanied her morning quickie, while Brent worked away below. He did have some serious oral skills, which fortunately made up for his deficits in other areas. Whoever said that black men didn't eat at the Y had obviously never met nor heard of Brent Smith. He spent so much time down yonder that you'd think he was a starving man who'd just discovered a free buffet, and that suited her just fine. As far as Joie was concerned, it was definitely an all-you-can-eat affair.

While he feasted, she closed her eyes, completely enjoying what was building up to be a nice, lazy midmorning orgasm. He lay on his stomach, holding her thighs wide apart with both hands so nothing came between him and his meal, and like a woman on a mission, she maneuvered her hips purposefully against his full lips and his hot, probing tongue, ensuring that each of his laps met its mark. She could feel that building sensation that she loved simmering in her groin, and grabbed her breasts, squeezing her nipples to intensify the feeling. As she approached the brink of nirvana, he slid three fingers into her wet, throbbing sex without missing one lick. Though it occurred to her to prolong the intense pleasure, she couldn't keep from tightening her thighs, locking him in for the ride as she slid over the edge.

She shook her dreads free. "That was a nice way to start the day," she said, stretching fully, like a cat finished napping in the sun.

"I'm glad I could be of service." Brent rolled over onto his back, his steel hard-on pointed northward.

"Do you need some help with that?" Joie was already on her knees crawling toward him, hoping for a good ride.

He smiled like the winner of the school spelling bee. Brent was pretty-boy handsome, light brown with curly dark hair that he wore cut low; there was nothing remotely roughneck about him. "Oh, yeah." He guided her down his shaft with both hands gripping her hips. After a few quick, powerful thrusts, he shuddered spastically, groaned out loud, and emptied his seed into her body. She climbed off and headed to the shower. It no longer bothered her that he came so quickly, as long as he took care of business orally beforehand; besides, there was another means of release at her disposal and it was only a phone call away.

She stepped into the shower and lathered up, using her loofah sponge to clean her body, running it between her full, firm breasts, down her flat stomach, letting the soft but rough material wake up her nerve endings. Joie was not the model-thin type; instead she was voluptuous and proud of it, loving the fact that she adequately filled out a pair of jeans and did not need the wonders from any bra. After rinsing her dreads under the shower-head she ran her hands down her body, enjoying the smooth feel of her skin. When they brushed over her breasts she found herself becoming aroused all over again. A devilish thought occurred to her and she smiled wickedly, knowing that one phone call could finish the job that Brent had only started. After all, what she needed now was a really good fuck, and unfortunately Brent wasn't capable of giving it to her. Now horny, she stepped out of the shower, toweled off, and walked past a satisfied Brent to the kitchen, where she picked up the phone and punched in eleven digits.

"Hey, baby, are you hungry this morning?" she purred when a male voice answered the phone.

She could tell by his lusty response that her timing couldn't be better. She could imagine him lying in bed stroking his big, hard dick. The thought of it made her even wetter, as her flowing juices mixed with those just left behind courtesy of Brent.

"Meet me in an hour at our usual spot." She hung up, dressed, and ran out, telling Brent that she was meeting a friend for brunch. She just failed to tell him that she was the dessert.

4

HE LOVES ME NOT

According to some, high tea at the Plaza's Palm Court was one of the few remaining bastions of old-world civility. It was a haven for the immaculately clad "women who lunch" after an exhausting day traipsing up and down Madison Avenue finding creative new ways to spend their husbands' money.

Though Kiernan was impressively turned out in a Chanel day suit, completely decked out with pearl earrings, a pearl necklace, and a bracelet, her assistant looked as out of place as George W. Bush would at a gangster rap concert. She wore a nitpicked wool skirt with a visibly home-sewn hemline, a nearly threadbare polyester blouse, and worn-down black pumps with heels that were covered with scuff marks, each one bearing testament to the many miles she'd traveled. This was LaTeesha's dressy look. Usually she wore outdated pants, one of her six blouses, and the same pair of black flats.

Once they were seated in beautifully upholstered chairs they were presented with a selection of teas and a three-tiered tray full of mouthwatering bite-size sandwiches, scones, and an assortment of sweet breads and pastries.

LaTeesha looked over the table of delicacies and remarked, "You know, I'd really rather have a hamburger."

Kiernan leaned toward the young girl and touched her arm.

"Honey, this is known as high tea, or more accurately, afternoon tea. It isn't meant to be a meal, only a bite to sustain you until dinner hour." She then patiently explained the origin and rituals of the Victorian-era tradition, while LaTeesha looked on with wide-eyed fascination at the stories of Anna, a duchess and lady-in-waiting from Queen Victoria's court, who began the practice of tea and a snack to hold her over between a big breakfast and small lunch to a very late dinner, as was the practice during that time. Little did she know that she would start a movement that evolved from a need for sustenance to a time for formal socializing, meeting, or just plain old gossiping.

Kiernan enjoyed schooling her young apprentice with bits and pieces of culture and social etiquette, and watching her soak it all up like a dry sponge, much as she herself had years ago, when she too was naive, and very rough around the edges. LaTeesha was enthralled that someone like Kiernan would bother teaching her anything, since she'd never had an adult take any interest in her beyond that which was necessary.

"You must learn to pour tea like a lady," Kiernan insisted as she gracefully reached for the delicate bone-china kettle, lightly touching its lid as she filled both cups with the perfectly brewed tea.

LaTeesha looked at the various utensils and contraptions, confused. She never knew so many were necessary to pour and drink a simple cup of tea, but Kiernan carefully explained the purpose of each one. In LaTeesha's house all that was required was a mug, a microwave, and a Lipton tea bag. This experience provided LaTeesha with an afternoon she would never forget. Every day she marveled over all that she didn't know, and was thirsty to learn.

After settling the bill, they headed west to view the newly purchased eight-thousand-square-foot apartment owned by a music-industry heavyweight who wanted it decorated in full entertainment-business regalia, and money was no object. It was located on the fiftieth floor of one of Donald Trump's apartment buildings. Kiernan walked around the empty, cavernous space, marveling at its simple but elegant design, imagining how to capture its essence and maximize its aesthetic appeal. Kiernan's company, By Design, and two competing design firms were bidding on the lucrative job, and she needed it badly. She'd just finished her last job and had none in the pipeline, while her bank balance was hovering dangerously low.

"Let me have the digital," she asked, holding her hand out to LaTeesha for her camera. Part of her process was to take digital pictures of the space and electronically alter them based upon her vision for its design. This enabled her to visually illustrate her proposal.

"I don't have it."

Kiernan looked as if she were struggling not to explode. "How am I supposed to write an interior-design proposal with no pictures?" She demanded incredulously.

LaTeesha really didn't know how to respond, since Kiernan had never asked her to bring the camera to begin with; but that didn't matter, so she braced herself for one of her boss's tirades. She didn't understand why Kiernan's moods swung so unexpectedly in the space of minutes. She did realize that she had a lot on her mind. She ran a booming business and an elegant household, and took care of a husband. LaTeesha's only comparison was her mom, who didn't yell at her, but also didn't do much of anything else, except collect food stamps and try to sweet-talk money from a long line of men who walked in and out of their lives. For LaTeesha, Kiernan's outbursts were a small price to pay to learn from someone like her. Someone who, in her estimation, had it all together. Kiernan even promised to give her a loan for school after she'd worked for her for one full year. There was another incentive to stay with Kiernan: Her probation officer had made it clear that if she didn't keep this job, she could serve out the rest of her three-year shoplifting sentence behind bars.

Kiernan huffed on. "What are you waiting for? Go get the thing, would you?"

"Could you tell me where to find it?" she asked meekly. She'd learned that the best way to weather the storm was to remain quiet and hope that it passed quickly.

Kiernan expelled a gust of air, which blew her bangs upward. "It's in my Prada portfolio back in the office," she said, rolling her eyes as though LaTeesha were a blithering idiot for not knowing exactly where Kiernan had left it.

After LaTeesha had scampered off, Kiernan yanked her cell phone from her purse and dialed her voice-mail number. She had three unheard messages. The first was from her sister, Thelma, letting her know that she was expecting a delivery in the next few days and would call to arrange to meet. Kiernan smirked. The two women had a classic love-hate relationship. Thelma loved Kiernan's money, and Kiernan hated Thelma for being a reminder of her past, one that she'd worked hard to forget.

Upon arriving in New York six years ago, Kiernan had reinvented herself as artfully as she might redecorate a house, with the "after" bearing no resemblance to the "before." When she met her husband at a swanky charity event for the Studio Museum in Harlem, she'd charmed him easily. She had an alluring, seductive quality about her that caused men to drown in the twin pools of her rich brown eyes, while she mesmerized them with batting lashes, good looks, witty repartee, and a convincing show of sophistication, from wines to travel and art. Theirs was a whirlwind affair that came to a screeching halt literally at the end of the wedding aisle. Soon after the "I dos" the groom saw a much different side of his new bride. According to the fictional account of her life, she was raised in an upper-middle-class household and orphaned just before leaving for college. Kiernan knew that no black people to speak of lived in Oregon, so it became the state from which the new she hailed. Aside from Thelma, no one else knew the truth about Kiernan's life.

The second call was from the assistant to the CFO of a large
media firm in the city, regretfully informing Kiernan that they
would not be awarding her the lucrative contract to design their
new luxury office space in Midtown. Kiernan was seething
when she heard the message. Not only did she really need the
job, but the nerve of them to have a lowly assistant call to tell
her she didn't get it.

She angrily punched the seven key on the dial pad to delete
the message, but the next call made her even more upset. It was
from her husband, calling to say that he'd be home late again because he had another meeting with a client. He was beginning to
sound like a broken record. She sank to the hardwood floor, un-
concerned about soiling her pricey designer suit, and tossed the
phone across the room. The sound echoed throughout the va-
cant space and up into the fifteen-foot-high ceilings. Though
she'd worked hard to delude herself and others into believing
the fairy-tale life she'd designed, she was being forced to realize
the obvious: Her husband was having an affair. All of the clues
were right in front of her face: the unexplained and frequent ab-
sences, his total lack of interest in sex (at least with her), and his
emotional vacancy even when he was physically present. She felt
a heavy pressure settle on her chest, as if a two-ton weight had
been placed there, constricting her diaphragm, making it harder
and harder for her to breathe.

Though she had been trying desperately to ignore it, they
were on a collision course that would likely end in divorce court.
The only miracle that could possible derail it was a baby, and it
was pretty hard to pull that off without his help. The timing
couldn't be worse, given her bleak financial outlook. But her real
problem was that she'd told him when they met that she was financially independent, due to the insurance policy left by her fic-
titious parents, so he'd always kept his financial affairs separate
from hers. She didn't even know the access code to his ATM
card. While he sat on what she was sure was a fat bank account,
she was barely getting by, living from one job to the next. And

now the jobs were coming few and farther between, leaving her resources stretched paper thin. She had to figure out a way to right this egregious wrong, but she couldn't tell him that she didn't have any money. He would know that she'd lied from the beginning and would likely uncover even more of her lies. Once she did ask for access to his accounts, and he'd responded by having his lawyer and best friend, Max, contact her to arrange things. But the smarmy bastard had promptly asked for access to her own nonexistent accounts, so that ended that conversation.

The longer she sat there, the more pissed off she became, simmering in her toxic brew of anger, when suddenly an idea bubbled to the surface. She sat up, wondering why she hadn't thought of it before.

Just then, a huffing and puffing LaTeesha stumbled back into the apartment toting the derelict digital camera. To her dismay, Kiernan got up from her stupor on the floor, grabbed her handbag, and headed toward the door.

"What about the pictures?"

Kiernan wore a blank expression on her face. "What pictures?"

"You know. Of the space . . . for the proposal," she helpfully prompted.

"Oh, yeah. Those. You go ahead and take them. I'll see you in the office tomorrow." She grabbed her bag. "Oh, and lock up on your way out." Before the bewildered girl could respond, Kiernan was out the door.

LaTeesha cocked her head, wondering how she could have so quickly dismissed what was so important only thirty minutes ago.

Kiernan commandeered the first empty cab she saw, nearly shoving aside a young mother and child as she jumped into the backseat and immediately gave the driver her home address. She needed to get there in plenty of time to go through his things. She was convinced there had to be proof of an affair somewhere in that house. With proof in hand, she'd be able to get a divorce, along with a substantial chunk of his money to boot. She almost slapped herself for not thinking of this sooner. It would solve all of her problems, financial and otherwise.

When she reached the apartment, she was nearly out of breath, but the adrenaline drove her on. She peeled off her clothing and headed for his office in nothing but her bra and panties. She didn't have much time to waste. It was after five o'clock, and by some fluke he could decide to come home and change before his so-called dinner meeting. With her hands on her hips, she surveyed the well-appointed office, and her gaze landed on the filing cabinet, the most likely place for any secret correspondence between him and his lover. She charged at it like a prizefighter in a title bout, but it didn't budge. It was locked, which only confirmed her suspicions that she was looking in the right place. All she needed was to find the key. After searching through desk drawers, cuff link boxes, chests of drawers, and even his golf bag, she couldn't find one key that would fit the lock. Desperate, she rummaged through the tool cabinet and emerged with a hammer and a screwdriver. Before she could mangle the stubborn cabinet, the phone rang, startling her.

"Hello?" she answered tentatively.

"I'd like to speak with Mrs. Kiernan Malloy," a professional-sounding voice requested.

"Who's calling?"

"It's Mrs. Whitman from American Express."

"She's not here," Kiernan said.

"Would you please tell her that it's urgent that she contact me as soon as possible? My number is 1-888-555-6213, extension 452."

"I surely will," Kiernan said, hanging up the phone more furious than ever. She knew the woman was calling to tell her that her payment was past due, something that she obviously already knew.

She dropped to the floor, dejected. All of her bills were late, and there was no financial relief in sight, except for the file cabinet that sat before her. She was about to assail it for all she was worth when another thought crossed her mind. It might not be the best time for a brute show of strength, she reasoned, since she was always told that you caught more flies with honey than with vinegar. She could lull him into a false sense of security instead, and then begin building her case, step by step, against the smug son of a bitch. So she smoothed out her hair, straightened the office, and headed to the bar, needing something a bit stronger than a cup of Darjeeling tea to soothe her.

5

A MEETING OF THE MINDS

Brooke listened patiently as her client unloaded a week's worth of angst. He lay on the tacked leather sofa in her office, with a pillow carefully propped under his head. His pin-striped, hand-tailored blue Brooks Brothers suit was carefully smoothed over his thick, middle-aged body. As his attire suggested, during *his* office hours he was a confident, take-no-prisoners corporate executive, who raked in a cool million-dollar yearly salary and a generous annual bonus running a five-billion-dollar division of a Fortune 100 company. He was suitably feared by employees and competitors alike. But during *her* office hours, he was an insecure basket case who was convinced that the whole world was implementing a stealthily coordinated attack against him.

"What makes you believe that your CEO is listening in on your calls?" Brooke asked as she leaned back into her swivel chair, closely observing his body language, tone, and even the dilation of his pupils for clues into his state of mind. When she had begun seeing him three months ago, his problems seemed far from serious. In fact, he appeared to be one of those patients who needed only a confidential ear, someone he could successfully sue if he was ever betrayed—which was typical paranoid thinking—not to mention someone he could be completely vulnerable with while not compromising his head-honcho image. But over the last few weeks his take on reality had shifted, and she was seriously wondering whether his treatment plan might also require medication, in which case she'd need to consult with a psychiatrist as well.

"I don't think he's been eavesdropping—I know it." His carotid artery bulged as his blood pressure rose.

"How can you be so certain?" she asked in an even tone, careful not to let doubt register in her voice. Sometimes when a patient's ideas were questioned they reflexively dug deeper into their convictions.

He was quiet for a few seconds, as though contemplating whether to divulge the next piece of information. His face became serious, somber even. "I hear him breathing on the line," he said quietly. When she didn't comment, he continued. "He gets louder and louder as the day goes on. In the morning I can hardly hear him—he's just a faint pesky noise—but by five o'clock he's so loud I can barely hear the person I'm talking to," he insisted as he raised himself up onto one elbow.

"He listens in on your phone calls all day?" Brooke hid the incredulousness from her voice. It was important for patients to know they were being taken seriously, even when they talked utter nonsense.

"I know it's hard to believe that he'd do such a thing, isn't it?" He reclined again, convinced his point had been made. Even as he lay there, his body seemed tense, as if he were braced for a frontal assault.

"How long has this been going on, Daniel?" He was really beginning to concern her. Though he had borderline paranoid tendencies, she had had no idea that he was at the stage of actually hearing voices or breathing, as it were.

"It's been a few weeks now," he said, interlocking his hands tightly over his stomach.

"Doesn't he have a lot of responsibility in the company? Things that would prevent him from having time to listen in on

your calls all day?" Her tack was to gently lead him to the conclusion that his scenario was improbable, rather than to say so
herself.

He huffed at her insinuation. "Not really. He has everybody
else doing his job. You know, people like me." He became more
agitated, clasping his hands together even tighter.

Brooke thought for a moment. "Didn't you say that he was at
a golf outing last Monday? One that you weren't invited to?"
This slight had been taken personally; in fact, they had spent all
of last week's session discussing it.

He squinted his eyes. "Yeah," he finally said.

Brooke leaned back in her chair again, twirling her pencil
thoughtfully between her fingers. "If he played eighteen holes of
golf . . . what's that? At least four and a half hours. How could
he have been listening in on your calls at the same time?"

He suddenly sat up straight. "You know, you're right!" he
said, staring straight ahead, his pupils dilated.

Brooke exhaled slowly, relieved that she had led him down
the path to logic.

"It can't be him." He slapped his forehead with the heel of
his hand. She could see the wheels turning in his head as he put
two and two together, but unfortunately he came up with five.
"What was I thinking? It's probably not Bob. It's Eric! He's the
bastard who's wanted my job all along. That's who's listening in
on my calls!"

So much for progress, she thought. Just then the vibrating
alarm in her jacket pocket went off, signaling the end of their
time together. She leaned forward, pushing her chair away from
the desk. "Daniel, I want you to do something for me before
next week."

"Sure, Doc." He began straightening his tie, reassembling his
corporate-chief persona.

"Every time you take a call, I want you to write it in a log for
me. Document who you're talking to, what time it is, and what
the conversation is about." She figured if she helped him build a

logical case himself, he'd soon come to recognize his own paranoia. With some patients the best you could hope for was that
they would recognize their issues for exactly what they were and
behave accordingly, rather than trying to get rid of the impulses
altogether—especially in the short term.

He snapped his fingers. "You know, Doc, that's a really good
idea. That way I'll have solid documentation for when I get
ready to take those assholes to court." His eyes were gleaming
beacons.

"For now, let's not even think about that." She searched his
face for signs of comprehension. "Okay?" she prodded. The
last thing she wanted was for him to lose his job over a case of
paranoia.

When he was gone, she sat at her desk and began noting her
observations from the appointment into her office journal. She'd
review the audiotapes at the end of the month to help design her
strategy for his upcoming visits.

It was eleven thirty and she'd already seen two patients, and
her next one was scheduled for right after lunch. After making
her notes, she grabbed her bag and headed for the door.

Walking past André, her secretary, she said, "I'm going to
grab a sandwich. I should be back in a few minutes."

Her hand was on the doorknob, about to turn it, when he
called out, "There's a call for you. Should I take a message?"

"Who is it?"

"A Mr. Taylor Hudson. He says it's personal." André sup-
pressed a teasing smile. Like Joie, he was vigilant in his efforts
to find a man for his boss.

Her heart leaped in her chest. All morning she'd been feigning indifference to the man who'd consumed her thoughts since
Friday, chastising herself for acting like a schoolgirl with a
crush. In many ways that was exactly what she was. She couldn't
remember the last time the mere thought of a man made her temperature rise, or made her lose track of time while her thoughts
wandered into erotic new territory. Once there, she could smell

the clean, citrusy cologne he had worn that day, and could see that sexy smile and the warm gaze of his teasing brown eyes. It was a thrilling but troubling experience for a thirty-four-year-old who'd only just met the man in passing. Maybe there was something to be said for chemical reactions between men and women. In an effort to make analytical sense of her reaction, she recalled that people who met under stressful conditions often formed quicker bonds. Not necessarily lasting ones, however. But as a woman, she knew that she couldn't wait to see him again, yet she braced herself for the disappointment that always seemed to follow her romantic ill-suited attachments.

"I'll take the call," she said, turning to head back into her office. She closed the door behind her, took a deep breath, and picked up the receiver.

"Hello?"

"Good morning. It's Taylor. We met last Friday in the elevator." His voice was as clear as if he were standing next to her.

She felt her skin dampen and sat down without consciously making the decision to do so. "How could I forget?" she said.

He laughed. "I always hope to leave that impression with people, though I'm sure you're referring to the experience itself. After all, it was definitely unforgettable."

She lowered her head. "Not exactly me at my best."

"Well, in that case, I'd love to see that. You looked pretty good to me."

She blushed and ignored his compliment. "Thank you again for helping me through that. In case you hadn't figured it out yet, I have a pretty severe case of claustrophobia."

"You're welcome. In fact, if you're ever stuck in an elevator—or anywhere else, for that matter—I just hope that I'm around." He chuckled.

"I'll keep that in mind."

"But," he jumped in, "I'm hoping I don't have to wait for random happenstance and faulty equipment to see you again."

She was silent. Her brain wasn't sure what to tell her mouth to say. Brooke was so accustomed to saying no to guys that her vocabulary for saying yes was frighteningly sparse.

"Brooke?"

She was nearly paralyzed with fear—fear of the what-ifs. What if he already had a girlfriend? What if he were really some rampant Casanova? What if he were a psycho? On the other hand, what if she really ended up liking him? And he her? What if he broke her heart—again? "I'm here."

"I'm sure you must be busy, but I do want my rain check for drinks. Otherwise, I'll be forced to send you a bill for my rescue services, and they don't come cheap." He wasn't going to give up.

She noticed how his rain check had changed from coffee to drinks. He was a smooth one, she noted. The next thing she knew they'd be having breakfast—in bed. She took a deep breath and decided to take some of the advice that she so expertly doled out to her patients, mainly that a person couldn't be afraid to live life. "My schedule's pretty flexible this week." Her heart was pounding in her chest.

"In that case, what are you doing after work?"

"Nothing, really." She nibbled anxiously on her thumbnail.

"Then why don't we meet at six thirty at the Hudson Library Bar? You won't even have to get on an elevator," he teased her.

She smiled. "That sounds good." She'd been there several times and really liked the cozy bar.

"Great. I'll see you then."

She hung up the phone full of excitement and anxiety, so instead of grabbing a sandwich, she spent her lunch hour rushing home to change clothes for her big date. After trying on five different dresses in a hurry, she left her bedroom in a shambles and headed back to the office wearing a vintage Diane von Furstenberg wrap dress, and a pair of Jimmy Choos. Joie would have been proud of her. The outfit was figure flattering and sexy, but conservative enough not to alarm her patients.

When she walked back into the office after her quick wardrobe change, André wolf-whistled. "Wow! Don't you look hot. What's the occasion?" He appraised her from head to toe, clearly impressed with what he saw. She always dressed well, but he'd never seen her in man-catching gear. He hadn't thought she had any.

"Oh, nothing special."

"Then Nothing Special must be Mr. Hudson's nickname."

She smiled and headed to her office. Brooke would have sworn that André and Joie were coconspirators, both always angling to fix her up with one guy or another.

At six twenty she hailed a cab, and fifteen minutes later she stepped out at Fifty-eighth and Eighth Avenue. The doorman nodded appreciatively, boosting her confidence. Riding the neon-accented escalator up to the Hudson, she felt a knot of nervousness tighten in her chest. Calm down, she told herself. It's just drinks, not even a real date. There's nothing to worry about, she insisted. She thought, when I see him, I'll probably immediately question what the big fuss was all about. In fact, her nurtured memory of him was likely to be much better than the reality of the man himself.

As soon as she caught sight of him, sitting back in a brown leather club chair with his leg casually crossed ankle on knee, she knew that she was dead wrong on that account. His physical presence was even more powerful and seductive than her recollection of him had been. The man was as fine a specimen as she remembered seeing. She smoothed her dress and walked toward him.

He stood up when he saw her enter the room, reaching out to greet her with a quick hug and a kiss on the cheek. She was thankful she was holding on to him, or she certainly would have swooned. He was so fine.

They sat in matching chairs that were angled toward one another. "What would you like to drink?" he asked, signaling for the waitress.

"I'll have a glass of French chardonnay," Brooke said. Taylor picked out a nice chardonnay for her and ordered a Courvoisier for himself.

"So how was your day?" Taylor asked.

His smile was dangerous. It communicated a million messages even when he wasn't saying a word. "Fortunately it was not as eventful as Friday," she replied. Her smile matched his, but she added a hint of challenge in her eyes as she crossed her legs in his direction. Thanks to her profession, she was a pro at masking her feelings during the course of conversation. Otherwise, instead of coming across as confident and sexy, better adjectives for her demeanor would have been "nervous" and "scared."

"Well, I, for one, am very thankful for Friday. Otherwise I wouldn't be lucky enough to be sitting across from such a beautiful and intriguing woman on Monday." His eyes held hers, meeting the challenge that remained there.

That look was the same one she'd seen in her fantasies all weekend. How did one man manage to be so easily seductive? Did he realize his effect on her? Or was it all just pure God-given talent? As that thought crossed her mind the waitress returned with their drinks and another serving of her attitude.

When it was clear that Brooke wasn't going to comment on his flirtatious statement, he changed the subject. "Besides clearing out Manolo Blahnik shoe sales, and stopping elevators and men's hearts, what else do you do all day?"

"I'm a psychotherapist." She watched his reation. Some guys were put off by her profession, fearing she might possess some magical X-ray vision that would allow her to see straight through their mack-daddy bullshit. She only wished.

"Brains and beauty." He whistled. "You know that's a dangerous combination."

"Do tell?" She brought her hand below her chin in the classic therapist pose.

"I have to be careful what I tell you. Otherwise you might learn all of my secrets," he toyed, winking an eye.

"You? Secrets? No!" she teased back.

He spread both feet apart and leaned forward in his chair with his elbows on his knees. "I do have a few, but back to you. Your job," he said, watching her intently, "must be very interesting."

She took a sip of wine. "It has its moments. Sometimes it's a very heavy responsibility, you know, being privy to the inner workings of people's lives. They tell you so much in confidence, and the most important thing a therapist can do is never to betray that."

"Something tells me that you're the type to take confidences very seriously."

"I do."

"In your personal matters as well?"

"What are you asking? Do I kiss and tell?" She wondered for a second if he had something to hide and quickly realized that a man as attractive as he was had to be involved with someone else. The question was, How seriously?

He laughed.

"What about you?" she asked him, changing the course of the conversation. "What exactly do you do besides rescuing damsels in distress?" Now that she was relaxing, she gave him a coy smile of her own. She was enjoying their easy repartee. Who knew that Brooke remembered how to flirt? She was even surprising herself.

"Well . . ." He sat back in his chair. "I invest money for companies and organizations at a privately held investment bank on Wall Street."

She thought, I'd let him do just about anything he wanted, as sexy images from her weekend fantasies replayed themselves in her mind. She quickly composed herself and said, "That's a lot of responsibility too."

"But not as much as helping people with their deepest and darkest secrets."

"What are yours?"

"I'll tell you mine if you tell me yours."

"It sounds like we're playing doctor."

"We can if you want to."

"That's true, but remember I'm the doctor and you're the patient."

"Just show me the couch and I'm there."

They chatted for a while about their careers before the conversation took a more serious turn. "You are so beautiful," Taylor said, holding her gaze. "You must have a line of men at your door."

"To be honest, I really don't date much." She thought that saying "I don't date at all" might scare him off.

"Well, I hope you'll add me to your short list. I'd love to see you again."

She was flattered that he thought she had a list at all. "I'm sure that could be arranged." She gave him a sly smile. She was very glad that he wanted to see her again, though a part of her feared that once he did, he'd question what the big deal was, and move on.

After finishing their drinks, they headed downstairs. A taxi was waiting curbside. "Can we have dinner? Say, Wednesday night?" he asked hopefully.

"Thursday would be better," she said. Not that she had anything to do Wednesday either, but she thought it best not to seem too available, especially for a man like Taylor, who must have women lined up for blocks waiting at his beck and call. It may have been a long time, but she did have some dating instincts left.

"Thursday it is," he said. He smoothly took her into his arms for a hug and a quick kiss. His lips were so soft, and she could taste a hint of the pinot noir he'd consumed. That light kiss was even more intoxicating than the two glasses of wine she'd just had herself.

She was glad to be climbing into the backseat of the taxi. She didn't trust herself to stand on her shaky legs. This was definitely drifting into uncharted territory. She couldn't wait to talk to Joie, who she was sure would give her some pretty good directions. She'd just have to figure out for herself how far down the road to go. She might be the psychotherapist, but Joie was, without question, the love doctor.

6

COFFEE, TEA, AND ME

Joie's cell phone rang just as she finished giving the harried waiter her order for a grilled ribeye, cooked medium-rare, with rosemary mashed potatoes and broccoli. She retrieved it from the outside pocket of her Marc Jacobs tote, checked the caller ID, and opened it before the third ring. "Hello," she cooed seductively.

While the waiter scribbled down Brooke's order of grilled halibut and zucchini onto his pad, Joie listened for less than a minute before snapping the phone shut.

"Excuse me. Nature calls," she said to Brooke as she stood from the table. A smile filled out her heart-shaped lips as she headed downstairs to the restaurant's bathroom. Though she'd just ordered an entrée, at the moment dessert was at the top of her mind. She entered the ladies' room, and was pleased to see there was no one in sight. The heels of her stilettos clicked purposefully along the ceramic floor as she made her way to the last and largest of the bathroom stalls. When she reached for the door's handle, it suddenly flung open and a pair of strong, muscular arms pulled her into the small space.

"What took you so long?" he demanded. It was her lover, Evan.

Before she could answer, he kicked the door closed behind

them and pinned her against the cold, hard tile wall with the full weight of his hundred eighty pounds of lean muscle.

"From what I see here," she said, reaching down to handle his fully erect ten inches, "I'm right on time." The massive organ protruded lewdly from the zipper of his khaki pants. Joie licked her lips, handling his flesh as though it were made of twenty-four-karat gold. Unlike Brent, Evan was massive, thickly veined, and perpetually rock hard, made for just the kind of action that she liked best. Her first impulse was to drop to her knees and worship it. She craved the feel of its pulsing girth as it stroked the inside of her mouth, tickling the back of her throat. Before she could slide down the bathroom wall for a taste, Brent swung her around roughly and hiked her skirt up above her exposed bare ass. He roughly pulled her thong aside and without warning grabbed her hips to angle her sex just right, jamming himself deeply inside her. It was just what she needed. Her head rolled back as her dreads tickled her spine. She was starving for a good romp and he fed her thoroughly, thrust after thrust, intermittently slapping the pale flesh on her behind to the rhythm of his assault, happy to see his handprint linger there—branding her as he relentlessly stoked her hot, wet sex. Compared to him, Brent was a boring vegetarian snack, while Evan routinely served up double helpings of all beef.

Moans escaped her mouth as sweat prickled her brow. She was right there, a firm stroke or a clit brush away from total ecstasy. Sensing that she was on the brink, he bent her at the waist, grabbed a fistful of thick dreads, and began pumping her like a wild stallion who'd just caught up with a mare in heat. It was more than either of them could stand. His ass tightened as he emptied himself into her, and she arched her back, anxious to take as much as he was able give.

"That was amazing," she panted, swinging her dreads back over her shoulders, shaking them out for air.

He stuffed himself back inside his briefs. "Next time," he said, zipping his pants up, "don't wear any panties." Without

looking back, he walked out the door, leaving Joie still breathless and panting.

After tidying up, she freshened her makeup and headed
back to the table, where Brooke was already halfway through
her appetizer.

"Sorry it took so long," she said, smiling to herself.

Brooke eyed her closely, noticing the flushed cheeks and the
smeared eyeliner. "What have you been up to?" Better than anyone else, she knew the kind of antics that Joie was capable of.
Her friend had once joined the mile-high club along with a
stranger who had the good fortune of sitting next to her on an
overnight transatlantic flight. When they landed at Heathrow, he
went his way and she went hers, never once looking back.

"Let's just say I needed to whet my appetite before lunch."
Joie was unabashed about her sexuality and, in fact, reveled in it.
"Though I must confess, anything else is likely to be anticlimac-
tic." She laughed raucously at her own bad pun.

Brooke shook her head. "You are too much." A part of her
worried about Joie's inability to emotionally commit to a relationship and the potential for vulnerability that came with giving away so much of herself, but another part of her envied her
best friend. She craved the uninhibited sexuality that was at
once selfish and giving. She fantasized about the physical release
that was always close by, and most of all she marveled at the fact
that Joie was fearless in her desire for fulfillment, a trait that
Warren, Brooke's ex-husband, among others, had nearly
stripped away from her. Through therapy she was much better
emotionally, but she still couldn't imagine experiencing the complete freedom that her friend so easily took for granted.

"That man is amazing." Joie picked up her napkin from the
table and began fanning it across her face, her chin tilted upward.

"Now which man might that be?" Brooke asked. Though
she knew of Joie's lover, she still had to ask the question because
nothing was a given with Joie.

She exhaled his name: "Evan." Her cheeks burned brightly

at the thought of the wild scene she'd just played out. The memory brought a fresh flush to her cheeks, deepening her even, cinnamon complexion.

"What about Brent?" Brooke asked, taking a sip of her iced tea.

Joie stopped fanning and gave Brooke a bored expression. "What about him?"

"Isn't he supposed to be your boyfriend?"

The fanning resumed. "That's just a label that society places on people in order to control their actions. We live together, that's all. I never took a vow of chastity."

"What about commitment?"

"I am committed to paying half the rent and utilities, but other than that, I've not promised him anything else." As far as she was concerned she wasn't really cheating.

Brooke found herself slipping into therapist mode. "Do you think he assumes that you're faithful?"

She shrugged her shoulders nonchalantly. "You'd have to ask him that."

"Well, let me ask *you* this. What do you think he'd say if he found out that you were having an affair?" Brooke rested her chin in her hand with her elbow propped on the table.

"I can't say he'd be thrilled."

It was fascinating to Brooke that Joie was totally detached from his feelings. "You know, you need to stop before someone gets hurt," Brooke advised, pinning her with a firm look.

Joie set her glass down and pursed her lips in thought. "It's funny that you should say that. On one level, I would like to stop. It's so messy to have two different relationships. But on the other hand I really don't know if I can." She shrugged. "It's like I've found this perfect relationship. It just happens to involve two men instead of one." She shrugged her shoulders nonchalantly before going on to explain. "From Brent I get affection, intelligence, and devotion, but from Evan I get passion and mystery." She sat back in her chair, feeling like she really had a handle on things now. "Brent is like perfectly stacked firewood, and Evan is the lighter fluid that really makes the fire roar." She cocked her head to one side. "You know what I mean?"

Brooke shook her head at the analogy. "On some level I do, but you don't think that this can go on forever, now, do you?"

Brooke could tell that her friend had never seriously considered this question.

"I suppose not." She looked disappointed with the inevitable answer.

"How do you think it's likely to end?"

Joie took a sip of wine. "Well, there're probably three options." She ticked them off by holding up her thumb, followed by two fingers on her right hand. "One: Brent will find out and he'll leave me. Two: Evan will get tired of sneaking around, and end it himself. Or three: I'll find one man who does it all and leave them both, living hornily ever after." She cracked up laughing.

"Just remember that movie," Brooke warned her.

"What movie? *Unfaithful?*"

"No. *Looking for Mr. Goodbar.*"

"I don't have to look. I've already found him," she said, smiling slyly. "And he is good to the last drop." She still felt traces of their steamy coupling between her legs.

"You mixed your metaphors," Brooke corrected.

"But you get the point."

"No, it sounds like you did."

Joie laughed and sighed. "Now all I have to do is help you find one too. Speaking of which, how did things go with Mr. Elevator Man?"

Brooke smiled and her eyes took on a dreamy, faraway quality. "It went very well," she said. "We had drinks and great conversation at the Hudson, *and* he invited me to dinner Thursday night."

She couldn't supress the glow that burned her cheeks whenever she thought of him, which was turning out to be very often.

This morning he'd sent exotic flowers to her office with a note that read:

Had a great time last night, and I can't wait to get to know you a lot better. Have a great day.

Taylor Hudson

Just before she left for lunch he called, and they chatted for a few minutes before she realized that she had to run out to meet Joie. As they were hanging up, he said, "Unless you plan to give up your lunch hour every day, it'll probably be a good idea for you to give me your home number." And she happily obliged.

Joie suddenly perked up. "So what are you wearing on your next big date?" She never thought Mr. Elevator Man would make it past the first one, because no else had. This was turning into big news.

"I don't know. I haven't thought that far," Brooke admitted.

"I've got an idea. What are you doing later tonight?"

Brooke looked puzzled. "Nothing. Why?"

"I'll be over at eight. We'll have takeout and do a dress rehearsal. If this guy is as perfect as you say, we can't let him get away."

"Hey, he's not exactly mine to let get away. It was only drinks, Joie. For all I know he probably has a long string of second dates in the hopper, so I really don't want to make a big deal over this." She knew that the higher you climbed, the harder you fell, and she had no intention of setting herself up for the inevitable fall.

Joie wore a reflective look. It saddened her to see the lingering effects of the abusive relationship Brooke had endured. Though there were no physical traces, the emotional scars were painfully clear. There was no other way to explain how a woman as gorgeous as Brooke could possibly overlook her own sex appeal. "Just be there at eight. Let me take care of the rest."

They settled the check and reentered their own worlds.

While Brooke's calling was soothing souls, Joie's was capturing them on film.

Hours later, Joie stood fumbling at her own apartment door, bogged down by canvas bags of photography equipment. She had just completed a photo shoot with Beyoncé for the cover of *Essence* magazine. Though the creative process was exhilarating, it was also exhausting when it involved a celebrity who came with enough handlers to run a midsize company, from publicist, stylist, manicurist, and manager, to agent, nutritionist, and massage therapist. The list didn't include the many intruders from the magazine side, but Joie ignored them. One of the reasons she was so good at her job was because she always had such an imaginative vision, and never compromised it, even at the risk of losing a job.

When she finally opened the door, there stood Brent, wearing a towel tightly cinched at his waist.

"Hi. How was your day?" she asked, walking past him.

"Probably not as exciting as yours. Here, let me take that," he said, grabbing some of the bags. When she was empty-handed, he led her into the bedroom, dropped his towel, and pulled her onto the bed.

"Hey, can I at least shower first?" she protested. She could still feel traces of Evan between her legs.

He looked her right in the eyes. "No, I want you just the way you are," he said with an unusually strong show of passion.

She was put off by the notion of him eating her lover's left-overs—even she drew the line somewhere. "But—"

Before she could stop him she was laid out flat on the bed with his head buried between her legs. Oddly enough the taste of her lover didn't seem to bother him in the least. In fact, he didn't appear to even notice. He ate Joie as if her juices were left over from the Last Supper. Though her head was screaming, No, this isn't right, his probing tongue ended the argument, paving the way for her second delicious orgasm of the day.

7

NEW BEGINNINGS

Brooke felt like a teenage girl primping on prom night as she nervously applied and reapplied the final touches to her makeup. The only missing pieces were a limp wrist corsage and a tacky white stretch limousine. Trepidation aside, she nervously stepped into the elegant black slip dress that Joie had insisted she wear, also stepping over a symbolic threshold, from one life hopefully straight into another. Not an easy transition for her, but she decided—at least for one night—to take a chance and live life, rather than sitting quietly on the sidelines commentating while others did.

"Listen, girl, it's time you put the past where it belongs, and if this guy is as hot as you say he is, why not start now?" Joie had coached. Of course, that was easy advice from someone who didn't believe in denying herself any pleasures.

Brooke turned to face her. "Tell me what's wrong with this picture."

"What are you talking about?" She had continued going through Brooke's evening shoes searching for just the right pair.

"You sound more like a therapist than I do."

She smirked and kept looking. "Hey, if you won't take your own advice, maybe it'll sound more convincing coming from someone else."

After several wardrobe changes and much critiquing, Brooke had put away the tailored pantsuit that she'd contemplated wearing and agreed to the slip dress, along with a sexy Robert Clergerie sandal. "You're right," she finally relented. Why not take a chance? She had to admit, she always hung up wanting more after their telephone conversations. There was something about his deep, husky voice and gently probing questions that teased her mind and touched her soul. He was intriguing, passionate about life, and intense about work. She also admired his sense of right and wrong, and thought it funny that he was overly protective of his kid sister, who was twenty-six years old, though he treated her as if she were still a teenager. Getting to know him was like excavating a rare artifact: Only after carefully brushing away layers would the true nature of the prize be revealed.

She blushed, recalling their long talks, but her smile faded as memories of another past relationship surfaced: the less than fairy-tale ending of her marriage to Warren, her college sweetheart. They met while attending Harvard undergrad. Brooke was studying psychology, while he majored in government as a prelude to what he assumed would be a brilliant legal career, followed by an equally brilliant career in politics. These were lofty but achievable goals for someone like Warren, who was posterboy handsome, spawned from a prestigious, wealthy, and well-connected black family, and blessed with natural athletic ability. He was the kind of guy whom everyone cheered for—men and women, young and old, but most especially Brooke, who fell head over heels in love with him during their sophomore year, during a time in her young life when a rainbow followed every rainstorm. It was a magical time for them. The two attractive, gifted young black kids were living the American dream on the campus of the country's most revered institution. Life could not have been better for what many considered the perfect couple. They were expected by all accounts to live happily ever after.

On cue, they were married after graduation in front of

a chapel full of adoring family and friends, and things went according to the script until his career aspirations were derailed after being ousted from Harvard Law as a result of a borderline plagiarism charge. He was crushed, devastated—and worse, he became resentful of her continued success.

His dramatic shift from attentive, loving husband to an inconsolable tyrant was as subtle as the imperceptible changes in a sunset. It began predictably, with clouds of sadness, depression, and bitterness, followed by sporadic bouts of abusive, angry words, which eventually yielded to the darkest side of spousal abuse, both physical and emotional. She always knew that the next episode was as inevitable as the sunrise, but seemed unable to leave him, for doing so would validate the unthinkable. Her life felt like she was playing a character in a dark comedy, or being awakened during a bad nightmare, one viewed by others through a dreamlike rose-colored lens. As with most award-winning performances, no one ever suspected the chaos that went on backstage as soon as the curtains came down following a perfect public performance. Brooke didn't want to expose the naked emperor; she didn't want to disappoint the adoring fans who sat in the audience of their life, clapping and smiling through act after act.

His incessant pleas for forgiveness, coupled with her self-deluding fear of facing reality, held her a shackled prisoner throughout grad school and her doctoral studies. Only the haunting words of an emergency room nurse who had been where she was freed Brooke from Warren's gripping control. Family and friends were finally confronted with the ugly truth, as the gleam was stripped from everyone's favorite golden couple, leaving only a tarnished memory. The question that loomed large was how a psychology major could allow herself to be abused. It was a question Brooke spent years asking herself, and while the answers remained elusive, her human frailty provided a reservoir of empathy that many therapists didn't have. Putting those memories aside, Brooke walked out of her apartment and away from her past, prepared to embrace the possibilities of the future.

She arrived at Jean-Georges's Tribeca restaurant, 66, where she found Taylor lounging in the bar sipping a martini. His looks were a combination of Blair Underwood's chiseled features and Terrence Howard's amazing sex appeal. As she approached him, Brooke sensed all female eyes drawn like magnets his way, but he seemed oblivious to anyone but her. He stood up flashing that megawatt smile to greet her. "Hi, gorgeous."

She gave him a warm hug, and immediately felt the pull of sexual attraction. It made her spine tingle.

They settled next to each other on the cozy couch that looked out over Church Street. "What can I get you to drink?" he asked, motioning for the Asian waitress's attention.

"I'll have a glass of champagne," she said, already feeling in the mood to celebrate.

"Why not make it a bottle?" he said. He turned to the waitress. "The lady would like champagne, so we'll take a look at your list."

They leaned in together, their heads nearly touching. His physical presence was like a strong magnet drawing her in closer and closer. She inhaled his masculine scent, making her head lighter than any French champagne ever could. After settling on a bottle of Veuve Clicquot, they followed the hostess to their dinner table. As they walked through the restaurant, all eyes were drawn to them. For a moment she felt self-conscious, remembering how her ex had also seemed so flawless and how they had looked like the perfect couple. Just as quickly she shook the memory off.

Once they were seated, champagne was presented to Taylor and then opened by the waiter. Two glasses of perfectly chilled bubbly were poured, as air danced to the top of the crystal flutes in strings of floating bubbles. Taylor raised his glass. "I'd like to propose a toast: to new beginnings."

"I'll definitely toast that." She smiled, feeling like Cinderella before she lost the glass slipper. "To new beginnings." They touched the lips of their flutes and held each other's eyes until the toast was consummated with a satisfying sip.

After resting his glass on the table, Taylor leaned back in his chair. "Speaking of beginnings, you never told me much about yours." During their phone conversations, Brooke had carefully avoided talk of past relationships, dancing over the subject as though it were synonymous with hot coals.

She shifted in her seat. "What exactly do you want to know?"

"Everything," he said, leaning forward intently. "I want to know as much about you as possible."

She leaned back and took a slow sip of the frothy liquid. "Just remember, turnabout *is* fair play."

"Absolutely. In fact, that's why I proposed that toast. I think it's important to understand where someone is, or has been, before you can move forward. And, in case you haven't figured it out, I do want us to move forward." His face took on a seriousness that she hadn't seen there before.

She blushed in spite of her best effort not to and reached for her glass again, unsure of what to say.

He smiled at her shyness. Most women he knew would have reveled in the comment like a baby going at a warm bottle. "I didn't mean to embarrass you. Besides, for all I know you may not even be interested in me at all."

She was surprised that he had read her silence that way. She put her glass down. This was where the rubber met the road, so to speak. She had to admit to him and to herself how she felt. Otherwise she might as well stay locked in the past forever. She cleared her throat and the memories of the past, deciding to face the future. "No, I would very much like to get to know you."

His eyes narrowed, studying her closely.

"Someone hurt you, didn't they?" he asked. It was a statement and a question.

He seemed able to look right through to the heart of her. In him she saw the same calming concern and warm tenderness that she'd first glimpsed when they were stuck together in the elevator.

She lowered her head. "Yes."

"Do you want to tell me what happened?" He reached out to gently touch her hand, a simple gesture that made all the difference.

Over dinner, Brooke surprised herself by telling him everything. She painted enough of the details of her marriage that he most certainly got the picture. Once she began talking, the pain, anger, and hurt poured out as if someone had poked a hole in the dam that held her emotions at bay. It felt good to say so many of the things that she'd always thought best to leave unsaid. Though she often told her patients how important it was to be in touch with their feelings, and to express them, rather than keeping strong emotions bottled up, she didn't always practice what she preached.

Taylor listened attentively, not interrupting her once. He just listened, while holding her hand and shaking his head from time to time. At moments she could see anger heating his blood as the veins in his neck throbbed; at others she sensed a tension, as though he were living the nightmare right alongside her.

When she was finished taking him on her painful journey, he sighed. "I know there is nothing I could say to erase the pain you've suffered, but I am so sorry you ever had to go through it." He was unable to fathom how anyone could be so cruel, especially to a person as special as Brooke.

Brooke held back a stream of tears as his words sank in. At another time, in another place, she might have allowed herself a good, healthy, cleansing cry. "It's still hard for me to believe that I misjudged him so badly."

He looked thoughtful. "It's hard for any of us to ever completely know another person, especially when we are young. It's as if you lack a frame of reference that life gives you only after years of experience."

"You're right. It's just, as a psychotherapist, I should have known."

He patted her hand. "You're being too hard on yourself. You're not just a psychotherapist. You're also human."

"Very well said." She brightened after listening to his pep talk. "Maybe you should be the shrink, or maybe you just have a crystal ball somewhere."

He laughed. "If I had one, I sure hope I'd see you in it."

More than being touched by his words, she was also amazed by his empathy and willingness to communicate. She knew first-hand how difficult it was for men. In fact, that had been a part of Warren's problem—being unable to deal with his disappointment. Rather than discussing it, or at the very least acknowledging it, he stored it away deep inside, and with no room to breathe, his anger grew, eating away at him. In turn he aired it by unleashing its wrath on her.

After dinner, Taylor leaned in and held her hand. "There's another reason I brought up the past. There's something that I have to tell you."

His change in tone caught her by surprise. "What is it?" she asked. The night had been so emotional to this point, from the trip down memory lane as she dressed, all the way to her un-planned confession session, that she wasn't ready for another dramatic moment.

He looked into her eyes, unsure where to begin. "I really want to spend time with you, and get to know you, but I have to be completely honest with you too."

Her brow furrowed; he could see the wheels turning as she tried to anticipate where this conversation was headed. Wherever it was going, she knew it wouldn't be pleasant. Her stomach tensed, waiting for the other shoe to fall, as she'd feared it would all along. He was too good to be true.

Sensing her apprehension building, he held on to both of her hands. "What I have to tell you is that legally I am married." He felt her instinctively pull away and saw hurt and anger flicker through her eyes, but he held on to her, not letting go. "Please listen to me," he pleaded. "I realize that as a therapist you must hear this a thousand times, but you have to believe me when I tell you that I *am* planning to get a divorce." He knew how lame this must sound to her, of all people, but there was no other way to put it.

Brooke's heart had been opening slowly like a rose beginning to bloom. It quickly shut tight. She wanted to kick herself for ever believing the phrase "happily ever after" could apply to her. Hadn't she learned that lesson already? She reached for her purse and pulled her hand away from his. "I don't date married men," she snapped.

He pleaded with her. "I didn't know that I'd be lucky enough to meet you. Otherwise I'd already be divorced. I wasn't looking for a relationship. You have to believe me." He looked at her for signs that she did, and saw none.

Disappointment and hurt replaced the glow of early attraction. How many times had she heard this same sad and sorry tale from her own distraught clients—the one about the married man who was leaving his wife, but never did? Was she doomed to live out every patient's dilemma, to go from abuse to disillusionment? She stood up. "Well, call me when you are," she said sarcastically. "And I won't hold my breath." She turned to leave the room.

"Wait, please." He fumbled in his wallet, tossing a credit card on the table, and rushed behind her to the coat check, where he found her impatiently waiting for her wrap. "Brooke, please believe me, my marriage has been over for a while now. I just hadn't done anything about it." He held her arm, not wanting to let her go. "Brooke, I didn't plan for this to happen. I didn't plan to meet you. I—"

She interrupted him. "The bottom line is that you *are* married, and after many conversations you are just now finding it convenient to tell me. And if you don't respect your vows and what they mean, I do."

It troubled him to see the pain in her eyes, knowing that this time he'd caused it. "If I weren't married, would you see me?"

She folded her arms tightly across her chest. "I don't answer hypothetical questions, so go home to your wife."

"Just give us a chance," he pleaded.

"There is no us," she said as she took her wrap and quickly strolled out of the restaurant and into the night, like Cinderella escaping the ball. But this time there'd be no citywide search with a glass slipper in hand, because she didn't care to ever see him again. Thankfully she had learned her lesson much quicker than before. It was best to get out at the first sign of trouble, and this one was in neon.

When she walked back across the threshold into her clothing-strewn bedroom, she calmly removed the black dress that she and Joie had so painstakingly chosen, and tossed the designer sandals into a corner. Exhausted, she sat on the bed with her arms wrapped around her folded legs and her knees tightly pressed against her chest. Maybe her best friend had the right idea about men after all: love 'em and leave 'em, before they left you. Based on Brooke's spotty track record, every guy that looked picture-perfect to her also ended up being anything but, while no one would ever accuse Brent or Evan of being picture-perfect.

Once again, she'd sadly misjudged a man. Tired and disillusioned, she rested her head on her forearms. Taylor had seemed so nice, so kind, so sensitive, but how could she have guessed he was also so married—a double-crossing adulterer? But she couldn't necessarily call him a liar. He hadn't denied being married. She'd just assumed that he wasn't—again her fault. When would she ever learn not to trust men, or even more to the point, that she shouldn't trust herself where they were concerned? Without any effort on her part, she somehow attracted the wrong guy every time.

After enough self-analysis she picked herself up physically, dusted herself off emotionally, and counted her remaining blessings; after all, things could be much worse. She could've fallen in love with him, but as it stood, she was merely in love with his image. While she dressed for bed, Brooke thought about calling Joie to commiserate some more, but decided to talk to her tomorrow. Rehashing everything in detail would only prolong a night that she would just as soon forget. So she headed back over the imaginary border she'd crossed only hours earlier, to the safety of her past life, secure within the borders of her own isolation.

8

MEN BEHAVING BADLY

A therapist's office was like a mental sanctuary for patients. It was a safe haven where they were free to divulge their deepest, darkest secrets, their innermost fears, and their boldest ambitions without fear of judgment. The best part of the deal for the patient was that by law they were also assured of complete privacy, so those hidden fears were well protected from prying eyes or well-tuned ears, assurances that couldn't be promised in everyday social interactions. Sure, everyone had a best friend who swore on the grave of a deceased parent to keep a secret safe forever, or on a stack of Bibles never to betray a confidence, until one day—oops. That juicy tidbit just slipped past a loose tongue, or was spit out after a quick taste of revenge, or was simply traded away for a bigger or even juicier secret.

To encourage those feelings of uncompromised confidence and mental solace, Brooke had carefully designed her office to soothe souls. The walls were covered in a rich, thick Asian grass cloth, and her desk—a handsome dark wood of simple design—bore a warm patina brought out only by age and loving care. The sofa and oversize chairs were made of butter-soft tan leather, and large leafy plants surrounded the room, while a recirculating water garden and a slowly rotating rattan ceiling fan added to the overall serenity of the room.

But all of this did little to comfort Erin, a thirty-five-year-old housewife and mother who was generally one of those patients who needed only a responsive, impartial sounding board. Erin wanted someone to listen attentively to her diatribes on her fabulous apartment, her equally fabulous rich husband, and her even more fabulous two-year-old daughter, Meagan. Their sessions consisted of countless long hours detailing Meagan's first words, her latest bowel movement, the state of her potty training, and how generally talented, beautiful, and brilliant the child was for a two-year-old, or for any child, anywhere, ever in life. When she'd sufficiently worn that subject down to nothing, Erin would start in on her fabulous Fifth Avenue apartment, its many iterations of decorating, how she couldn't imagine living in New York without a car and driver, nanny, cook, and housekeeper, and how the Lord knew how hard it was for her to find good help. Listening to her, no one would ever know that she grew up barely lower middle-class. The last bastion of "me" territory was her husband, whom she worshiped solely because he had more money than God.

He loved the fact that she aspired to no life outside the one created within the confines of their walls, which meant he didn't have to compete with a job, career, hobby, or even close friends. The child was only a mild distraction, given the staff who stood at the ready when he walked through the door every evening to a freshly bathed, scented, and dressed wife with her hair neatly coiffed and her makeup perfectly applied. In return she had carte blanche access to his enormous wealth, and spent it lavishly up and down Madison and Fifty-seventh Avenues, from Hermès to Bulgari and Bergdorf's.

Brooke was expecting the usual flow of conversation and was thus unprepared for the woman who walked through the doorway. Instead of breezing into the office giddy from the high life, she wore an air of dismay that weighed down each and every step.

"Erin, are you okay?" Brooke asked once they were both seated.

"Yes, I'm fine," she said, but the wringing of her hands and her red-rimmed eyes said otherwise.

Brooke leaned forward. "I'm not sure what's happened, but you have to remember that I'm here to help you, and I can't if you don't confide in me."

Brooke could see her wrestling with her emotions. It was so against Erin's nature to admit or even entertain the possibility that her life wasn't picture-perfect, so she was afraid to even voice the obvious. How ironic. Now that she actually had a problem, she seemed incapable of discussing it with her therapist. A stream of tears ran silently down her cheeks, defying her will to ignore reality.

"Erin, it's okay to have problems. We all do, but we also have the power to do something about most of them. But you can't unless you face them, so I need you to tell me exactly what has happened," she implored.

"It's Lawrence," she finally said. Just uttering his name brought about a rush of tears.

"What happened?"

"There's another woman," she finally said before breaking down in a fit of body-racking sobs.

She finally told Brooke how she'd decided to surprise her husband the night before with takeout from his favorite Thai restaurant, since he had been working late at the office. She'd gotten all dolled-up, with only lingerie underneath her silk trench coat, and had her driver take her to his office. She strutted through the building's lobby carrying a gourmet Thai dinner and a bottle of his favorite champagne packed in a beautiful Ralph Lauren wicker basket. She headed up to the executive floor and breezed by his assistant with a quick wave. Before the woman could hop up from her desk to intercept her, Erin was walking into the shock of her life. When she opened the mahogany double doors to his office, she found her fabulous doting husband with his head deeply buried between the long, widely stretched legs of a busty brunette—he apparently already had dinner plans.

Erin was so shocked by the lurid scene that she dropped the picnic basket, spilling pot stickers, curry fish cakes, satay, and spring rolls everywhere. Her perfectly manicured, freshly painted, and paraffin-waxed hands flew to her mouth in horror as her hubby's head emerged from the comely pair of legs covered in *jus de femme.*

She backed out of the room, horrified, unable to face the shame and semipublic ridicule, since the entire spectacle was witnessed by his secretary, who'd followed Erin into the sex den. This made it harder for Erin to convince herself that it hadn't happened. Pushing past the red-faced woman, she fled the scene of the crime, expecting that her husband would be in hot pursuit behind her, begging, pleading, and groveling for her to forgive him, declaring his undying love, and promising that it would never happen again, if only she'd forgive him. But that wasn't the case. Though she listened, there were no sounds of shoes beating a quick path to catch her; nor was there one sign that he hadn't said, "Oh, well," and simply finished his meal.

Once back at her apartment she rushed past the nanny, the housekeeper, and her daughter's outstretched arms, heading straight to her boudoir, where she could break down in peace and wait for her wayward husband to come to her and back to his senses. She waited all night. He finally showed up the next morning at the breakfast table as though nothing unseemly had ever happened. Later, when they were alone, she confronted him, resurrecting her anger from the night before. He was as calm as if he'd been caught only with lipstick on his collar.

When she was finished telling the story, her face was flushed and her eyes were swollen orbs. Brooke appraised her client carefully and decided to get straight to the point, rather than skirting around it. Unless confronted dead-on, Erin was the type of patient who was masterful at not seeing those things that she chose to ignore. "Erin, given what happened, what do you want the outcome to be?"

She wiped her eyes and took a deep breath. "I want things back to normal."

"Describe normal."

"A loving and devoted husband," she answered indignantly.

"Given what just happened, is 'back to normal' possible? You have to face the fact that he isn't devoted—at least not sexually—and given his reaction, even his being loving is in question." Brooke crossed her legs, intently listening for Erin's response.

Erin seemed shocked by this harsh assessment of her marriage. "How can you say he isn't loving just because he made one slipup?" she defended.

"How do you know it's been only one slipup? Did he say that?"

Erin bowed her head and in a barely audible voice said, "No."

"In that case, you don't."

When Erin looked as though a fresh burst of tears was percolating, Brooke leaned toward her and said softly, "For your own well-being and your daughter's, you have got to look at things as they are, and throw away the rose-colored glasses." The timer in Brooke's pocket went off, indicating that their session was over. "I want to see you again in a couple of days." She didn't think that Erin could get through this crisis alone, and a week was far too long to begin rebuilding her self-esteem in preparation for the hardship that was sure to come.

When Brooke was alone, she buzzed André for her messages. "Mr. Hudson called twice," he said with a teasing smile in his voice.

"If he calls back I'm unavailable," she said curtly.

"For how long?" He sounded disappointed.

"Forever," she said, hanging up the phone.

NEVER KISS AND TELL

The nerve of the lousy cheat, she thought. She remembered how hurt Erin was by the exploits of her own unfaithful husband. Brooke wanted to tell her that it was highly unlikely that this was Lawrence's first extracurricular activity—just as unlikely as it was that she would have been Taylor's first had she been a willing participant. She decided to pick up the phone and call someone else who knew a thing or two firsthand about cheating.

When she reached Joie on her cell phone, her friend was downtown prepping for a photo shoot for Phat Farm.

"Hey, I was wondering when you'd call to give me the four-one-one on last night."

"Are you sitting down?"

"Don't tell me you gave him some," Joie whispered conspiratorially into the phone.

"Not likely, but what if I told you that he was married?"

"You're kidding me!" She sounded as disappointed as Brooke had been.

"Wish I were." Brooke went on to describe the disastrous outcome of their date with the professional clarity and distance that a night of sleep sometimes provided. She sounded as if it had happened to someone else, maybe one of her patients.

After a few seconds of silence, Joie ventured to say, "Maybe he's telling the truth. Maybe the marriage is over."

"Even if that is the case, he still should have told the truth from the beginning."

"If you think about it," Joie suggested, "this *is* the beginning. After all, nothing has happened yet. Besides, if he'd told you in the elevator, would you have ever gone out with him?"

"No."

"I rest my case."

"What are you saying? That I should date married men?"

"No, but I am saying that you shouldn't be so hard on him. For all you know he could really be a victim of a bad marriage."

In Brooke's experience, most of the victims of really bad marriages—including herself—were female. "Maybe so," she said, "but that's between him and his wife and has nothing to do with me."

"Your next patient is here," André announced through the intercom. By policy, he never said the patient's name in case someone else was in the office or passing through the waiting area.

"I've got to go. My next patient just arrived," she said to Joie, happy to get off the phone to end the conversation. Leave it to Joie to have an unorthodox opinion of what had happened. Anybody else would have agreed with her that the man was loathsome and dead wrong.

"Send her in," Brooke announced to André. She flipped through her calendar in search of a name to put with the face that would soon be walking through her door. She saw a note that this patient was new.

The door opened and in walked a tall, brown-skinned woman with shoulder-length hair and a smug attitude. She was turned out in the latest designer garb.

Brooke stood up after discreetly pressing the play button of the recorder mounted under her desk. She walked over and extended her hand. "Good afternoon, Mrs. Mathews. Please make yourself comfortable."

"Please call me Kate," the woman said before sitting stiffly on the edge of the sofa.

Brooke noticed that she was wound so tightly that she seemed ready to sprint for the door at any moment. Though her body language said "Flee," her facial expression was as relaxed as if she were lying poolside at Baccarat sipping a mojito without a care in the world. The incongruity intrigued Brooke; in fact, it brought to mind the possibility of substance use, which often produced schizophrenic body language.

"So, Kate, what brings you here today?"

"My husband," she said, crossing one leg over the other.

Here we go again, Brooke thought. "Tell me about it." She leaned back in her chair, watching her new client carefully.

Kate sucked her teeth, tossed her hair, and finally said, "We've been married for almost three years now, and he is a great catch. He's sucessful, he's gorgeous, and he's very intelligent."

"But . . ."

"But I know he's having an affair," she said adamantly. Her eyes burned brightly, and she seethed with anger. It ran just beneath the surface of her cool exterior. She paused a few seconds to check her composure before continuing. "We haven't been together intimately in over four months, and he doesn't even look at me anymore, except to make sure not to bump into me." She shook her head forlornly.

Not another one, Brooke thought. "What do you think brought this current state about, assuming that at one time things must have been different?" Brooke saw her patient preparing to deliver a prerehearsed response and quickly interrupted her. "You can be perfectly honest with me. I'm not here to judge you or to cast any aspersions. So tell me the truth, and together we'll be able to work through your problems."

This seemed to get the other woman's attention. She exhaled slowly and rolled her eyes to the ceiling, wringing her hands. "Things worked for a while, until he finally figured out that the painting he brought home was only a signed copy, so he goes to work, he comes home, and he goes to bed—on his side."

"Was it?" Brooke asked.

Kate looked at her as though she didn't understand the question.

"Was it a copy? Do you feel that way?"

"It's not important what I feel." She was visibly uncomfortable with this line of questioning.

"Of course it is. How you see yourself often influences how others see you." Seeing that Kate wasn't ready to go that deep,

Brooke returned to the surface. "Has your husband said anything to you about his feelings, about how or why things may have changed?"

"No. We don't really talk, but I'm sure he has a girlfriend."

"Why do you think so?"

"In case I didn't mention it, he's a very handsome man, and women throw themselves at him. Always have. Plus, I know men. If he's not getting it at home, he's damn well getting it somewhere."

Brooke spent the remainder of their session probing, trying to get to know the closed and angry woman who sat before her, trying to dig beneath the layers that hid a well of emotional turmoil.

After lunch she discovered that her third client of the day was Teresa Benson, yet another woman who was also dealing with a lying, cheating husband. She cried during the entire session, alternately hating his guts and loving his dirty drawers. Each emotion was right next to the other, so she alternated freely.

By the time Brooke left the office for the day, she was mentally exhausted from the emotional baggage that Kate, Erin, and Teresa had all checked with her. Normally it didn't feel as heavy, but after her run-in with Taylor, it felt like the weight of the world.

9
COCKTAIL FAVORS

Kiernan's penthouse was a hive of activity. Florists were flitting about, caterers were carting in delectable delicacies, and bartenders were setting up battle stations armed with everything from fine champagne and mint-infused mojitos to sidecars and the martini du jour. At the epicenter of this organized chaos stood Kiernan, the queen bee, wrapped in a leopard lounge jacket, with her hair coiled atop her head in yellow Ethel Mertz–style rollers. She was standing there smoking a cigarette and spitting out orders like a rapid-fire pistol in between drags.

"Henri, I'm sure that I told you *no white flowers* of any kind under any circumstances! I detest white flowers—they remind me of funerals." She frowned at the dainty little man and stomped her marabou-slippered foot several times to emphasize her displeasure with him and his flowers.

He looked at her blankly, sublimely unfazed by her theatrics. "You specifically asked for baby's breath as a bed for the piano display and, dahling, they only come in white." He pursed his lips together tightly.

"Then dye the little bastards some other color," she ordered, before moving her cloud of smoke and madness to another corner of the room, where LaTeesha toiled away making sure that the guest list was updated with the latest RSVPs.

Kiernan walked up and stopped within inches of the girl's face. "Where is the guest list?" she demanded, still rapidly puffing on the nicotine stick.

LaTeesha quickly handed her the neatly typed list. "These are all of the RSVP yeses."

Kiernan blew smoke directly into LaTeesha's face as she scanned the sheet quickly, making sure that the people on her A-list, in particular, were accounted for, but looking for one name specifically. "Are you certain Eva is coming?"

"I spoke to her personally, and she said she'd be here."

"What time is she arriving?"

"That she didn't say."

Kiernan squinted her eyes, turning them into angry little slits. "Well, why didn't you ask?"

"Wouldn't that seem a little desperate?" the girl dared to say.

"Yeah, you're right," Kiernan admitted as she stroked the girl's hair like she might a smart and loyal puppy. She was correct. Asking would have been utterly gauche, but the bottom line was that Kiernan *was* desperate. She badly needed Eva's project to keep her flailing company afloat. In fact, wooing Eva was the only reason she was having such a lavish cocktail party. She hadn't even finalized the date until LaTeesha had it cleared with Eva's schedule through the woman's secretary. Since the two women had met at the museum event, Kiernan had phoned the socialite twice, and each time the woman was off at an event and was unable to talk. That was when Kiernan got the bright idea to host a party at the penthouse, enabling her to pin Eva in a room for at least an hour and show off her own impressive home.

Bored with having the attention of such an unworthy audience as LaTeesha, Kiernan stubbed out her cigarette and sashayed into the master suite, where she found her hubby relaxing on the silk damask chaise longue with his head buried in the business section of the *Wall Street Journal*. He was oblivious to the ruckus going on throughout the rest of house. She walked over to him and yanked the paper down below his face.

There sat Taylor Hudson, wearing a most perturbed expression. "What is your problem?"

"Well, let's start with the fact that we are having a party in less than an hour, and all you can do is lie here with your head buried in the newspaper."

"Let's correct that. *You* are having a party here in an hour," he said, shaking the paper out and repositioning it in front of his face. She hadn't even mentioned it to him until two days ago, then insisted that he pay all the vendors.

"What are you saying? That you won't be here?" She suddenly looked stricken. He had to be there. Being married to a handsome investment banker was part of her designer package. People would begin to talk if he didn't show up. At the moment, it was of no consequence that their relationship was doomed. All that mattered to her was that it appeared in order to others.

"Kiernan, this is your show. Not mine." He was still pissed at her for the tantrum she'd thrown when he came in from dinner the night before.

After an exhausting night out entertaining clients, he had walked in to find Kiernan sprawled out on the living room couch, sucking down a cocktail that clearly wasn't her first. She lit into him, accusing him for the umpteenth time of having an affair, which was richly ironic to him, since before he met Brooke, an affair had been the farthest thing from his mind. And now that a relationship with her was all he could think about she wouldn't even take his phone calls. He'd called countless times, both at her home and at her office, but to no avail. He'd sent several bouquets of flowers and many boxes of Belgian chocolates, but had yet to get any response besides the "She's unavailable" that he got from her assistant, and her voice-mail message that he got at her home or on her cell phone. She was obviously screening her calls, and he'd been successfully

screened out. He was at a loss about what to do. His better judgment told him to move on, but the more he tried to put her out
of his mind, the more vivid his images of her became. He felt
like a schoolboy with a crush. As maddening as it was, it was
also refreshing. Taylor couldn't remember the last time he'd felt
so completely attracted to a woman. If only he could get her to
talk to him. He had to convince her that he was really getting a
divorce; in fact, he was meeting with his attorney and friend,
Max, this week to discuss it. He only regretted that he'd waited
so long to do it.

Kiernan dropped down to his side, resting her arms on his
legs. "Taylor, please. You've got to make an appearance. Otherwise I'll look like a complete fool. All this will be for nothing,"
she pleaded. "Besides, Eduard and Emily are coming." Eduard
was the president of Taylor's investment firm, and his direct
boss.

He put the paper down and looked at her cynically. "Kiernan, why are you doing this?" When she started to open her
mouth he stopped her, fearing a lie. "The truth."

"For business," she said. "There's an account that I'm trying
to land with a New York socialite. If I get the contract to decorate her town house, it would mean a slew of A-list referrals,
and I really need this business." She stopped short of telling him
just how desperately she needed it.

Taylor looked at her as though trying to see through the
shield of lies, hoping to get a glimpse of the truth. Why hadn't
she told him before now that she was inviting his boss, Eduard?
He realized that he'd best stick around to protect his future,
since Kiernan was turning into such a loose cannon that it was
crucial he be there to monitor her aim. Something else bothered
him. He of all people understood going after business—he often
courted potential investors—but what he didn't understand was
why she suddenly reeked of desperation. She was acting as
though she were on her last dime. "I'll make an appearance, but

I can't be up all night, I have an early breakfast meeting, and a stack of papers that I have to go through."

This seemed to satisfy her. The most important thing to Kiernan was that he be present when Eva showed up. And she knew from experience that having Taylor on her arm was definitely impressive, even though lately it was more for show than anything else. She could feel him pulling away from her each day, which reminded her of her next problem.

Though Kiernan hadn't gotten the file cabinet open yet, she had rummaged through every other inch of the apartment, trawling for evidence, but hadn't found any proof of an indiscretion. There had to be someone else; she had only to figure out who the bitch was. She'd be damned if she'd stand idly by and watch him and some floozy waltz away with what should be her money. No, she had to find out who the slut was, quick and in a hurry, so she could prove adultery. Then all bets were off; half of his money would take up new residence—in her pocket. That was certainly one way to soothe a broken heart, with a nice, thick wad of cold, hard cash.

She stood up and headed into her room-sized boudoir, closing the door behind her. Taylor's head was already buried back into his paper. After perusing her assortment of hostess-appropriate cocktail dresses, she settled on a teal green Valentino number, which she accented with four strands of pearls, Coco Chanel style, before stepping into a pair of jewel-encrusted mules. She looked every inch the rich New York socialite herself. If only she felt as good as the designer garb made her look. But she could fix that too.

She dug deep into her lingerie drawer and pulled out a magenta silk drawstring pouch, opening it to reveal a myriad of multicolored pills of various sizes. It was a virtual pharmaceutical candy store. Using the long nail of her first finger, she stirred the little jewels around and around, like a bartender mixing up a specialty cocktail, deciding which combination was best suited for her happy-and-gracious-hostess-meets-deal-closer mood. Ultimately she swallowed a Zoloft and an Ativan, washing them both down with a glass of white Bordeaux, which she poured from the private bar that she kept behind wood paneling in the elaborately decorated dressing room.

By the time she finished her hair and makeup, Kiernan was floating on a thick, lofty cloud, feeling as though she could conquer the world single-handedly. She swooped back into the living room with swaths of the teal fabric sailing in her wake, and a cloud of Eau du Soir trailing behind it. After ordering the pianist to "get to playin' " and lighting fires under the caterer, the bartender, and LaTeesha, she helped herself to another glass of white wine to finish taking the edge off.

In short order her guests began to arrive, all dressed elegantly and decked out in cocktail-hour jewels, which pleased Kiernan. It was important to her that people made an effort to impress her. She welcomed them all with her most effervescent, drug-induced personality: eyes sparkling, teeth gleaming, and lips perpetually set for the quick double air kiss. Within half an hour the glass-walled room was full of fashionistas—gay, straight, male, female, and those in transit—publishing mavens, journalists, artists, and even the occasional Wall Streeter. All were sipping from delicate leaded crystal, nibbling on caviar toast points and other assorted delicacies, and eagerly gobbling up the latest gossip as they watched the brilliant sunset over the East River.

"Darrrling, did you hear about Mimi's latest face-lift? I hear she's officially reached that one-too-many mark. It's something akin to Michael Jackson meets Jocelyn Wildenstein." The deliverer of these tidings shuddered in fright to add theatrics to the story. "A real train wreck . . ."

"Don't tell her I told you, but I heard that Lita has been servicing her chauffeur lately, rather than the other way around. Brings new meaning to the term 'stretch limo,' wouldn't you say? Ah-ha-ha-ha."

"Great party, but where is Kiernan's handsome hubby? I hear he is a dreamboat."

Kiernan reveled in the buzz generated by a roomful of social animals, all in heat. As she jumped merrily from one social pod to another, bullshitting and glad-handing the whole way, it still amazed her that she, a little black girl from Oklahoma, had risen to such a lofty status on New York's social ladder. The dizzying height both excited and scared the hell out of her. Her fear was based on the steepness of any potential slipup. The execution of her skilled performance was like walking a tightrope strung high across Madison Square Garden, with the spotlight amplifying her every move, while thousands of pairs of eyes looked on. Just one misstep or tiny stumble and she could be facing wholesale embarrassment—or worse yet, devastation. The pills helped steady her nerve-racking climb, enabling her to navigate safely from one side to the other, high above the fray of reality. They also helped her cope with knowing that while a roomful of millionaires milled about her penthouse eating Beluga caviar and drinking French champagne, she had only a little over three thousand dollars left to her very name, which wouldn't pay the monthly floral bills alone for most of her guests, and all of her credit cards were now maxed out.

Kiernan had discovered this yesterday when she was humiliated in Barneys, the chicest of chic boutiques. The surly salesclerk had gleefully told her that her card had been declined. Why, oh, why should she be in such a fix when her hubby was one of the best investment bankers on Wall Street? But the time had long passed when he might have shared his finances. Their relationship had run ashore, causing enough permanent damage to ensure that it would never again set sail on the high seas, so any money she got from him would have to be awarded in a court of law. She had to find the evidence in order to get her fair share, but meanwhile she had to land this job with Eva. Incidentally, where the hell was she anyway? Kiernan wondered.

"Excuse me." Kiernan cut off a gushing gay dress designer in midsentence and headed off in search of LaTeesha.

She found her staring at the guests and the apartment in unabashed awe.

Never had the girl seen a room so lavish that wasn't either in a hotel, on TV, or in a magazine, and to think that a black person actually lived here.

"LaTeesha, where the hell is Eva?"

LaTeesha was snapped out of her reverie. "She isn't here yet?" she answered, deciding it was best under the circumstances to play stupid.

"If she were here, do you honestly think I'd be wasting my time in here talking to you?"

"Kiernan, enough already." Taylor had just come through the serving doors into the kitchen, looking ravishing in an Italian-cut blazer, crisp open-collared shirt, flat-front pants, and a pair of black suede Gucci lounging loafers. He turned to address LaTeesha, who was as much in awe of him as she was of the apartment. "LaTeesha, how are you?" he asked.

LaTeesha's heart almost stopped at the sight of him. He was gorgeous and debonair, and seemed like a really nice man. She'd met him only briefly once before, when she and Kiernan had swung by his office to pick up some papers. She wanted to say something smart and sophisticated to him, but found herself unable to form a string of words, so she simply said, "I'm fine."

"Have a good night," he said, before taking a glaring Kiernan by the arm and leading her away from the young girl. Passing through the living room, they approached a group of guests who parted their ranks to include the host and hostess in their gossipy little circle, but before they closed it, Kiernan spied Eva, who'd just arrived. She made a beeline for the woman, dragging a startled Taylor along with her. "Eva, darling, how are you?" she crooned. The bitter taste from the unpleasant encounter in the kitchen had been swallowed whole, and replaced with a thick dose of honey.

"I couldn't be better," the glamour puss answered, swinging her long blond hair out behind her as if to emphasize the point. Eva dripped with money, both old and new. One could tell from a glance that she and Harry Winston were old friends.

Kiernan stuck out her chest proudly and gestured toward Taylor, who she was thankful was still on her arm. "Let me introduce you to my—"

"Oh, don't bother," Eva said, fixing Taylor with a sexy look. "We are already very well acquainted." Though Eva was a flirt by nature, and generally meant nothing by it, the insinuation of something salacious hung heavy in the air.

To her credit, Kiernan absorbed the shock and kept right on rolling along. "Oh, really, now? And how might that be?" She studied Taylor carefully, resisting the urge to scratch both his eyes out of his head.

"We met last month to discuss the Guggenheim Museum's investment account," Taylor said matter-of-factly, as he kissed Eva's upturned cheek. "The firm has handled it for years now."

Kiernan turned to Eva. "Why didn't you tell me you knew my husband?"

"Who's to say I knew he was your husband? After all, you two do use different last names. Makes things a little more complicated, wouldn't you say?" she drawled, looping her arm through Taylor's. She turned to face him directly. "Why don't you get a girl a drink? I'm feeling like hard liquor tonight; maybe a sidecar would quench my thirst." With that, she walked arm in arm with him, away from his wife and in the direction of the bar, chatting and smiling every step of the way.

Kiernan stood in place, boiling. She was furious at Taylor for letting that hussy play him like a string quartet, and she could spit nails at Ms. Hussy for being so blatantly in heat. And she was no less angry at herself for simply standing by watching the humiliating fiasco as though it were an episode of *Days of Our Lives*. Her lips pursed as her eyes darted in their direction, stealing a sly glimpse of the twosome. Taylor was obviously taken with some clever witticism that Eva had uttered, for he was laughing full throttle, head thrown way back, his Adam's apple bobbing up and down freely, while Ms. Hussy coyly rubbed his firm biceps and continued her cacophony of sweet nothings very close to his earlobe. When was the last time Taylor had laughed at anything she'd said? The whole thing was unseemly and humiliating; and to make matters worse, everyone in the room had witnessed it.

Kiernan felt physically ill. To think that she had gone to so much trouble to drag Taylor—who was soooo busy—out into the party, and who got to showboat him but Eva Rupert? The same Eva who'd yet to utter a single word about hiring Kiernan. Suddenly the tightrope that Kiernan walked masterfully seemed to sway a tad, throwing her off-kilter. She exited the room and swept through the master suite and into the boudoir in search of her little magenta bag. This was obviously going to be a very long night.

When she reemerged fifteen minutes later, she bumped right into Eduard, who she'd forgotten would be there.

"Kiernan, my dear, what a wonderful party." Eduard took her hand and kissed the back of it.

If she'd been capable of swooning without hitting the floor, she might have done so, and came perilously close, helped by the combination of pharmaceuticals and alcohol.

"Eduard, I'm so glad you could come," she replied, latching on to his arm to be escorted through the room. Her hold was as much for balance as it was to make an impression, being seen with the distinguished white-haired gentleman. Not to mention that it would serve Taylor right to see her cozied up to his boss after his distasteful display with that tramp Eva. "Is Emily with you?"

"No, I'm afraid I'm alone tonight. She had a previous engagement."

"Sorry to hear that," Keirnan lied. "Come. Let me get you a

drink. What would you like?" she asked, giving him her most seductive look.

"What about something spicy and wet?"

She looked up suddenly and caught a hint of twinkle in his blue eyes. If she didn't know better, she would swear he was flirting with her. "How about a single-malt scotch?"

"That sounds perfect."

They headed toward the bar with his hand resting in the small of her back. What exactly did he have in mind? she wondered. As rich as he was he could have just about anything he wanted; besides, she'd always liked that Sean Connery look, distinguished with a dash of danger.

Once they had drinks in hand and found a cozy nook, nestled away from the fray of other guests, Kiernan stepped closer, allowing her breasts to tease his forearm. When he moved it back and forth it created a delicious friction, and she felt herself go moist below. She barely stopped a moan from escaping her throat. It had been so long since she'd had sex that the feeling caught her by surprise. "I guess it is time that we got to know each other better," she said, all the while making it clear that if he wanted to, they could get to know each other *very* well indeed.

"We'd better join the others," he said, taking her elbow and guiding her toward the main room. They ran into Taylor, who seemed to be looking for someone, presumably them—or more accurately, Eduard.

"There you are," he said, reaching to shake Eduard's hand. "I heard that you had arrived. I trust that Kiernan's been taking good care of you?"

"Indeed she has," he said, raising his drink. "If you'll excuse us," he said to Kiernan, "I wouldn't want to bore you with office talk."

"Why, certainly." She smiled conspiratorially. "I'll attend to my other guests."

Eduard and Taylor strolled toward the window overlooking

the city, both holding drinks, looking like masters of the universe. "I'm really glad that Kiernan invited me, because I needed to talk to you about something very important."

"Oh. And what might that be?" Taylor asked.

"I'll just cut right to the chase. I've nominated you for a promotion to partner of the firm."

Taylor was shocked. "Excuse me?"

Eduard smiled. "It's no secret how pleased we've been with your performance over the years, and your expertise in the foreign markets is priceless. And I just think it's about time that we had our first African-American partner."

Taylor bristled at the mention of race. He'd always hoped—perhaps naively—that his performance alone was all that counted. "I'm honored," he said. Like any aggressive and successful banker in a prestigious firm, he'd harbored dreams of one day making partner, but given the blue-blooded, WASPy nature of his firm, he'd never hung his hat on it.

"Let's not celebrate too soon. There are a couple of things that have to be tended to first."

"Oh? What might they be?"

"First of all, the vote will take place at our quarterly meeting next month, so it's very important that you keep your nose clean between now and then. Don't give anyone any excuse not to vote yes."

Taylor nodded in agreement. He knew all too well that some of the board members would be looking for any reason to exclude him.

Eduard rocked softly on the toes of his handcrafted shoes. "And the second has to do with a deal that needs to be done."

"A deal? What kind of deal?" Generally speaking, Taylor and the other investment bankers in the firm structured their own deals, though it wasn't unheard of for one of the partners to assign one under special circumstances. Generally it happened when they were too busy to handle the deal, or it required a special expertise that the junior member might possess.

"There is a consortium out of England. They call themselves Beacon Hill, and they are interested in spreading investments across some of the American biotech and technology firms. This deal would open up significant overseas revenues for the firm that would ultimately be quite lucrative, and because of your expertise in foreign currencies, and the euro in particular, I'd like for you to handle it." He rattled the ice in his highball glass.

Taylor absorbed this information and decided to close the deal right now. "Let me understand. Are you saying that if I close this deal and keep a tight profile that I'll make partner? Is that right?"

"You've got my assurances."

That was good enough for Taylor. Everyone at the firm knew that as senior partner Eduard definitely had enough clout to swing the necessary votes, so his assurance was as good as money in the bank.

The two men shook hands on the deal, then joined the others, who were in full party mode by now. They were tossing back cocktails and champagne as though prohibition were on the way, and freely swapping gossip like valuable trading cards—all, that was, except for Eva, who'd made her exit minutes before Kiernan left Eduard in hot pursuit of her and a check.

10

THE LION'S DEN

The world in which Taylor operated was one of expensive dinners, two-martini lunches, exclusive country clubs, and rich wood-paneled offices. He had grown up in a lower-middle-class family from Hyattsville, Maryland—his mother was a high school principal, and his father a postal worker—planets away from the enormous wealth that his current position gave him access to. There were days when he was still amazed to be included among the "good ol' boys' club," even after fifteen years. It was at those times that he reminded himself that they weren't doing him any favors, and that his membership was a direct function of his near-genius ability with matters of finance. When Taylor was in the fifth grade he'd assumed the household duty of balancing the checkbook; he'd always loved manipulating numbers and the perfect symmetry they represented, an attribute not always applicable to life.

He later graduated from Columbia University magna cum laude, with master's degrees in both finance and economics, and upon graduation began his career as a stock trader at one of New York City's small investment firms. Soon he caught the attention of Eduard Wentworth II, the senior partner at Mayer, Jones, and Wentworth. Now, fifteen years and billions of dollars in lucrative deals later, Taylor was finally being invited into the inner sanctum of the prestigious old-money firm. Now it was only a matter of time before he would be a bona fide, card-carrying member.

The only downside to his promotion was that he'd need to wait until after the board meeting and vote before he filed for divorce. Based on Eduard's warning, a nasty divorce could potentially derail his nomination. Given Kiernan's antics, he'd have to believe that nasty was certainly possible, which would give some of the more conservative members just the stockpile of ammunition they'd need to shoot him down. But fortunately the quarterly meeting was only weeks away.

His mother had tried to warn him not to marry Kiernan to begin with. She always said, "There's something that's just not quite right about that girl." He'd ignored her protests, knowing that she never thought any girl was good enough for her only son. She always told him that he was special, and though she loved her daughter, they both knew he was her favorite, which explained why he in turned doted on Jennifer to make up the difference. After meeting Kiernan and hearing about her orphaned childhood, he now realized, part of his initial draw to her was a result of that same streak of sympathy.

She was also very charming back then. On their first date she invited him to a picnic on the beach in the Hamptons. It was a production straight out of one of Martha Stewart's handbooks: antique linen napkins, crystal flutes filled with a crisp rosé champagne, homemade egg-salad sandwiches, fresh fruit, an assortment of cheeses, chocolate, and pâté de foie gras. They stuffed themselves while listening to Ella Fitzgerald and later waded in the cool water before building an impressive interior designer's version of a sandcastle, with shells, twigs, and algae for adornment. They discussed everything from New York politics and the national health care crisis to global warming. When they got around to discussing their families, she told him she was an only child and had been orphaned when her parents were killed during a charter plane crash while on vacation in

Fiji. Though she had money from two lucrative life-insurance policies, that was all she had left, so there was a sad vulnerability in her that made him want to protect her from the rest of the world.

After they'd been dating six months Kiernan told him she was pregnant, and naturally Taylor's sense of duty led him straight down the aisle to the altar. They were wed in a civil ceremony, with no one in attendance except for Max. A month later Kiernan called his office in midafternoon, frantic; she'd had a miscarriage. The other shoe really fell when he was going through paperwork from his medical benefits carrier and didn't see any mention of the gynecological visits she claimed to have been making. He realized that she'd never been pregnant at all. Of course, she insisted that she thought she was at first and didn't know until after they got married that she wasn't, and by then it was too late. But every time he thought about the faked morning sickness and assorted lies about doctor visits, he knew that he'd never completely trust her again, which changed the tone of their relationship forever. That was when her mood swings began. Oftentimes he looked at her and wondered out loud, "How the hell did I end up with her for a wife?" It almost seemed like a bad dream, except that when he woke up, she was right there beside him.

The phone rang, interrupting his thoughts. "Mr. Wentworth would like to see you now," Janice, his secretary, said.

This was just the call he'd been waiting for all morning. "Tell him I'll be right there." He stood up, slid into his suit jacket, grabbed his portfolio, and headed out the door to a private elevator for the ride up to the company's top floor.

Once he was there, the smell of money was intoxicating. From the original oil paintings and crystal chandeliers to the rich silk wallpaper, the executive suites were a shrine to the twin gods of power and prestige. Eduard's male assistant–butler, Stuart, met Taylor just as his foot hit the thickly napped carpet. No one, except for partners, was allowed to wander these hallowed halls unescorted. "If you'll follow me, Mr. Hudson, I'll take you right in to see him."

Taylor smiled discreetly as he walked behind Stuart. There was only one deal between him and his partnership, and only the partnership between him and a divorce, and only a divorce—hopefully—between him and Brooke.

Stuart rapped on one of the huge double oak doors before turning a heavy brass handle to gain entrance. Behind a massive mahogany desk sat Eduard like a king atop his throne. "Come in, Taylor." His voice boomed across the spacious room. "It's good to see you." His smile was as perfect as any actor's in Hollywood, and his deep tan was the kind acquired only under a tropical sun.

"How are you, sir?" Taylor greeted him as he shook the man's pillow-soft hand. A fifty-thousand-dollar Audemars Piquet watch peeked out from under his custom-tailored, French-cuffed shirt.

"If I were any better the Democrats would pass a law against it." He laughed heartily at his own humor, which Taylor didn't find very funny at all but chose to ignore. Eduard was the kind of rich man who saw nothing morally or economically wrong with men, women, and children in his own city starving while he spent enough on one watch to support a family of four for a year. "Come, have a seat," he said, gesturing to a cove of richly upholstered chairs nestled near a fireplace that was large enough for Taylor to stand inside.

Eduard reached into a silver box on the coffee table, extracted a Cuban cigar, and began rolling the thick shaft slowly between his fingers as he took a seat. "Care for a smoke?"

"No, thanks," Taylor said. He pulled his pants up a tad before sitting and resting his ankle on his knee.

"About this deal," Eduard began, getting right to the point. "As I said before, there's a consortium of English chaps with loads of money who're interested in entering the American market in a big way."

"Given the strength of the pound, why bother?" Taylor asked. The British currency, a holdout from the unified European conversion to the euro, had remained strong, while the dollar had been on a long-term slide.

"Let's just say they are interested in global diversification."

"Who exactly are they?"

"As I said, they are a consortium of individuals formed to hedge losses and retain anonymity."

"Have we done business with them in the past?"

"We haven't been so fortunate, but thanks to a few strong connections they've agreed to give us this shot."

"Interesting." Taylor stroked his chin thoughtfully.

"They are very unlike us Americans, who believe in publicizing our weath at every opportunity."

Yeah, like buying fifty-thousand-dollar watches, Taylor thought. "How did you come across them?" he asked.

"One of the principals, Maurice Worthington, was an exchange student from Oxford when I attended Princeton. So I've known him for decades. He'll be your contact, and he's waiting for your call. Meanwhile, I'll have Stuart type up my notes in this file and then get it to you right away," he explained as he gestured to a folder lying on the table between them.

"As soon as I get it, I'll start." Taylor edged forward in his chair, preparing to leave. "Any suggestions for background or reference checks in London?" Though he was the in-house expert on foreign currency, he'd yet to do a deal that originated in London.

"No need to bother," Eduard said. "Maurice is a close personal friend whom I'd vouch for anyday." As Taylor stood to leave he added, "This one is very important, not only for you and your promotion, but for the firm as well, so be sure to tie up all loose ends."

"Consider it done," Taylor said as he headed for the door.

* * *

"Man, you're lookin' good," Max said as he met Taylor at Asiate at the Mandarin Oriental in the Time Warner building.

"You don't look too bad yourself for an old man," Taylor teased. Max was a year older. When they were kids he never let Taylor forget it, and now Taylor never let him forget it.

"Let's hit the courts and see who's older," Max challenged. They hugged each other with clasped fists, the way guys who really liked each other but couldn't show it publicly did.

Once they were seated at a window table with an expansive thirty-fifth-floor view and had ordered glasses of Courvoisier, Max leaned forward with his elbows on the table. "So what's up with you? You know I get nervous when you have your secretary call to set up lunch. That tells me that it's business, and the lawyer in me starts to worry about you."

Taylor smiled. Max always had his back. "It's nothing too heavy."

"Well, don't keep me in suspense." He leaned back in his chair and crossed his arms, lawyer-style.

"I want a divorce, Max."

The other man nearly spit his drink out of his mouth. "It's about time," he finally sputtered. When Taylor looked at him strangely, he added, "I know that's not very professional of me, but I never thought Kiernan was the one for you, pregnant or not. There was just something not quite right about her."

"There you go, sounding like my mother."

"Hey, Ma Hudson didn't live to be eighty by being stupid."

Taylor leaned back in his chair. "So how much is this going to cost me?"

Max chuckled. "Always the money man."

"It's not that. I really just want out of it, but I also don't want to lose my shirt in the process."

"Since you were smart enough to follow my advice about the prenup and there're no kids, no jointly owned property, or allegations of affairs, it shouldn't be bad at all." He thought again, setting his glass down. "There *aren't* any allegations of affairs, are there?"

"Kiernan is so paranoid that there have been allegations since the marriage hit the skids, but no, I haven't been involved with anyone," he said regretfully, as he thought again about Brooke.

Max knew him all too well. "What *aren't* you telling me?"

Taylor shook his head and smiled. He should have known better than ever to try keeping anything from Max, so he told him all about Brooke, starting with their accidental meeting in the elevator, followed by their two dates, and how she unceremoniously dumped him the minute he told her he was married.

"She sounds like a smart girl to me."

"Hey, whose side are you on?" Taylor asked.

"All kidding aside, my best advice to you is not to get caught with anyone, because *then* it may cost you."

Taylor nodded his head. "Okay."

"One more thing."

"What is it?"

"Does she have any friends?"

Taylor sighed. "Some things never change."

"But fortunately for you, others do."

11

A PERFECT WORLD

The constant pretending drained Kiernan little by little, like sap slowly seeping through the bark of an old maple tree. Her problems stemmed from the fact that her entire existence was one big, fat lie. Her first few tales starting out were just blips on the radar, though in time they'd fed on one another and grown, taking on a life of their own. In her fantasy world, she was the perfect wife, with the perfect husband, the perfect career, and of course, the perfect home. What woman wouldn't want to be married to a successful investment banker, live on Central Park West, and decorate lavish homes for a living? In truth, she was more of a large stately tree that fell like chopped timber during a storm—seemingly proud and stable on the outside, but rotten to the core and falling apart underneath it all. The unrest brewing in her life now had all of the elements for a serious storm: a shaky marriage, a disintegrating business, and self-esteem that was withering daily.

Kiernan looked up from the bank statement she'd been lamenting to find LaTeesha standing just outside her office. "There's a call for you on line one."

Though she liked having LaTeesha around, she hated the way the girl seemed to lurk like a mouse leery of a hungry cat—or worse, as though she were studying Kiernan's every move. An acquaintance and board member with Big Brothers, Big Sisters had suggested she hire her, and back then Kiernan had seen it as a way to get in good with the New York charity scene. And of course it was cheap labor, since she worked the girl like a slave for nearly minimum wage. "Who is it?" she snapped, taking a drag from her cigarette.

"A Ms. Whitman from American Express." LaTeesha was proud that she'd remembered to ask the caller her name and the company that she worked for.

Kiernan expelled a puff of air and rolled her eyes skyward in exasperation. This was the third call from the woman this week. She was relentless and annoying in the way only pit bulls and bill collectors knew how to be. With AmEx and Citibank at her door she felt like a fox with a slim head start on a ravenous pack of hounds. She didn't need to pick up the phone to know what Ms. Whitman wanted; that was the easy part, since Kiernan was close to ninety days past due on her platinum card, and facing a daunting balance of twenty-three thousand dollars. The hard part was figuring out how to pay it.

Since she didn't have the answer to that particular question, there was no need to upset herself further by actually having to speak to the woman. "Tell her I'm not here," she mumbled. It was so embarrassing for her to be seen by lowly LaTeesha squirming like bait caught on a fisherman's hook.

Now LaTeesha was confused. "But I already told her that you were."

"Well, I suggest you tell her you were wrong." Kiernan returned her attention to the bleak bank records, leaving a frazzled LaTeesha to handle the persistent collection representative herself.

According to those papers, her personal checking account was overdrawn by over four thousand dollars, and what remained of her savings account hovered under five grand. Even worse, all of her bills were behind, including the office lease.

Lately she'd even taken to coming into the loft space from a side entrance, hoping not to run into the building's pesky landlord.

Unfortunately, the real world was sticking its nose where it didn't belong, threatening to poke holes into the carefully constructed fairy tale that she'd painstakingly built. It was all quite depressing really, not to mention humiliating. The stress made it hard for her to even breathe.

Call it a sixth sense, a funny feeling—anything but paranoia—but Kiernan also knew without question that there was something different about her husband lately. Never mind the affair that she was sure he'd been having; whatever was going on now was much more dangerous than a few romps in the hay. In her lucid moments she'd always known that their marriage had deteriorated into a sad farce that she was helpless to do anything about, except to witness it the way one might watch a bad movie. Even Taylor seemed to accept it as their private doom, resigned to his fate in the way one who stuttered accepted it as a way of life. But lately her finely honed sense of danger had detected a shifting of the landscape, small, yet seismic enough for her to register its change. It seemed to her that the very sight, sound, and smell of her was too much for him to bear, as though revulsion had usurped his customary acquiescence.

What if *he* left *her*? She'd never really considered that before now. She figured that when the time was right, she'd leave him and take with her what she wanted, especially after she had proof of his affair, which was her only detour around the prenup that she'd signed. But what if she never got proof—and worse, what if he left her instead, and without any money?

LaTeesha once more interrupted her thoughts. "Eva just called." This time she only poked her head in the door.

The name beckoned her like a bright light piercing through the darkness. She lunged for the phone. "Put her through."

An apprehensive look drifted across the girl's features. "I just told her you weren't here."

Kiernan rolled her eyes and pounded the desk with her balled fist. "You did what?" How could anyone be that stupid? She wanted to get up and slap the dumb, stunned expression off La-Teesha's face.

The girl looked genuinely puzzled. "You said just a few minutes ago that you weren't here."

"Were you born stupid, or was it something that you learned?"

LaTeesha's hurt feelings were visible all over her face. She was close to tears. "I'm sorry."

"So am I. I'm sorry I ever hired you."

"I promise it won't happen again," LaTeesha said, even though she still wasn't completely sure what she'd done wrong. All she could think of was having to explain to her probation officer that she'd gotten fired.

"Just get her back on the phone," Kiernan barked, grinding out a cigarette stub in a crystal ashtray. "Now!" How did I end up with such a dumb, dim-witted assistant? Favor or not, I need to get rid of that girl, Kiernan thought, but in the back of her mind she knew that she wouldn't. She could barely afford to pay her, and certainly wouldn't be able to pay anyone else. Because of LaTeesha's dire circumstances she also knew that she could treat the girl like dirt and get away with it.

She'd been desperately trying to catch up with Eva for over two weeks now. To her dismay, after Eva had finished flirting shamelessly with her husband, she'd left Kiernan's cocktail party, talking about another, more important function that she had to get to. Now, just when the woman finally decided to return a phone call, Kiernan's stupid-ass assistant told her she wasn't in. How was that for perpetuating bad luck? She couldn't help but laugh at it, but the sound came out more like a raving cackle.

Eva was her one-way ticket out of her calamitous financial nightmare. If she could just land the commission, she could begin repairing the torn pieces of her life. "Eva! Darling, how are you?" she cooed once the call was put through. Sweetness dripped from her voice. Over the phone line, one would never have known how deeply troubled she was—Kiernan sounded as if life were, in fact, a walk in the park. Central Park, that was.

Eva got right to the point. "I was just returning your call."

"Yes, of course. I wanted to make an appointment to come by and look at your place. As we discussed, I'd like to give you a proposal for the interior design work." She hated herself for sounding so cloying and desperate, but a string of creditor calls sometimes had that effect on a girl.

"Sure." Not exactly a resounding affirmation, but it would do. "How does your schedule look?"

"Why don't you come by Friday at, say, one o'clock," the woman tossed out absently. She sounded distant, as though she were busy at work, maybe filing her nails—much more interested in the state of her cuticles. Except that women like Eva didn't file their own nails, nor tend to their own cuticles.

"Great. I'll see you then." Kiernan hung up the phone feeling a touch better, though her nerves still felt raw and exposed, as if a coarse grade of sandpaper had been brusquely rubbed across them. In any regard, it was nothing that a couple of Prozac wouldn't take care of, she thought as she reached for her handbag to dig out her pillbox.

After work LaTeesha took the subway home to the Bronx, and worlds away from Kiernan's chic downtown habitat. When she walked in the front door of her family's two-bedroom apartment, it was indeed like landing on another planet. Instead of a slick art-deco decor, theirs could best be described as thrift-store survival. As far as LaTeesha knew, they'd never had a brand-new piece of furniture. Instead of high-gloss hardwood, the floors were covered in a dingy linoleum that bore decades of grimy buildup, so much that the residents could only guess at the original color. Bare bulbs cast a depressed film of light over dirty walls, and the air smelled perpetually of Hamburger Helper, regardless of what had been cooked in the last seventy-two hours.

As grateful as LaTeesha was for the opportunity to see how the other half lived, there were times when she would rather not have known. Sometimes ignorance was bliss. The spit-polished shine of Kiernan's world served only to illuminate the bleakness of her own. In fact, it wasn't until recently that she realized that she and her family were very poor. Prior to that she had assumed that they lived pretty much like everyone else; only now did she understand the depressing reality that everyone else she knew was also poor. It made her sad, as if her innocence had been robbed and replaced by a harsh reality. It was sad to her that some people had so much, that some things meant nothing to them, while others had so little that most things meant the world, like the sight of a refrigerator full of food. She didn't know which world she resented most: her own, or the one that Kiernan lived in.

She'd learned with Kiernan that things ran hot and cold, feast or famine. One day she'd treat her to lunch at the fanciest restaurant in the city, and the next she barked like a guard dog if LaTeesha took a Hershey's Kiss from the crystal bowl in the foyer. Today was a famine; LaTeesha hadn't eaten since she left the apartment that morning. At minimum wage she barely made enough money to pay for her daily commute and her share of the household bills, let alone buy lunch at the trendy and expensive restaurants in SoHo.

She dropped her bag on the kitchen table and headed straight to the fridge. The icebox contained slim pickings; there were a few slices of bologna, some half-molded cheese, half a carton of sour milk, a few dried-out condiments, and not much else. LaTeesha took out a loaf of bread, slathered mayo and mustard on two slices, and sandwiched a piece of pale bologna between them. Not quite the Plaza, but it would have to do. From the sound of the TV coming from the bedroom, she deduced that her mother was in another of her bed-confining depressions.

Just as she was taking her first bite, her mother's voice called out to her from the back bedroom. "LaTeesha?"

She often wondered why she always had to scream her name. Why couldn't she just say it? It wasn't as if they lived in some spacious apartment where the walls weren't paper-thin. "Yes, ma'am?"

"That probation officer of yours called here today." She said this in an accusatory tone, as if it were an inconvenience to her that he'd called. LaTeesha's arrest was more of an annoyance to her mother than anything else. Out of seven kids, three were already in jail, for assorted offenses, but her mother figured her success rate wasn't too bad. It was better than many of the other families in the projects.

LaTeesha immediately tensed up. Why was he calling her at home? She'd kept all of her appointments and done everything she was supposed to. Fear gripped her chest, because it could only be bad news. Nobody's probation officer ever called with good news. She couldn't help but think of Lenora, a woman down the block who neighbors said used to be a looker, but you'd never know it now. She looked like death warmed over. They said that she'd gone to jail initially for selling drugs for some no-good man, and by the time she came out three years later, she was hooked on them herself and started working the streets to feed her habit. She was so bad off now that she couldn't even give it away. Just the thought of Lenora was enough to scare LaTeesha straight for life, and that was all she could think of when they had hauled her downtown after her arrest.

After pacing the floor for five minutes she finally found the courage to call her probation officer at the number she found scrawled on the back of an envelope. She took a deep breath and dialed the number. "Hello, Mr. Perkins, this is LaTeesha."

"I was calling to reschedule our appointment tomorrow morning."

She had wrongly assumed the worst. "Oh, no problem, Mr. Perkins," she said, finally exhaling.

"How is Wednesday at eight?"

"That's fine, sir."

She was about to say good-bye when he said, "Oh, by the way, would you tell your employer that I'll be calling this week to do a follow-up report?"

She began to pace. "A follow-up report?"

"Yes, I need to complete two with your employer before your probation period is up." When she was silent, he said, "You do still work there, don't you?" For the first time menace entered his voice.

"Yes, sir. I do."

"Good. Then let's keep it that way." And he hung up.

LaTeesha sank onto one of the flimsy vinyl-covered kitchen chairs, suddenly losing her appetite. Though she had no intention of leaving her job, the call to Kiernan worried her. The woman was so unpredictable, she could either be sugar and spice, or sour as spoiled vinegar, depending on what, exactly, LaTeesha still didn't know. She knew why her mother was troubled and could hardly get out of bed some days, but for the life of her she couldn't figure out why someone with everything in the world, including a rich and handsome husband, could be so mad sometimes. She just prayed that her probation officer called when Kiernan was in one of her good moods.

12

HAVE PATIENTS

"So who's the secret lover?" Joie asked.

Brooke grabbed her coat off the coatrack. "What are you talking about?"

"The mini garden here," Joie answered, pointing to an enormous vase of beautiful exotic flowers that were almost as large as the coffee table on which they sat.

"Oh, those," Brooke huffed. "I asked André to get rid of them," she said, eyeing him, "but he insists on keeping them around." Taylor had sent yet another beautiful bouquet of flowers. It had been over a month since she had walked out of the restaurant and his life, but he'd still refused to give up.

"Well, if you don't appreciate beauty, I certainly do," he retorted.

She rolled her eyes. "It's not the flowers that I have a problem with," she mumbled under her breath as she and Joie left the office and headed to lunch.

Joie shook her head. "You know, you need to loosen up."

Brooke looked straight ahead as they walked toward Madison Avenue, barely acknowledging the comment. "I'm just fine."

"I know what you need," Joie said, skipping backward in front of Brooke.

"Oh, and what's that?"

"The one thing that you are sure not to get, the way you carry on: laid."

"Joie, sex isn't the answer to everything."

"Maybe not, but neither is celibacy." She turned around and continued walking alongside Brooke.

"Sex isn't exactly something that you give away like, say, a raffle ticket," Brooke said, tossing her hands in the air to emphasize her point. "At least not for most of us," she finished, giving Joie a knowing look.

They were walking up Madison Avenue on the way to Amaranth, a quaint Italian restaurant on Sixty-first between Madison and Fifth Avenues. It was a beautiful autumn day, the perfect afternoon to sit outside of the hip sidewalk café, have a light lunch, and people-watch. "Suit yourself," Joie said, swinging her dreads. "I certainly do."

"I can't deny that."

Just as they walked up to the café a nattily dressed gay couple were abandoning a prime outdoor table. Joie made a dash for it, nearly butting heads with an attractive Italian guy who had the same idea. "Excuse me," he said in a very sexy accent.

"Excuse *me*," Joie answered, giving eyes as good as she was getting them. She gave him the once-over and immediately decided that she liked what she saw.

"Of course, I would be a gentleman and let you have the table, but then I might not have the pleasure of talking to you." He was a smooth one, from the sexy, glazed-over hood of his eyes, to the thick, perfectly knotted tie that sat between his widespread collar. The man knew how to dress and was probably just as adept at undressing.

"Who said that I liked gentlemen?" Joie winked at him, enjoying the look of surprise her response garnered.

Brooke shook her head. Joie was a one-woman episode of *Sex and the City*. She had Carrie, Samantha, Charlotte, and Miranda beat by a long shot. Within minutes the two soon-to-be lovers were seated side by side, huddling like littermates. When the waiter came over for their drink orders, Casanova took charge and ordered a round of Bellinis for the table. While he and Joie fantasized about the journey from the table to the bedroom, Brooke soaked up the warm sun and her thoughts ventured to Taylor Hudson and how great it had felt to be involved with a man, however briefly.

She was sitting there wearing a lazy smile when Joie's voice intruded. "Earth to Brooke, Earth to Brooke."

She looked around and found that Mr. Lover Man was gone. "What happened to your Italian stallion?"

"We're meeting later for a little foreign exchange." She giggled.

"Exchange of what?"

"Don't ask, and I won't tell."

"You are *so* out of control."

"Au contraire, my dear," Joie said, sipping her drink. "Unlike most women, I am very much *in* control. You'll never catch me sitting around waiting on some guy to give me what I want. If I want sex, it's not about 'giving it up.' I go get it." She nodded her head slowly, as if this were the only way to live. And for her it was.

Brooke considered Joie to be an anomaly among women. That was not necessarily a good thing, nor a bad one—just very, very different. Her belief system went against everything that women had ever been taught, from the cradle to the grave. She thought more like a man than any woman, and was the complete polar opposite of Brooke.

"What about Brent?"

She shrugged her shoulders. "What about him?"

Brooke changed tack. "What exactly is it that you want out of a relationship?"

"Who said I wanted a relationship? Maybe I want several."

Brooke took a sip. "There goes an interesting idea," she said sarcastically.

Joie turned to face her. "Listen, it makes perfect sense," she insisted, holding up a finger to stop Brooke's predictable protest. "How could anyone expect another person to give her everything she needs? It's too much pressure." She shrugged. "So why not have several people who, combined, give you everything you want?"

Some forms of logic just weren't worth arguing, so Brooke changed the subject. "Have you ever been in love?"

"Now you're sounding like a shrink."

"I *am* a shrink."

"But you're also a woman."

"Answer my question," Brooke challenged.

"Define love," Joie challenged back.

Brooke thought for a second. "Of course, loving someone and being in love are two different things. And I don't know that there is one concrete description for either, but one way to look at it is that when you love someone, your decisions and feelings are inextricably linked to theirs, and when you are in love, you are connected to that person even when you're alone, like wearing a second skin that fits just right." She sighed as she thought of Taylor. For weeks now she'd been forcing him out of her mind, pretending that their encounters had never happened, but for some reason—maybe it was timing, the flowers, the Italian, or the beautiful day, who knew?—he seemed to be haunting her thoughts today.

Joie watched her carefully, reading her thoughts. "You know, everything doesn't have to be according to some premeditated plan. Don't you ever break your society-imposed rules?"

Brooke bristled. "They aren't 'society-imposed.' They're my own. Not everybody flies by the seat of their pants, landing wherever the wind—or their libido—takes them."

"Ouch." Joie frowned.

Brooke reached out to gently touch her hand. "I'm sorry. I shouldn't have been so judgmental. As a therapist you'd think I'd know better."

"Yeah, but guess what. Everything isn't always by the book." Joie held her gaze with a knowing look.

"You're right. Maybe I'm just more jealous of your lifestyle than I care to admit."

Joie laughed. "Now there's an original thought."

At that moment the sky darkened and opened up as dime-sized drops of rain fell in heavy sheets from the sky. Fortunately the canopy over the restaurant's sidewalk protected them from the onslaught, so they sat there together, as different as night and day, or sunshine and rain, enjoying each other's company and the sight of chicly dressed New Yorkers scampering for cover.

After lunch Brooke headed back to work. When she walked through the door, heading to her office, André stopped her. "Your next appointment is here," he said.

She looked at him, puzzled. "I thought my schedule was clear until three."

"This is an emergency patient."

"Emergency? Who—" She turned to face her office door.

It opened and there stood Taylor. "Brooke, it's me."

She spun on her heel to confront André, who was now sporting a sheepish look.

"It's not his fault," Taylor said. "I insisted."

She glared at André and walked past Taylor into her office, closing the door behind her. "What do you think you're doing, coming here like this?"

"You won't see me or even speak to me any other way, so you left me no choice."

"There's a good reason I didn't want to see you, remember?" She crossed her arms tightly across her chest.

"I do, and in fact, that's why I'm here." When she failed to say anything, he kept talking, taking advantage of the fact that he hadn't been thrown out yet. "Brooke, I'm getting a divorce. I wanted you to know that." He hung his head. "Like I said that night, my marriage has long been over, but I had my head buried in my work and just ignored it. I didn't think about Kiernan—or any other woman, for that matter—until I met you, and now I can't get you out of my mind. Please don't think that I'm doing this as a knee-jerk reaction. I'm simply burying something that's long been dead."

Brooke was speechless; she was completely unprepared for his physical presence. It was much easier to ignore her attraction to him when it was only a figment of her memory, and not in the form of a handsome, sexy man standing inches away from her. "Taylor, I'm happy for you, but it really doesn't have anything to do with me," she told him—and herself.

"But it does. I know I'm not crazy and that you have feelings for me, just as I have them for you. The only thing standing in the way of us is a marriage that's long since been over, unless you're simply too scared to trust yourself," he challenged.

That comment hit home, because deep down she knew that fear was the fertilizer that fed many of her actions, or lack thereof.

"Listen, we can take it slowly. I met with my attorney, who will be handling my divorce. He's preparing papers and will file them as soon as I wrap up a deal out of London." He went on to explain the partnership offer, and the deal that would precede it.

"Congratulations, Taylor. You deserve it."

"What I deserve is you."

Her intercom buzzed. "Sorry to interrupt, but Dr. Spindell is on the line for you. He says it's important."

"I'll be right there," she answered.

"Why don't we finish this over dinner tonight?"

She took a deep breath, and a big plunge. "Okay."

After he left the office and she was off the phone, André walked in and placed the bouquet of flowers where they belonged, on her desk.

"That was pretty sneaky," she said, cutting her eyes at him as he carefully arranged the stems of hibiscus, ginger, and tiger lilies.

"Well, somebody's got to look out for you," he said curtly.

Just then her private line rang. "Hello," she said.

"So how do you like your new patient?" It was Joie.

No wonder Joie had insisted on lunch today. "You two are banned from speaking to each other anymore," she said, smiling as she looked at André, who winked as he left her office.

"Somebody's got to—"

"I know, I know. 'Somebody's got to look out for me,'" Brooke interrupted her, repeating the line that André had just said. She should have known that the two of them would collude against her to get her with a man.

"Well, I'm glad you agree," Joie said. "Now give me all the juicy details."

13

AN EXCHANGE OF FAVORS

LaTeesha's daily trek from the bowels of the Bronx to the hip and stylish streets of SoHo could just as easily have been a commute from the North Pole to the South, so far apart were the two destinations. At times when she and Kiernan were popping in and out of chic boutiques and ordering exotic dishes from expensive menus, she secretly fantasized that Kiernan was her real mother, and that the glitz and glamour were her real life, instead of the sad, pathetic one she left behind every day by subway. In her fantasy world her current existence was simply a tragic mistake, like being accidentally switched at birth. What would her life be like, she wondered, had she been born with the privileges that Kiernan took for granted?

LaTeesha hated herself for wishing that her fantasy were truly a reality and that her own life were simply a bad dream. She felt guilty. Her mother's circumstances weren't her fault; she was simply playing out the weak hand of cards that she'd been dealt. Bessie Ingram had grown up in South Carolina working twelve-hour days tending a near-barren farm, toiling from sunup to sundown, rather than learning to read or write in a classroom. Her escape route from the fields was straight up Interstate 95 to New York at a time when all black people thought the streets up north were paved in gold. Many found out that the city was full of hustlers, and being attractive at that time she was quickly sucked up by one jive-talking wannabe after another. She was now only forty-five years old but looked nearly twice that. She'd been ridden hard by life and hung up wet. One of LaTeesha's biggest fears when she saw her mother was that she was actually looking into the future at herself.

She walked into By Design's office and immediately realized that Kiernan was in one of her moods: fidgety, surly, and unfocused. She could tell by the tight knit of brows and the disheveled appearance of her normally perfectly appointed hair and makeup. So LaTeesha wisely decided to stay out of the line of fire today. She waved good-morning and quickly retreated behind her desk in the outer room to begin filling out return slips for unused merchandise left over from their last job.

"Would you come in here for a minute?" Kiernan yelled from inside her office.

LaTeesha cringed and reluctantly got up from behind her desk. "Yes, ma'am?"

She eyed LaTeesha like a testy cat eyeing a weary mouse. "Your probation officer called me," Kiernan announced matter-of-factly.

Her heart rate quickened at the mention of Mr. Perkins. "S-so what did he say?" She began fidgeting. She had hardly slept the past few nights, knowing that whatever Kiernan chose to tell him could affect the rest of her life, and with Kiernan being so unpredictable, there was no telling what she would say.

Kiernan took a cigarette from the silver holder that graced her desk, and tapped it rapidly against the lid. "Nothing yet," she said before sticking it between her teeth. She went rifling through her desk drawer in search of a match.

When LaTeesha gave her a puzzled look, she continued on. "I haven't called him back yet, but what you *should* be asking is what am I *going* to say." She lit the cigarette and inhaled deeply. Her threat hung in the air like a cloud of dark smoke. She was enjoying her game of cat and mouse.

"What do you mean?"

Kiernan shrugged as if to dismiss the conversation. "Oh, nothing. It's just that I hope you'll continue to do as you're told, because I'd hate to have to give him a bad report." She took another deep drag and expelled the smoke upward as she waved LaTeesha back out the door, as if she'd suddenly grown bored with her.

Just before lunch Kiernan again summoned LaTeesha into her office. "I need you to run an errand for me," she said, not bothering to look up from the photos that were spread all over her desk.

LaTeesha shrugged her shoulders. "Sure."

"I'm supposed to meet someone in twenty minutes, but I just got an emergency call from a client—a problem with some furniture that was just delivered—so I need you to go for me." She picked up a cigarette and lit it with the burning butt of another. When Kiernan had picked up her first cigarette in her late teens she'd nearly gagged to death on the foul-tasting smoke. Even though she hated the taste, she suffered through it until she was sucessfully addicted, only because she thought smoking was chic.

LaTeesha hated the disgusting habit. The stench of stale cigarette smoke reminded her of the run-down prostitutes in her neighborhood who leaned against streetlights for hours at a time dragging on smokes while waiting to be picked up by anybody with a spare twenty. "No problem," she said.

"You'll be meeting a woman named Thelma," she said. "She'll meet you at the Starbucks at the corner of Broadway and Grand." She handed a thick manila envelope to LaTeesha. "You can't miss her. She has short black hair, dark skin, and a gap between her teeth. And she's a little taller than I am."

LaTeesha hid her enthusiasm. She was thrilled to get out of the office. "What am I picking up?"

Kiernan waved her hand. "Just some jewelry that I ordered

from an uptown designer. But don't open it. I'll check it out later."

LaTeesha headed out the door, glad to be gone for a while. It was such a gorgeous day, which tempted her to walk the long way to soak up the flavor of SoHo. She loved the artsy, hip, urban people who wandered the quaint cobblestone streets, the avant-garde fashions that beckoned to passersby from store windows, and the raw energy that made New York unlike any other city in the world. Not that she'd ever traveled outside of the tri-state area, at least not physically, but more and more lately, she had in her mind. For the first time in her life LaTeesha felt a desire to explore the world beyond her neighborhood and see what it had to offer besides poverty.

This new attitude, she knew, was all due to Kiernan. In the six months that she'd worked for her she'd found not only an employer, but a role model and a window to a world beyond the narrow one she'd seen. The glitzy photo shoots, the rich, beautiful, and famous clients, and the thrill of seeing a project go from mere concept to masterpiece were all intoxicating to her. Though Kiernan could be a challenge, her antics were still a small price to pay to learn the ropes and see firsthand that black people did live just like the white people she saw on TV. Just like a lot of people in America, LaTeesha had bought into the media's pervasive depiction of her own race.

When she walked into Starbucks she immediately saw a woman who fit the description that Kiernan had given her. She was surprised. The woman wasn't spit-polished and carefully coiffed like most of Kiernan's friends and associates; in fact, she looked more like the people in her own neighborhood.

She held out her hand. "Hi, I'm LaTeesha. I work for Kiernan." LaTeesha detected a whiff of alcohol as the woman looked her up and down.

"Where is she?" The woman didn't seem too pleased with Kiernan's absence.

"S-something came up, so she asked me to come by to meet you instead." She reached into her bag. "Oh, and she gave me this." LaTeesha handed the woman the envelope.

"Tell Miss Kiernan I'll be callin' her later," she said, handing LaTeesha a small shopping bag.

Inside was a box that Kiernan figured must contain earrings. She wondered why Kiernan needed any more—she had so many—but then she remembered that rich people never really needed anything; it was usually only a matter of wanting.

When she returned to the office Kiernan was still there, just where she'd left her, parked behind her messy desk.

"What happened to your meeting?" she asked, handing over the bag.

"Oh, she called right after you left and canceled." Kiernan took the bag. "Why don't you take the rest of the day off?" she offered.

This was right on time, since today was the perfect day to play hooky. "Are you sure? What about the HBO proposal?"

Kiernan had rolled in a favor in order to be considered for the redesign of the cable company's office space.

"We can start on it tomorrow."

"Cool." LaTeesha turned and headed out the door. "I'll see you in the morning."

Kiernan took the box into her office and ripped it open. She smiled when she saw a magenta drawstring bag bulging with an assortment of goodies.

"Did you want me to pick up some lunch for you first?"

Kiernan was surprised to see LaTeesha back in the doorway. She quickly put the stash back into the shopping bag.

"No, I'll pick something up later."

LaTeesha continued to stand in the doorway, as if looking to see what was being put away. In fact, she was very curious about what was inside the beautiful silk bag. She imagined the jewelry inside must be exquisite, since everything in Kiernan's life was perfect, except for her attitude. She wondered if the woman she'd met was the jewelry designer, but she didn't appear to be the type. Maybe she was an assistant who'd been sent on an errand, just as LaTeesha had been.

"You'd better go now, before I change my mind and put you to work."

"In that case, I'm out. See you later." She turned and bounded out the door, eager to enjoy the rest of the day, and happy that Kiernan seemed to be feeling better. She certainly didn't want her returning Mr. Perkins's call while she was in one of her funky moods. Maybe the jewels in the bag had helped.

When she was gone, Kiernan locked the door behind her. She was anxious to be alone with her multitude of new friends, all courtesy of Thelma. At least her sister was good for something, but she would really have to manage her contact with her from now on. Recently she had found out that Thelma had been arrested for drug possession just hours after Kiernan had hooked up with her to buy some. That was way too close for comfort. Suppose she'd been with her then? She shuddered to think of the consequences of having her name and face smeared across the pages of the New York newspapers. Her social and professional connections would dry up faster than she could blink a false eyelash, not to mention what was left of her marriage, which was already on life support with a "do not resuscitate" order.

No, she had to stay as far away from Thelma as possible, which was why LaTeesha would continue to come in handy. Why not let her do the pickups? Even if she were caught she'd just be another delinquent girl who couldn't stay out of trouble. And if she dared to tell the authorities that Kiernan sent her, she'd simply deny it. Who were they more likely to believe, a delinquent on probation, or an upstanding member of the community?

14

COUCH CONFESSIONS

After several seconds, Brooke finally realized that the ringing she heard wasn't part of her dream, but was interrupting it; so she fumbled for the phone before dragging the receiver between the sheets.

"Hello," she answered. She didn't even bother to try sounding awake. If it was Joie—Ms. Early Bird—Brooke would hang up the phone right away, unless she had news of another fabulous sample sale.

"Wake up, Sleeping Beauty." It was Taylor. In contrast to her semiconscious grumbling, he was as wide-awake as if it were high noon. The sound of his voice brought a lazy smile to her face as she remembered their time together the night before.

He had told her about his marriage, beginning with Kiernan's faked pregnancy, up to its current irreparable state. Brooke was convinced that he was telling her the truth and wasn't simply a married man looking for a fling. She carefully watched the steady gaze of his eyes, and heard the tremble of emotion in his voice. He was honest about his part in the failure, how he'd married for the wrong reasons, and now felt as though he were living with a stranger who bore no resemblance to the woman he'd picnicked with on the beach in the Hamptons.

"Good morning." She yawned. "What time is it?" She

peered from under the covers and caught the glow from her digital alarm clock; it was seven ten, twenty minutes before it was set to go off. Rolling onto her back, she decided this was a much better wake-up call, and worth the lost sleep.

"I know it's early and you're still getting your unneeded beauty sleep, but I'm about to board a flight to London and needed to hear your sexy voice before I left."

"For the sexy voice, you have to call after my first cup of coffee."

"Your voice sounds sexy to me anytime. In fact, everything about you is sexy."

She smiled and stretched, thinking about their first real kiss, which they had shared last night. Under the glow of a streetlamp, just outside the door to her apartment, he had held her in his arms and given her the sweetest, most seductive kiss that she'd ever had. The teasing of his tongue made her knees weak, and chased away any lingering images of any long-suffering wife. How quickly we forget.

When their lips parted he had taken the key from her hand. "May I?" he asked, reaching for the lock.

Still breathless, she nodded, and moments later they were inside her apartment, alone together.

"Can I get you something?" she asked. She felt nervous about where this might lead, not at all sure that she wanted to go there. She had to take things slowly.

"The only thing I want is you," he answered, again pulling her into his arms.

He kissed her eyelids and stroked her face gently. This simple gesture said so much that no words were necessary. His touch was electrifying, opening circuits in her that had long been seared shut.

He slowly pulled away. "I should probably say good night now," he said softly.

Though part of her didn't want him to go, she was very relieved that he was.

"I don't want you to do anything you'll regret, and if I'm right, we'll have lots of time together. And when we do, I want it to be right—no second thoughts. Okay?"

"Okay." She smiled, happy that he was as patient as he was understanding.

He straightened his jacket and kissed her good night before disappearing through the door. She locked it behind him, and leaned back against it, letting the sparks of passion subside, thankful that Taylor was smart enough to not let them burn too quickly.

This morning the sound of his voice and the vivid memory made her flesh tingle. "Uhhhmmm." A moan of contentment escaped her throat. "I'm going to miss you," she purred. He was off to London to close the Beacon Hill deal. He was planning to file for divorce as soon as it was done and his partnership was confirmed.

"I'll miss you too, babe, but hopefully I should only be gone a couple of days."

She could hear the sound of flights being called in the background, and wished she were there with him, ready to board a transatlantic flight for a few days of oblivion and adventure.

"Well, travel safe, and call me later."

"I'll call you tonight before you go to bed."

"That'll be three o'clock in the morning for you."

"A small price to pay to make sure that you don't forget about me," he teased.

As if I could, she thought. It seemed as if the minute she let her guard down with him, she was filled with strong emotions that had little to do with reason, logic, or common sense. "I don't think you have to worry about that." The yearning and passion that she thought she'd never experience again were now ingrained in her DNA. Even as a therapist, she was amazed that such intense feelings could sneak up and consume her before she'd even had a chance to react.

"Do you trust me?" His tone had changed. This was a serious

question. They'd come a long way since that bumpy ride in the elevator, but he wanted to know she was still in it for the distance.

Her heart fluttered in her chest. "Yes, I do."

She hung up the phone feeling hopeful. Hopping out of bed, she danced around the room pretending to pluck petals from a daisy. "He loves me. He loves me not. He loves me. He loves me not. He loves me!" she squealed as she pulled the last make-believe petal from the make-believe daisy. She finally fell back onto the bed with a bounce and stared up at the ceiling as though waiting for a dream that was too good to be true to end. After a strong shot of Italian coffee she forced herself to stop daydreaming and get on with the day.

"Good morning, André." She breezed by him into her office; purposely ignoring the questioning glance he threw her way. She knew he was dying to know what happened last night between her and Taylor. He'd just have to wait. It served him right for tricking her in the first place.

He appeared in her doorway. "Don't you look chipper today." When she didn't respond, except to stifle a smile, he gave up and handed her a printout of the day's appointments. He was so efficient. She wondered what she'd do without him. Sure, she was great with patients, but it was André who kept the wheels churning at East Side Associates. If she were left to her own devices, there would be no billing, no accounting, and hence no phones or lights.

She took the paper from him and headed into her office, a cup of Starbucks in hand. This was a two-cups-before-nine-o'clock kind of day. She reviewed the list of names, mentally preparing for her day's journey through the minds and souls of her patients.

A few minutes later he buzzed her line to let her know that her first patient was there. Brooke downed the rest of the coffee, turned on her recorder, dimmed the lights slightly, and lit a Diptyque candle just in time to welcome her at the door.

"Make yourself comfortable," Brooke said as she greeted

Kate. The woman wore nervous energy around her like a sheath of static electricity. Though Brooke couldn't see it, the force was only a touch away.

Kate took a seat on the couch opposite Brooke and immediately crossed her legs tightly, clasping her hands firmly in her lap, barely concealing her agitation. Brooke leaned forward, sensing the woman's distress. "Are you all right?" There was something unsettling about her. Maybe, Brooke thought, it was the emptiness. She seemed unwhole, like a body walking around without a soul that fit properly. Brooke set aside her personal impressions, instead focusing on assessing professional observations that might be of help to her patient.

Her question seemed to pull the woman out of a mental fog. "If I were all right, I wouldn't be here, now, would I?" she snapped.

Brooke let the snide remark go by, not acknowledging it at all. "Why don't you tell me what's bothering you today?" She sat back in her chair, intending to disarm her tightly wound patient.

Flashes of anger burned brightly in Kate's eyes as tears eased down her cheeks. She made no effort to wipe them away. She seemed to be in a trance, as though seeing and feeling things that were too elusive for her to grip firmly. This was not an uncommon state for people with mental illness, because anger was an easily assessable substitute for more deeply hidden and more troubling emotions.

From experience Brooke realized that regardless of what reasons Kate might give—even to herself—for her inner turmoil, other, deeper emotional issues would lie buried at the bottom of the well. In cases like this it often took lots of time to unearth root causes, since patients usually fooled themselves as successfully as they fooled others.

"He's leaving me. I know it," she spit out.

"What makes you so sure of that?" Brooke asked calmly, determined not to feed her patient's simmering anger. Sometimes doing so was an effective tool to excavate the layers of denial often piled too high to plow through. Even though she and Kate had made progress over their sessions, she didn't think that now was the time to go digging around.

Kate closed her eyes tight, stanching the flow of tears. She spoke in a low, detached voice. "I just know." She wiped the corners of her eyes with the back of her hand and began to tremble with a silent rage.

"Have you discussed your suspicions with him?" Brooke kept her voice even, her disposition cool. After years of hearing every admission possible—short of murder—she was expert at keeping her reactions absent from her voice or her facial expressions. She also kept her guilt at bay. Here she was counseling a woman whose husband was cheating on her, when she was seeing another woman's husband.

Kate looked at her as though she'd asked her to strip naked and dance down Broadway. She had no intention of confronting her husband. In her mind that would only prompt him to leave that much sooner. And given her fragile condition, she wasn't sure that she could survive without him.

"I can't," Kate finally answered, slumping back against the sofa's cushions. She looked like a helium balloon that had been popped, its air dissipating suddenly as it fell to earth.

Brooke regarded her quick change in demeanor. "Why not?" she asked.

"I just can't."

"Do you love him?"

The question appeared to catch Kate off guard, as though she'd never really considered whether she truly loved him before now. It gave her pause for thought. She shrugged her shoulders. "I suppose I do."

Brooke regarded her solemnly. What an awful marriage this one must be, she thought. The angry wife didn't seem to love the husband, but didn't want to let him go either. Who knew what Mr. Mathews's issues were. Though she didn't know him, and he certainly wasn't her patient, she still couldn't help but felt sorry for him too. "Kate, let's step back for a minute," Brooke said. "Let's talk about your childhood." She leaned back in her chair, concentrating on what the woman would say—and more important, what she wouldn't say.

Kate shifted uncomfortably in her seat, as though the cushions had suddenly grown hot. "What do you want to know?"

"What are your earliest childhood memories?" When she hesitated, Brooke said, "You can lie down if it will make you more comfortable."

Kate swung her feet up awkwardly onto the sofa and reclined her head onto the pillow at the end facing the door. "That's a hard question for me to answer," she finally said, exhaling deeply.

"What do you mean?"

"Well, I didn't really have a childhood."

"What do you remember about your preschool years?"

For what seemed an eternity, Kate said nothing, perhaps hoping the silence would consume her, along with her pain. Brooke, having long ago learned to be comfortable with prolonged silences, also said nothing; she simply watched the internal battle that her patient waged within. Finally she said, "Pain," in a tiny voice.

"What kind of pain?" Brooke probed.

There was something about Brooke's unflappability that made her patient feel that it was okay to admit something out loud that she'd never admitted before even to herself. "Down there," she said, pointing to her crotch the way a toddler might if asked where her private parts were. She'd never planned to tell anyone the awful truth, but after being buried for so long, the tormented memory won the battle against her battered ego and bubbled to the surface before she could hold it down. The story she told was one of a father's despicable betrayal of a daughter, and a mother's cowardly response to the vile abuse.

All at once, Brooke understood what lay beneath her patient's anger and self-hatred. She put her notepad aside and leaned forward. "Kate, it's important that you understand that what happened to you was not your fault. You are and always have been a worthy person. Someone capable of and entitled to love and respect. No one else can take that away from you, but you can take it from yourself. You have to understand that before you can address and repair your marriage, or any other relationship."

Kate simply shook her head as the tears began to flow again, this time unchecked.

"What happened all those years ago is a reflection of your father's weaknesses and cruelty. As a child you didn't have—and couldn't have had—any control over the situation, and more important, you have to know that what he did does not make you any less of a person. Just like anyone else, you are worthy of love, but you have to put aside your father's flaws and embrace yourself."

When the session was over, Brooke pulled out her handheld tape recorder. "Adult female patient Kate Mathews has symptoms consistent with early childhood sexual abuse that has significantly diminished her self-image. Recommended course: continued therapy twice a week for the time being."

Meanwhile, her patient had safely tucked away those unchecked emotions, along with the weakness associated with being Kate Mathews, and headed toward Central Park South ready to face the world as Kiernan Malloy.

15

A ROCK AND A HARD PLACE

"**A**re you okay?" Brent asked. They were being bounced around the backseat of a taxi, driven by a kamikaze driver who was playing bumper cars as he careened down Broadway at a breakneck speed on the way to Butter, where Brent and Joie were meeting friends for drinks.

"This is *not* roller derby," Joie shouted into the front seat. The driver feigned deafness and nonchalantly cut off another cab as he continued to bob and weave through the throng of city traffic.

Brent looked at her questioningly. "What's wrong with you?"

You don't want to know, she thought. "Nothing," Joie lied, then turned to stare out the window, anywhere but at him, as she stifled the urge to snap at him, in addition to throwing another barb at the manic driver. It must be hormones—how else could she explain the fact that most everything Brent said or did grated on her nerves. The mere sound of his voice was like nails raking down a chalkboard. Not even the thought of sex was enough to calm her down. Even when he went down on her this morning—the part she usually loved—she only wanted him to stop. He was licking her clit when he should have been lapping her labia, or he was lapping when he should've been probing.

After he left for work, she lay in bed debating whether to finish the job that he couldn't with her trusty butterfly vibrator, when the phone rang.

"Hello," she answered, distracted.

"May I speak with Joie Blanchard?"

She was reaching for the night table drawer where she stashed her toys, balancing the phone between her ear and shoulder. "Speaking."

"It's Julie with Dr. Young's office."

Joie immediately snapped to attention, almost dropping the phone in the process. Why on earth would they be calling her? She'd just gone in last week for a routine annual physical, but they never called unless something was wrong. "What is it?"

"We just got the results from your tests."

Joie immediately felt light-headed. This did not sound like good news. Did she have AIDS, or some other deadly disease? "And?" She sat on the edge of the bed with her heart throbbing in her chest.

"According to our results, you're pregnant." Though the woman's tone was even, Joie could tell that she thought this might be good news. Little did she know.

"Pregnant? What do you mean, pregnant?" Joie couldn't have been more surprised if space aliens had landed in her bedroom. She didn't even remember hanging up the telephone, and certainly didn't say good-bye. She lay back in bed in a zombielike position for a full fifteen minutes in shock.

How could this have happened? She was on the pill, though she was admittedly careless about taking it from time to time. While she tried to absorb the implications of one shock, another one detonated. She wasn't even sure who the father was! She and Evan usually used a condom, but there were too many occasions when they would forgo the precaution in haste or lust. She smacked her forehead with the heel of her palm. How stupid could she be?

Given all of the possibilities, she realized, pregnancy wasn't the worst news. She'd seen the results of AIDS firsthand from colleagues in the fashion industry; in fact, she'd lost several friends to the insidious disease.

She finally emerged from her stupor and called her assistant to let him know that she would not be in that day. He could scout locations by himself. She had to get some answers, so she hauled herself out of bed and quickly showered and dressed before hopping a taxi to her gynecologist's office. But instead of answering questions, the visit only raised another big one. She'd thought that the obvious solution was an abortion, and she was ready and willing to schedule one until her gynecologist told her that if she had another one—especially at her age—her chances of ever conceiving in the future would not be good. Worse, she didn't have much time to consider it. According to the doctor's estimation she was already ten weeks pregnant, and an abortion should be done within the next couple of weeks. But did she want to give up what might be her last chance to ever have a child?

The funny thing was, she wasn't sure she even wanted kids, *ever,* but on the other hand she didn't like the idea of not having the option should, by some miracle, she wake up one day with a maternal instinct, something she was sure she didn't have at the moment. Her daydreams had never included a white picket fence, a knight in shining armor, a pack of sniveling brats, or any of the usual makings of a young girl's fantasies. Instead, she always dreamed of faraway places, exotic adventures, and a cast of characters whom she directed. Her script didn't call for dirty diapers, sticky fingers, car seats, cribs, or any of the other baby gear that came along with a horde of rug rats.

"You look like you're going to a wake instead of a party," Brent said, cutting into her thoughts.

"I didn't think it was a party. I thought we were just meeting a few people for a couple of drinks."

"Still, it should be fun." No doubt it would be for Brent,

who loved hanging out with his best friend and his crew of models, mainly because their world was so different from his own buttoned-down corporate job at Time Warner. He envied the hip, creative bad-boy appeal of the fashion business. For him, it sure beat sitting in boring strategy meetings with a group of stuffy MBAs.

At that moment, Joie envied Barbara Eden's character from *I Dream of Jeannie*, who could fold her arms in front of her chin, nod her head, and instantly be transported to anyplace she wanted. Some trick, but not one that could save Joie from a night of hell. She wished desperately to be going anywhere else other than where they were headed. She'd given Brent every excuse she could think of to avoid going out, but he wouldn't hear of it, so she finally agreed just to shut him up.

When the taxi ended its solo high-speed chase, they got out and walked into the lounge, where they found the group perched on chairs, chaises, and sofas, preening and sipping on brightly colored cocktails.

"Long time no see," Evan said as he pulled her into a tight hug.

So here Joie was, stuck between her boyfriend and her lover, pregnant by one, but not having a single clue which. How the hell had she managed to get herself into such a sticky mess? The real question was, how would she get out of it? There was a time when she'd have been amused by the way her boyfriend's friend would sneak over and rub his hard-on (which he seemed capable of summoning at will) on her thigh, and if positioned just right during an "innocent" hug, it would hit that magical place between her legs, giving her an even greater thrill. On those nights when the cheating twosome were feeling particularly naughty, their coup de grace would be to conveniently disappear together, meeting in a bathroom or any other clandestine, out-of-the-way spot for one of those quickie cocktails that didn't come from behind a bar. Evan was hard for Joie to resist, and in fact was one of the few top black male models in the business who actually made a good living at it. Clad in nothing but a pair of skintight Calvins, he'd even graced a billboard in Times Square that was practically larger than the size of the small town in Ohio where he was born.

"I've been pretty tied up," she told him as she disengaged herself from his embrace. The last thing she was in the mood for was wild, uninhibited sex; after all, look where it had gotten her.

Evan greeted Brent with a warm hug, winking slyly at Joie, who stood behind Brent's back. It was at times like this when she occasionally felt a twinge of guilt for their betrayal, but God knew it was only a fleeting sensation, quickly replaced by her body's fresh recollection of mind-blowing orgasms. The whole thing never seemed to bother Evan at all; the two friends were closer than ever.

"Hi, guys." It was Lorrie, Evan's on-again, off-again girl-friend, who looked like a French poodle right before showtime at Westminster. Joie just ignored her greeting, but did refrain from rolling her eyes. Lorrie was one of those white girls who went to every length possible to try to be black. She was what some might call a Wigger. When she began dating Evan, in her mind she'd received an honorary "black card," and she carried it proudly.

Evan signaled a cocktail waitress over. "What are you guys drinking tonight?" He flashed his cover-boy smile. All of his teeth were Chiclet even and porcelain white, framed by lips that were designed for oral seduction. They were thick and inviting and, Joie thought, one of his best assets. Apparently so did he, since he was constantly licking them, drawing attention from any who might otherwise miss their appeal.

"What are you drinking?" Brent asked Evan.

"A Harvey Wallbanger."

"I'll have the same."

"What about you, Joie? What's your pleasure?" Evan asked Joie, licking his lips seductively.

"Just a caffeine-free diet Coke," she said, directing her answer to the waitress. Brent and Evan looked at her strangely. Joie normally kept up with them drink for drink.

"Don't be a party poop," Lorrie chimed in sounding very white. Just then the DJ mixed in Beyoncé's "Crazy in Love," the let's-get-busy party song, and Lorrie got on the table, dancing in a feeble attempt to do the booty-shake dance that the singer did in the video. Without booty or rhythm, instead she looked like an epileptic in the throes of a fatal seizure.

Joie looked at Evan and said, "You really should do something about your girl before she breaks something." He could only try to hide his embarrassment.

She and Brent sat on an empty love seat, and Evan squeezed in next to her. Perfect, she thought. Here she was sandwiched between the two sperm donors with no idea which one was "it." She laughed cynically at the cruel irony of her pathetic situation.

"What's so funny?" Brent asked, putting his arm around the sofa behind her. "Please share."

She hadn't even realized that she'd laughed out loud. "Oh, it's nothing, just thinking about a funny story I heard."

"I'll tell you a funny story," offered Elan, the requisite fashion queen, complete with a self-imposed lisp. "My brother got married last weekend," he said, looking around the group to make sure that everyone was hanging on his every word, even Lorrie, who'd given up the go-go-girl act since it hadn't produced rave, indifferent, or even any reviews. "Since I was the best bride of honor"—he stopped again and beamed at his little joke—"I had to go with him and his beer-swilling buddies to the most dreadful bachelor thingy." He waved his limp wrist in the air in front of him, as though he couldn't be bothered to think of the name of such a barbaric, antiquated custom as a bachelor party. "Anywho, I'm in there carefully avoiding the boobs, butts, and tacky weaves, when who do I see getting ground through a lap dance but a guy I'd just been out with a few days earlier." He paused for dramatic effect, with his eyes wide and his hand placed demurely at his mouth. When he got a chorus of "Oh, my Gods," "You've gotta be kidding," and "Oh, shits," he continued. "Now you know I had to show my ass up in there. So I got up." He stood now to act out the rest of his story. "And I twisted right over in front of him and grabbed Ms. Silicone Alley up from his lap and finished his lap dance for her right there in front of his macho friends." He slapped his thigh and roared with laughter.

"You are out of control," one of the other models said.

"Oh, but I was in control all right," he said proudly. "I worked him over so tough, he was seconds away from losing his load, but of course he tried to play it cool. And don't you know when the song finished, I had people giving *me* tips." Happy with himself, he sat back down gingerly and crossed his legs.

Brent laughed and said, "Well, if this modeling thing doesn't work out, I guess you have a career as a stripper ahead of you."

"I'd rather drink muddy water," Elan said, turning up his nose.

"You know, it's really fucked-up the way these gay guys on the DL pretend to be straight," Lorrie announced. You could tell that she was proud of the fact that she'd cursed and used a slang word in the same sentence. That should definitely chalk up some points toward her lifetime membership.

"They don't consider themselves gay," Elan explained. "They just like a little 'extra' on the side every now and then. Most of them have a wife and kids at home."

Brent jumped into the conversation. "Anytime one dude touches another dude's dick, he's gay," he said adamantly.

"Don't knock it until you've tried it," Elan teased.

"I'm only swingin' one way, and that's right down the middle, ain't that right, baby?" he said, hugging Joie closer.

Sick of the whole conversation, Joie didn't answer. She just got up to go to the bathroom. "I'll be right back," she said.

She was tempted to walk straight out the front door, but headed to the ladies' room instead. She went to the sink, wet her hands with cold water, and dabbed them on her face. The pregnancy definitely explained the feeling of fatigue that she'd been experiencing lately, as well as the ten extra pounds that she'd been trying to ignore. Most of those must have gone to her boobs, she thought as she hoisted them up, enjoying the extra weight. Too bad it was temporary. She reapplied lip gloss, fingered her dreads, and walked out the door, right into Evan. He grabbed her around the waist and pulled her close, leaning in for a kiss. She turned her head and yanked away from him.

"What's wrong?" he asked.

"I'm just tired," she said, giving him a bored look.

"Then let me do all the work," he said, reaching for her again.

"I've got to go." She pulled free from him and hurried back to the table. Once settled she braced herself for another barrage of inane conversation, quickly coming to the conclusion that alcohol must surely anesthetize people's brains to this sort of mindless drivel. To bad she couldn't drink, but she'd been warned by her doctor to abstain unless she was sure that she wasn't keeping the baby. And right now she wasn't sure about anything. Her teetotaling did nothing to quell anyone else's thirst, including Brent's—he was already three sheets to the wind. Eventually she told him that she was heading home and he could catch up later, or stay the night at Evan's downtown apartment. She honestly didn't care one way or the other at that moment.

When she settled into the back of a taxi, she gave the driver her address and pulled out her cell phone, calling Brooke. "Can I come over?" she asked, fighting back tears.

"Joie, are you okay?" Brooke heard an unfamiliar sadness in her friend's voice.

"Not exactly."

"What's wrong?"

"I don't want to talk about it over the phone. I'll be there in ten minutes."

She hung up and gave Brooke's address to the cabdriver, who grunted his displeasure for having to go someplace other than where he'd planned to. What difference could it possibly make,

Joie thought, except that it gave him something to grumble about? Joie was convinced that a bad attitude was a prerequisite for getting the medallions that allowed cabdrivers to work in the city. There had to be some kind of attitude-aptitude test, and those who scored the highest with the most attitude were hired on the spot; driving skills were a distant second.

Wearing a concerned expression, Brooke opened the door the minute Joie got out of the car and tossed the driver a ten-dollar bill through the window.

"Come on in," Brooke said as she stepped to the side, letting Joie in.

"Thanks."

"You don't sound so good, and you don't look so good either." She stood in front of Joie, watching her carefully, wondering what could have happened to cause her normally effervescent friend to be so sullen.

"Nor would you if you'd just spent an hour trapped between a rock and a hard place."

"I take it that means Brent and Evan." Joie followed Brooke down the hall into her bedroom, where all serious girlfriend conversations took place.

"Bingo," she said, removing her coat and tossing it at the foot of the bed.

"What happened? Did Brent find out about Evan?" Brooke feared that this was inevitable and was surprised that it hadn't happened sooner.

"Not likely," Joie said. "As long as Evan doesn't kiss and tell—which he won't; he's having way too much fun—then I don't have to worry about that."

"So what's wrong?"

Joie smiled weakly, and a tear fell down her cheek as Brooke looked on in shock. She'd never seen Joie cry in all of the years they'd known each other. After a minute of silence Joie quietly said, "I'm pregnant."

"Oh, Joie." Brooke's hand flew involuntarily to her mouth.

That was the last thing that she had expected to hear from her friend.

Tears streamed down Joie's face as she told Brooke what her doctor had said and how torn she was about what to do.

Brooke handed her a tissue from the nightstand and hugged her close. As much as she hated to do it, the next question had to be asked. "Do you know who the father is?"

"That's my other problem. I can't say that I do." There was a sad little smile on her face, followed by another stream of tears.

"It's going to be okay. We'll get through this. I promise."

Brooke's tone was so soothing and authoritative that Joie felt better than she had all day. She wondered why she hadn't called Brooke right away, although she knew the answer to that question. She was so afraid that Brooke would give her a list of "I told you so"s. But she should have known better, because a good friend wouldn't do that, and Brooke was nothing if not a very good friend.

16

THE UNINVITED GUEST

Kiernan was an expert at keeping secrets, but the toll of carrying excess baggage around year after year was steep. Maintaining her many lies was like bailing water from a sinking boat with a bottom full of holes. But hers had long since left the dock, and there was no turning back now. Not without drowning in the truth.

Deep down inside, Kiernan believed there could be no happily-ever-after for people like her, but out of habit she continued her ruse, sometimes even fooling herself into believing that all was right in her make-believe world. The effort took an emotional toll, one that she hoped therapy would help to repair. After reading an article in O magazine about the benefits of psychotherapy, and seeing Brooke's name on a list of recommended African-American therapists, she decided to give it a try. At this point she had nothing to lose; she'd do just about anything to feel better.

Lately she'd been plagued by sleepless nights and awful nightmares on the rare occasions when she did manage to sleep. The accumulating stress was causing bouts of depression, and she had recently experienced panic attacks. Her only concern about seeking therapy was protecting her privacy, since it wouldn't help her carefully crafted reputation or career if her secrets were to seep out. The thought of those people whom she revered in New York society learning the truth about her was more frightening than actually living with it. After reading up on client-patient confidentiality she felt better, but still decided to go under an alias—just in case.

Like many days lately, Kiernan's day started with a frightful migraine headache after she was jolted awake in a cold sweat. Shards of intense pain radiated from the center of her brain between swollen red eyes, shooting angry daggers with each stab of light or bit of movement. She swallowed two Extra Strength Excedrins the minute she could make it to the master bathroom. Twenty minutes later she was back in front of the well-stocked medicine cabinet, but this time she ignored the over-the-counter drugs and went straight for the hard stuff. She rummaged through her arsenal, pulling out a Percocet, which she downed with a handful of New York City tap water, something she'd never admit to consuming. She'd sooner tell the world that she popped pills. Now that she was sufficiently medicated, she lay back on the bed and replaced the pair of eye covers that hung around her neck, hoping to block out the blinding light that shone stubbornly through her silk venetian blinds.

Lying perfectly still surrounded by pitch blackness, with her arms parallel at her sides, Kiernan's thoughts turned to death, and how much easier everything would be for her if she just swallowed a fistful of pills. There'd be no more threats of humiliating poverty, no haunting memories of a drunken abusive father, no long list of lies to remember so she could retell them accurately, and best of all, no looming threat of exposure hanging over her like a guillotine with a trick switch. There'd be nothing but total darkness, perfect quiet, just like now.

While she lay prone with her mind worlds away, the door to the bedroom opened. Startled, she snatched the eye cover down over her nose to find Taylor standing before the mirror loosening his tie.

"What are *you* doing here?" she snapped. She'd forgotten

that he was due back from his "business trip" this morning. She was sure that he had probably really been away on some rendezvous with his lover.

Taylor had come home only to take a shower and change his clothes. With his contracts signed he was anxious to get back to the office to execute his deal, locking up his promotion to partner, and thus his divorce.

"The last time I checked, I lived here." He turned and caught a whiff of alcohol, along with the sight of the empty vodka bottle and the clothes that were strewn about the room. Looking at her directly wasn't any prettier. Kiernan's hair looked like an angry bird's nest, her nail polish was chipped, and it appeared as though she'd gone to bed with her makeup still on.

"Don't get smart with me. I know what you're up to," she spewed angrily. "What do you think I am, some fool? I know you are having an affair."

"You have no idea what you're talking about." Taylor turned his back to her dismissively and continued to undress.

She jumped up from the bed, tossing the tangled mess of bed linen aside angrily, and stood in front of him. "I'll take you for everything you've got," she spit.

He could smell the stench of liquor, which was mixed with a sour dose of morning breath and stale cigarettes. His goal was to quickly shower and get out of there as fast as possible.

"Do you think I'm fuckin' crazy?" she asked.

"Kiernan, you really should just go back to bed and sleep it off."

By now she was in his face, with her hands planted on her hips, in full bitch mode. "Don't play me like I'm some drunk ho." Her spittle sprayed his face as she continued her ranting. "I know what the fuck is going on around here."

"Yeah, well, I know one thing, too. You need to get out of my face."

She cut him off. "Or you'll what?" she taunted, rotating her neck from side to side. "You won't do a goddamned thing." She grabbed his arm to keep him from leaving.

He snatched it away, unleashing her grip, fighting off the urge to throw her across the room and out of his sight. "Don't be so sure, Kiernan." Though he remained calm on the outside—which infuriated her more—he was itching to tell her that he was getting a divorce. But why have that conversation with a drugged-out alcoholic? It would be much better to wait and let Max deal with her. In fact that was something else he needed to get from the apartment: a list of financial records necessary to lay the groundwork for his divorce. He'd get them from his office file cabinet on the way out of the door.

Kiernan followed his thoughts as they passed across his face. And she didn't like what she saw. "You smug bastard! Do you think you can just walk out on me? Nigga, I'll take everything!"

He walked away from her toward the bathroom.

"Don't you walk away from me!" The veins in her neck bulged as she screamed at his retreating back. He didn't stop, which angered her so much that she found herself lunging for him with her nails bared. He closed the door just in time, but couldn't shut out the angry pounding of her fists.

When he walked out of the bathroom fully dressed thirty minutes later, she was nowhere to be seen. She was probably in the guest bedroom, he thought. So he took full advantage of her absence and headed to his office, where he quickly went through his files, looking for his latest financial records for Max. Once they were in hand, he hastily repacked his briefcase and headed out the door, but in his haste to escape another angry encounter with Kiernan, he failed to lock the file cabinet.

She heard the door when it closed behind him and bolted into the office on a mission. Now, more than ever, she had to find proof of his affair. Without it she wouldn't be able to survive a long, drawn-out divorce, one in which she'd surely be nickel-and-dimed all the way to the poorhouse. She was about to go through some boxes she'd spotted in the closet the day before when her eyes fell on the file cabinet, the same one that she'd been unable to get into before, but now she saw that it was un-locked. Bingo! She immediately set about the business of poring and sifting through every file and piece of paper there. An hour later she knew his net worth from his accounting statement—over $9 million, including all assets. She knew that he sent a monthly check for five grand to his mother and that he was scheduled for a dental checkup next Thursday, but still had no proof of his adulterous affair.

Feeling desolate, she took an Ambien and climbed back into bed, hoping to wake up feeling better. An hour later she barely heard the phone ring through the haze of drugs that coursed through her bloodstream. It started as a dull and distant sound that insinuated itself slowly into her consciousness, becoming brighter with each long ring.

With effort, she lifted her head from the pillow. It felt like a bale of wet lumber. Her eyes were swollen orbs amidst a face that was a bloated mess, highlighted with traces of smeared mascara, remnants of a drug-induced sleep. She reached for the phone. "Hello," she managed to utter in a thick, raspy voice.

"Mrs. Malloy, there's a woman—a Ms. Thelma Pitts—here to see you." It was Frank, her doorman.

Alarmed at the mention of her sister's name, Kiernan felt the heavy fog that surrounded her begin to lift, pushed aside by the approach of a bigger weather pattern that was headed her way. Trying to ward off the inevitable, she said, "Tell her I'm unavailable."

"Yes, ma'am."

She sat up in bed and ran her fingers through a thatch of tan-gled weave. She pulled the covers up around her shoulders, and began to concentrate on inhaling and exhaling one breath at a time. What the hell was Thelma doing here? she wondered. She'd always made sure never to mention where she lived, so she had no idea how Thelma even knew her address. Before she could come up with a plausible explanation, the phone rang again. This time it was shrill, demanding, and defiant.

"Hello?" She held her breath.

"I'm sorry to bother you again, Mrs. Malloy," Frank whispered, "but she refuses to leave. She's insisting on seeing you and is making quite a scene."

Kiernan rolled her eyes to the ceiling, clearly imagining the embarrassing spectacle that her sister was probably making of herself, while smearing Kiernan's good name in the process. She could tell that Frank wanted nothing more than to have someone take the unruly woman off his hands. Kiernan was sure that dealing with people like Thelma was not in his doorman's etiquette training guide. "Oh, go ahead and send her up." Thelma was one of those buried secrets that somehow kept clawing its way back to the surface.

Kiernan dragged herself out of bed, ran her fingers through her tangled hair, slid her feet into house slippers, and put on the bathrobe that lay bunched at the foot of her bed. Like a surly inmate trudging off to see the warden, she walked through the spacious apartment to the front door. What waited on the other side was a waking nightmare. Thelma looked like death barely warmed over. She was rail thin—and not in a runway-model sort of way—with an ashen walnut complexion and a dual set of dark bags that hung like drooping sacks underneath her eyes. She reeked of stale alcohol and fresh cigarettes. It scared Kiernan to think that she could be looking at a mirror image of herself in a few years.

"What are you doing here?" she hissed, pulling the other woman into the apartment before one of her neighbors caught a glimpse or a whiff of her. She only wished she could find another source for her drugs; then she would never have to see her sister again. But that wasn't the sort of service she could very well look up in the phone book or solicit referrals for; she had too much to lose.

Thelma yanked her arm free and entered the apartment. "It's

good to see you too," she said sarcastically. She shrugged off her act of indignation as her eyes bulged from their sockets when they drank in the display of wealth that surrounded her. She felt as if she'd suddenly materialized onto the pages of one of those thick, glossy decorating magazines. The place was spectacular, a far cry from the one-room crack house she shared with three other addicts in the Bronx. "I didn't know you was rollin' like this." After her last exchange with Kiernan, she'd secretly followed her home, and after Kiernan had failed to show for the last exchange, Thelma figured that a house call was in order.

Kiernan was fuming. "Thelma, what do you want?"

A nasty smile spread across her sister's hardened face. "I'm sure that's not the way you greet yo seditty high-society friends, so how you gon' treat yo' own blood like dat? Besides, you ack all friendly when you wants a package, but you too good to meet me fo' that now too, huh? Sendin' yo' flunky to meet me." Thelma hadn't taken too kindly to being stood up by Kiernan, especially since she'd been counting on seeing her to pinch a few extra dollars. Usually when she handed over the drugs she'd give her sister a sob story in return for an extra fifty or a hundred dollars. And this time she really needed the money. She owed four hundred dollars to a nasty drug dealer in the Bronx and had no way to pay him. He wasn't the type of guy who'd settle this score in court. So while she was running and ducking for cover, here her sister was living the life of Riley. What kind of shit was that?

Kiernan crossed her arms over her chest, preparing for battle. "I was busy. Just tell me what you're doing here."

Thelma walked uninvited down the hall to the living room, counting Kiernan's money along the way, adding up the cost of the original art that hung beneath custom lighting on the walls, the furniture that looked as though it were lifted from the pages of the some ritzy home magazine, a Steinway grand piano that sat in the corner, and beyond that the most expensive detail of all: a priceless view of the New York City skyline. Thelma didn't need a degree in interior design to know that her sister was lying in the lap of luxury. All this time Sister Dearest had led her to believe that she was hardly getting by in the Big Apple, when obviously she'd been living in the land of milk and honey. Thelma flopped down on the suede couch, running her fingers over the luscious material of the cushions.

Originally she had stopped by only to give Kiernan a piece of her mind, but after stumbling across Fort Knox, she'd changed her mind. "I needs me a loan."

Kiernan knew that when Thelma asked for a loan, what she really meant was a gift. "What do I look like, an ATM?" Kiernan turned toward the hallway, anxious to put an end to this little chat.

"You can give me five hundred dollars, or I'll have to call my brother-in-law and ask him for it personally." Thelma had no idea who he was, but her instincts told her that Kiernan hadn't bothered to tell him about her either.

Kiernan stopped midstride. Having Thelma show up now was the last thing on Earth that she needed, since Taylor had no idea that she even existed. She thought quickly. "Wait. I don't have any money, b-but I'll see what I can come up with." She needed to buy some time.

Thelma smelled her sudden desperation. She stood up and walked over to her. "I know you got some money somewhere, and I also know that you haven't told your obviously rich hubby about me, so unless you want me to plan a family reunion I suggest you get me some cash real quick." She showed her dingy yellowing teeth in a sad semblance of a smile as she shifted from side to side on her grimy, run-down shoes.

Kiernan could feel the return of her migraine as it marched up her temples and took up residence. It repulsed and shamed her that she should even have to know the trifling woman who stood before her, let alone that they shared a bloodline. She'd spent most of her adult life convincing herself and others that she was someone else, someone civilized and well-bred, but it took only one phone call, a stubborn memory, or worse, an ill-timed knock at the door for her self-esteem to crack like shattered glass.

Feeling cornered she said, "I'll try, but I'll need some time."

"How much time?"

"Give me a week and I'll see what I can come up with." Again she started out of the living room, headed toward the door, hoping that Thelma would get the hint and follow her through it.

"Unless you want your hubby knowin' more'n you tellin', I suggest you work quicker than that, Norma." It was about time that her sister was brought back down to Earth, Thelma decided. She'd been flying way too high.

Kiernan cringed at the mention of her given name. She'd been running from the sound of it for decades, and to have Thelma stand in her own home spitting it in her face was unconscionable. She spun around and shouted, "You bitch!"

"Don't go git nasty with me. Remember I know all yo' dirty little secrets." At that moment Thelma looked very self-satisfied, standing there with the hollows of her cheeks sucked in—like a third grader jiggling a pocketful of marbles recently won on the playground's battlefield.

Kiernan's hand flew to her mouth as her body heat spiked. The vileness in Tulsa all those years ago had happened to someone else, to a sullied little girl who'd experienced the unthinkable at the hands of someone who should have been her protector instead. Those memories and others that followed after she eventually ran away from home were like lurking land mines she'd usually successfully avoided, but now she was pushed onto a trip wire, losing bits and pieces of herself in the aftermath. "No, no, no," she pleaded. "Please don't tell."

Thelma's response was to stand up and put her hand out. "Well, pay up."

Kiernan grabbed her hand between her own. "Thelma, listen to me. I don't have it right now. I'm broke."

"Who do you think I am? Boo-boo the fool?" She swiveled around looking at Kiernan's expensive worldly possessions as if they represented the promised land. "Where did all this come from, your fairy godmotha?"

"I know how it looks, but I have no money. Taylor pays for all of this," Kiernan said, spreading her arms wide. "My business hasn't been doing well for a while now. You have to believe me," she pleaded.

"In that case, you can jes' get the money from him," she said, heaving her dirty canvas bag higher up her shoulder, as though ready to leave now that all the details had been worked out. "I'll be back for it in a few days." She turned to leave the apartment, pleased that she'd taken the time to drop by.

Just when Kiernan thought things couldn't possibly get any worse, they had. When Thelma was gone she sank to the floor, overburdened with the added weight that her sister had added to her already monumental load. She barely had enough in her bank accounts for a week's expenses; she had no idea where she'd get money to pay Thelma off. And the bigger problem was her certainty that this was only the beginning of Thelma's reign of extortion. Once her sister began milking this cow, Kiernan knew that there would be no stopping her. For now she had to find a way to pay her or all the therapy in the world would do her no good! But where would she find five hundred dollars?

From her seat on the hall's glossy hardwood floor, she had a direct view into Taylor's office and the file cabinet that she'd recently pillaged. Suddenly she got a bright idea, one that actually lit up her face and quickened her heart. Why hadn't she thought of it sooner? She scrambled up from the floor and headed for the cabinet like a drowning man scrambling for a life buoy.

17

THE LAND OF MILK AND MONEY

Champagne spewed through the air like the trail of a comet, as waiters wearing tailored white uniforms uncorked three bottles of 1961 vintage Dom Pérignon for the fifteen members of Mayer, Jones, and Wentworth's inner circle who were opening their ranks to include Taylor Hudson. He was the first minority man to be made partner of the prestigious investment banking firm. Though he'd been informed of the vote immediately following the board meeting that afternoon, Taylor still had difficulty believing his name would now be among those with offices on the elite firm's top floor. Sure, he had the success to warrant the position, but he well knew that was hardly enough, especially for a black man.

Holding his flute by its stem, Eduard raised it into the air. "Gentlemen, I'd like to propose a toast." As the others dutifully fell quiet, he turned in Taylor's direction. "To Taylor Hudson, who is a bright star in our galaxy, and a young man whose enormous talent, unwavering dedication, and resourcefulness will continue to make our company a benchmark for others to follow." He faced Taylor. "Congratulations, Taylor, on making partner," he said, before taking a sip of his champagne. The others murmured their good wishes as they all sipped the bubbly in honor of their newly minted member. It was all very surreal.

"Thank you," Taylor replied through a broad smile. After raising his glass around the room he took a sip of champagne, swallowing and savoring his sweet success. He was intoxicated already from the exhilarating thrill of victory. This moment represented the dream that he'd worked for years to see become a reality, but had never really expected to.

"So how does it feel?"

Taylor turned to find Eduard standing at his side.

"Indescribable," he answered, still smiling broadly.

"I'm really proud of you," the older man said, patting Taylor on his back. "You really did an outstanding job on the Beacon Hill project, as usual. In fact," he said, reaching into his inside breast pocket, "I have your commission here." He handed Taylor a check for two hundred fifty thousand dollars.

"There must be some mistake," Taylor said, looking over the figure with a frown.

"Mistake?"

"This doesn't reflect your percentage." It was their policy that a partner who referred a project to an associate would receive 25 percent of the commission. Since Eduard had passed the Beacon Hill deal on to Taylor, the check should have been 25 percent less.

"Consider it a bonus," Eduard said, reaching back into his pocket for his ever-present cigar as he rocked back on his heels.

Taylor had heard rumors that Eduard was worth over three-quarters of a billion dollars, so sixty-three thousand would definitely be pocket change to a man like him. His compounded daily interest was more than that. "In that case, I guess it really is my lucky day." Taylor decided on the spot that he would give his sister money to open the restaurant in Atlanta that she'd dreamed of.

"That it is," Eduard replied. "That it is."

The next day when Taylor arrived in the office, his new status was clearly evident. It was as if he'd stepped through a magical looking glass and come out the other side suddenly someone else: a VIP. Not only was he given computer-coded key access to the executive elevator, but he was also met by an interior decorator who would begin designing his own personal haven on the illustrious top floor. His new domain would include a spa, a steam shower, a closet, a fully stocked kitchen and bar, as well as a fireplace. Not bad, he thought. If he didn't find an apartment quickly enough he could simply move into his office, especially given the fact that it would be larger than the majority of New York City dwellings.

At eleven fifteen Janice buzzed his line. "Mr. Hudson, don't forget your noon appointment with Mr. Johnson." In addition to having his salary tripled, his promotion was quickly reflected in how he was addressed by the rest of the office staff. Just yesterday the assistants had referred to him by his first name, but overnight they'd all gotten the memo that he was now Mr. Hudson.

"Have my car meet me out front at a quarter till." Last, but certainly not least, his favorite perk was the twenty-four-hour on-call access to a personal car and driver. If only his mother could see him now. He was tempted to call her, but didn't. All of the money and prestige meant very little to her. Her measure of success was the impact that one person had on others. By that scale, Taylor wasn't so sure how he stacked up. He'd always wanted to get involved with underprivileged children, but somehow had never found the time to do it. He vowed to fix that. If Kiernan could help LaTeesha, certainly he could do something for someone, even though he often disapproved of how his wife treated the girl, at least she was trying. He had to give her that.

When his chauffeur jumped out to open the door of his Mercedes Maybach with a cheerful "Afternoon, Mr. Hudson," Taylor smiled to himself. Not that he was materialistic or even elitist, but he could certainly get used to this. The $350,000 car was the automotive equivalent of the *Queen Mary II*. No more schlepping around New York, or scrambling like a rat on a sinking ship for taxis when it poured rain. He settled into the back

of the luxiourously appointed car and pulled out his cell phone
to call Brooke.

He caught her just before she left the office for lunch. "Hey,
baby."

"Hey, partner."

He could hear the smile in her voice. "I like the sound of
that."

"So do I have to reapply now that you are officially a big-
wig?" she teased him.

"You're entitled to preferential treatment."

"What exactly does that entail?" she purred.

"Anything you want," he said.

"Now, I like the sound of that."

Changing the subject, he asked, "What are you doing next
weekend?"

"The usual, why?"

"I thought it would be nice if we got away for a couple of
days to celebrate my promotion." He could hear her wheels
spinning over the phone. "Brooke?"

"I'm here."

"What do you think? Maybe we could head down to Half
Moon for a couple days. Get some sun and relax. What do you
say?"

"I don't know."

"What if I told you that Max is filing for my divorce tomorrow?" he asked. He'd already checked into a suite at the Four
Seasons, but had yet to remove many of his things from the
apartment.

"Are you serious?"

"As a heart attack."

He could hear her intake of breath. "In that case, it's sounding better," she admitted.

"I'll call my travel agent," he said, closing the deal before he
got a no.

"If you insist."

"I insist." He hung up the phone, truly feeling on top of the world.

When the car pulled up to Balthazar, Max was standing outside, just about to go in. "So you rollin' like that," he said, giving Taylor a closed-fist hug and a look of respect as the driver closed the door of the Maybach behind him. "I'm just proud to say I know somebody with that ride."

"Ain't nothing but a thang," Taylor said, grinning as he slipped into the urban vernacular that he and his friend sometimes shared.

"How you doin', man?" Max had a beautiful dark brown complexion with a thick closely cropped black beard, which he stroked whenever he was deep in thought. He was a no-nonsense type of guy who was somewhat shy with the fairer sex, not one to pursue women, so consequently he always ended up with those who went after him, and was never really satisfied. At the age of thirty-seven he was still a bachelor.

"It's the best of times, and the worst of times," Taylor quipped.

"From where I'm standing, I can only see the 'best' part."

"You only have to go as far as Central Park to see the 'worst.'"

"Don't worry, man. We'll get you through this divorce relatively unscathed."

The hostess came over and checked their names from her reservation list, then proceeded to show them to a table in the center of the popular French brasserie. Once they were seated, Max said, "You really should be okay. As I said before, you have an iron-clad prenup, you guys don't have any children, you owned the apartment before you ever met her, and as far as I know there are no accusations of cruelty or adultery. Are there?"

The waitress came over to take their drink orders, interrupting the moment. They both decided that it was a dirty martini–lunch kind of day.

After the tall brunette left, Taylor leaned in and asked, "How long will this take?"

"I'll have papers served immediately, but the length of the whole process will depend a lot on how she reacts."

"How so?"

"Let's put it this way: The best-case scenario is one year for it to become final."

"But?"

"But she could drag things out for much longer, depending on whether—and how—she fights back, so if I were you, I'd be very careful." Max knew Kiernan perhaps better than Taylor ever had since he'd always somehow seen beneath the lies. He'd tried desperately to keep his friend from marrying her in the first place, so executing this divorce would be his pleasure. In his mind he was simply undoing something that never should have been done in the first place.

"If you're talking about Brooke, I'll be discreet."

"I'm sure you will, but from what I know about Kiernan, I think we should come prepared for any- and everything." He vividly remembered how she had suddenly balked when he asked for her financials after she'd asked for access to Taylor's accounts. And she was supposed to be so independently wealthy. It was enough to make him wonder.

"What do you mean by that?"

"I'm going to hire a private investigator."

"A private investigator? For what?"

"Just in case she comes with some surprises, we need to have a few of our own. I just don't trust her."

"Personally, I don't care if she is having an affair." At this point Taylor just wanted out so that he could get on with his life.

"Neither do I, but a judge might. So why don't we just see what we can find?"

Taylor raised his hands in surrender. "Only if you think it's necessary."

"Given what you have to lose, I'd say it's very necessary."

18

CHICKENS COMING HOME TO ROOST

Kiernan and LaTeesha shuffled back and forth between the building and a small U-Haul parked at the back entrance as they hauled the last of the files, fabrics, and other furnishings out of her trendy SoHo office. It was six o'clock in the morning, so there'd be no chance that she'd run into the testy landlord, to whom she now owed three months of back rent. Kiernan figured it was best to bail out now under her own steam, rather than being served with an eviction notice and thrown out, which would be unbearably humiliating. She could almost hear the nosy biddy who ran the advertising agency next door gossiping about it the minute she found out. The thought nearly brought tears to her eyes; the prospect of people making fun of her hurt much more than the reality of abandoning her office. If only she could have closed the deal with Eva by now, things would be much different. Instead the woman was as elusive as ever. That commission alone would be near six figures, so the 50 percent deposit would have been enough to sustain her, at least for a while. Instead here she was scraping to get by, with barely enough money to pay LaTeesha and cover her personal expenses from week to week. For that, at least, she thanked Taylor.

The week before, when she sat commiserating in the hallway,

trying to figure out how to pay Thelma, a brilliant idea had occurred to her. She bolted up, ran into the office, yanked open
Taylor's file cabinet, and struck gold: a box full of Taylor's unused checkbooks.

After gleefully tearing a check out, she immediately made it
payable to herself for three thousand dollars—she knew from
her forays through his papers that his balances were high
enough that he might not even notice the money missing, at least
not for a while.

"Hurry up. Let's get out of here," she ordered LaTeesha. To
save some modicum of respect she'd told LaTeesha they were
moving because of a dispute over new leasing terms. She
couldn't admit to the one person who still looked up to her that
she couldn't pay her rent.

Kiernan closed the door for the last time, bravely holding
back her tears. In addition to this latest setback, Taylor had
moved most of his personal things out of the apartment. There
were now empty spaces where rows of hand-tailored suits and
fine cotton shirts once hung. Though she'd known for a while
where their marriage was headed, the finality of seeing gaps
where his clothes once hung still felt like the horrifying seconds
before a head-on collision: it was physically painless, but terri-
fying nonetheless.

"Where should I put these?" LaTeesha asked as she stumbled
into the apartment buried under a stack of boxed files.

"Put everything in Taylor's office." She wanted to get it all
done quickly, before her neighbors saw what was going on.

"What about Mr. Hudson? Will he mind?" LaTeesha remembered how meticulous he'd seemed about his office at other
times when she'd been at the apartment. She couldn't imagine
him wanting a load of boxes cluttering things up.

Kiernan glared at her. She hadn't told LaTeesha that he'd
moved out; she had to maintain some dignity. "Let me worry

about Mr. Hudson, and you worry about getting those boxes in here." She couldn't believe the girl had the nerve to question her about her own husband, absent though he was.

Honestly, he was now the least of her worries, since he wouldn't be using that office anytime soon, and if she had things her way, he'd never step foot in this apartment again. So what if he'd owned it before they got married? She'd sooner commit hara-kiri than give up her Central Park West address. He'd have to pry her dead, clutching, rigor mortis–afflicted digits from the doorway; in fact, a locksmith was coming this very afternoon to change the door locks to secure her fortress.

She headed into Taylor's office and eased into the chair that sat behind his desk, running her hand across the smooth, rich mahogany.

Her cell phone rang, jarring her from her thoughts. "Hello?" she answered tentatively. It wasn't often these days that she got good news—in person or on the phone.

"Hey, sis." It was Thelma, the last person on Earth—or in heaven and hell—that she wanted to talk to. In fact, she hadn't heard a peep from her since her surprise visit last week. Kiernan had been desperately hoping that it had all been a really bad dream, or that Thelma had found a conscience and decided to give her a break.

"What do you want?" Though she knew it was best not to provoke her sister, she still couldn't manage to keep the edge out of her voice.

"Do I have to spell it out? M-O-N-E-Y."

So much for dreams or a conscience. "I need more time."

"You have until four o'clock today, or I'll start making phone calls."

"But—" *Click.* Dial tone.

Kiernan slammed the phone down and slumped dejectedly onto the desk with her head resting on her folded arms. At times if felt as though the weight of the whole world were getting comfortable on her shoulders. She didn't think she could take much more. She'd spent most of the money from the last check of Taylor's she'd cashed, so it was time to take another one from her stash. She started to write it out for seven hundred dollars—enough to cover Thelma and leave a little extra for herself—but figured, What the hell? And instead she wrote it for another two grand. If she had to give Thelma money anyway, she might as well give her enough for a supply of drugs—she was running dangerously low.

As she was forging Taylor's name to the document, LaTeesha walked back into the room carrying a box containing desk supplies. Kiernan tried to cover up what she was doing, so to divert her attention she yelled at the girl: "What are you doing in here?"

"You asked me to bring the boxes in here, didn't you?"

"Well, put them down, would you?" She got up to leave, slipping the check into her pants pocket. She had to get to the bank as quickly as possible in order to have Thelma's money by the afternoon. "And get this room straightened out before I get back." The room was cluttered with files left behind by Taylor, files that she'd rummaged through and those that they'd just hauled in, but she'd let LaTeesha deal with that mess.

Kiernan was at the door to Chase Manhattan when the doors opened at nine o'clock. Since she also had an account there, she was able to cash the check right away, leaving with a grand in her checking account, and walking out of the branch with the rest. When she got back to the apartment, LaTeesha was still hard at work sorting through files and putting things away. Kiernan went into the bedroom to phone Thelma to arrange a time and place to meet.

As the morning passed, she realized that she'd been up since five and hadn't had one bite to eat, so she picked up the phone and ordered Thai food for delivery from a place just blocks away.

At twelve forty-five Frank called up. "Ma'am, there's a gentleman here to see—"

"Send him up," she said, cutting Frank off.

A minute later there was a knock at her door. When she opened it, fully expecting to see a deliveryman wearing a white jacket, she was surprised to find a well-dressed white man standing there with a document in hand. "Are you Kiernan Malloy?"

"I am," she answered defensively.

"This is for you," he said, shoving the papers into her hand and turning quickly to leave.

Still planted in the same spot in the doorway, Kiernan read the divorce papers as the color drained from her face and her blood slowly boiled. Angrily, she stepped back into the apartment and slammed the door shut behind her. This last salvo had lit a fire in her ass. An old, familiar anger began to simmer in the pit of her stomach. Tossing the papers onto a Chippendale foyer table, she twisted a fist menacingly inside the palm of her hand. If he wants to play hardball, she thought, I'm just warming up.

19

MOTHER'S BABY, DADDY'S MAYBE

Late Saturday morning Joie waited at Sarabeth's restaurant, nervously twirling the ends of her dreads, not sure exactly what she would say when Evan finally arrived to meet her. She was certain of one thing: She would have to make a decision soon about whether to keep the baby she was carrying, since in another week it might be too late for her to consider an abortion. After pinpointing her last period and figuring out when she'd had sex with whom, she was still no closer to knowing which man was the father of her child.

Aside from being pissed at herself for plain stupidity and carelessness, she was also terribly conflicted about the future. On one hand the thought of having a child held no special allure for her, but on the other—for some strange and inexplicable reason—she was becoming attached to the one she now carried; she even found herself talking to the baby on occasion. These one-sided dialogues always provided her with amazing clarity, so she figured it must be a girl, because only conversations with other women were so fulfilling. So in her mind's eye it was a little girl with sparkling brown eyes and dimples like her own.

"Hi, sweetcakes," Evan said, leaning over to kiss her on the cheek, no doubt believing that brunch would quickly lead him to dessert.

"Hey." They hadn't seen each other since that night at Butter, though he'd called several times wanting to "hook up." Under the circumstances she really wasn't in the mood for sex, not even good sex, which was certainly a first for her.

"Let's eat a quick brunch and then have each other." He flashed his million-dollar Colgate smile. Normally she would've already been wet between the legs.

Joie took a deep breath. She was not looking forward to this conversation. "We need to talk," she said, giving him a serious, all-jokes-aside expression. After long thought, it seemed reasonable to tell the man she would most want to be with first. Though she didn't love either one, at least she did feel passionately about Evan. So for lack of any other criteria she was telling him about her pregnancy before telling Brent.

"That's what you've been sayin'. So what's up?" He leaned back into his chair, now looking slightly bored as he crossed one Prada street shoe casually over his knee.

There was no need to beat around the bush, so she just came right out with it. There was no subtle, delicate, or diplomatic way to say what she had to say; she simply blurted it out: "I'm pregnant."

He looked stunned, as though he wasn't sure what action was required of him. "So what's that got to do with me?" he asked defensively. He'd turned into the bad pretty boy that some people found so attractive, but at the moment seemed very ugly.

Joie was crushed by his crass, insensitive comment, made worse by his insolent tone. Her first reaction was anger. "Considering that you've been fucking me on the regular for a while now, I'd say quite a bit." She pinned him with a look that said, Now you can go fuck yourself.

"Me, Brent, and God only knows who else." He stifled a smirk and gave her a return look that placed her barely above a streetwalker.

She felt like she'd been slapped hard across her face. As the shock of his comment wore off, she realized what he'd really thought of her all along. It was so unfair that a man who enjoyed his sexuality was simply "sowing wild oats," while a woman doing the same thing was just a whore. She hadn't foolishly thought that he harbored any feelings of undying love, but she didn't know that he considered her a slut either. Well, if he wanted to play hardball, they both could.

Joie glared at him with ice in her veins and fire in her eyes. "You can say whatever you want, but the fact is that the odds are fifty-fifty in your favor or against you, however you'd like to look at it."

He leaned forward, gripping the table. "Now wait a fucking min—"

"No, you wait a minute, asshole." She jabbed a finger within inches of a spot between his eyes. "It was all fun and games when we were having freaky sex all over town, but the minute I have a problem you want to dissociate yourself. Well, for your information it doesn't quite work like that, so you'd just better hope this kid isn't yours, because if it is, I'll drag your sorry ass to court so quick that your dick'll spin." She grabbed her bag and stood to leave, tossing her napkin down onto the table.

Evan stood too. "Let's talk about this," he pleaded, holding her by the shoulders. It suddenly occurred to him that she wasn't one to fuck with, and that so far he'd handled this situation all wrong.

"That was my plan, until you decided to be a bastard instead. Just remember, two can play that game."

He hung his head low. "Listen, I'm sorry, I was just shocked. I had no idea."

"Do you think that I haven't been shocked?"

He shuffled his feet back and forth, trying to find some empathy where none existed. "I'm sure this must be hard for you."

"You don't know the half of it." She rolled her eyes as tears threatened her tough exterior.

"So what are you gonna do?" he asked hopefully.

"What do you mean?"

"I mean, if you need some money to take care of this, I can give you that." He quickly reached into his back pocket, anxious to rid himself of this problem.

She stared at him, for the second time amazed. "Is that why you think I'm telling you this? So I can get a few hundred dollars to kill my baby?" she huffed. "If it were that simple I wouldn't need to tell you at all. It'd already be done."

He stepped back, truly stunned now. "So what are you saying? That you're keeping the baby?" The blood drained from his face as quickly as water from an unclogged drain.

"I'm not sure exactly what I'm going to do. I just thought you might want to know, that's all." She turned to leave.

"Wait. Does Brent know?" He stood there pouting like a six-year-old who had just gotten kicked off the Little League team. All he needed was a stone to throw.

"No."

He grabbed her arm and swung her back around. "Oh, so you just decided to pin the little bastard on me."

She yanked her arm away. "The only bastard in this situation is you." With that, she turned and walked out.

An hour later she found herself at Brooke's front door, hoping that her friend was home and not jogging through the park. On the third ring, Brooke finally opened the door holding a mug of coffee and the morning paper.

"What brings you this way?" Brooke asked as she stood aside for Joie to enter.

"I just had a very unpleasant conversation with candidate number one. He's not taking the possibility of impending fatherhood too well. I don't know what I expected, but it wasn't to be treated like Typhoid Mary." She looked dejected.

"Come on in. I'll fix you some herbal tea."

Joie settled in the kitchen's bay window, soaking up some sunlight, while Brooke set about making her a lavender herbal blend, letting Joie enjoy the silence and her thoughts. Once

Brooke had a steaming mug ready, she joined Joie on the bench in the window, handing it to her. "So tell me what happened."

Joie took a deep breath. "Well, he all but called me a whore, and informed me—in no uncertain terms—that this had nothing to do with him. When he finally calmed down a little he reached into his pocket, ready to pull out enough cash to pay for an abortion. A real winner, that one." She shook her head in disgust.

Brooke reached over to hug her friend. "I'm sorry it had to be that way." She was also surprised that Joie expected anything better from a man who slept with his best friend's girlfriend. The harder question for Joie, she thought, was what could be expected from the girlfriend.

"Yeah, well, so am I. I'm sorry about a lot of things, but it's all water under the bridge now."

"You're right. Now you have to focus on what's best for you—and the child, should you decide to keep it." Brooke was careful to qualify her statement. The last thing she wanted to do was to influence Joie's decision about whether to keep her baby. That was one call that her friend had to make all alone.

"The only problem is that I have no idea what *is* best." She shrugged her shoulders and sighed. "I'm not the best-qualified person to make important decisions. You know that." She smiled lightly at Brooke. "I've always ventured through life taking one day at a time, doing what I damn well pleased. So long-term planning isn't exactly my strong suit." She took a sip of the hot tea. It felt good in her stomach, which was a tad queasy today.

"Joie, you've got to lighten up on yourself. All of that is in the past now. You are more than capable of taking care of yourself and a baby, but only if you choose to."

"You think so?"

Brooke had never seen her friend so uncertain and vulnerable. "Of course. It'll take a lot of time, focus, and yes, money to raise a child, but the rewards can be priceless. You just have to weigh all the pros and cons."

Tears began to stream down Joie's face. She'd never in her life felt so alone, lost, and incapable. "Now I'm really afraid to tell Brent. There's no telling what his reaction will be, especially if he learns the whole truth."

"First of all, you have to remember that this isn't about Brent. Or Evan, for that matter. It's about you and your baby. Tell him that you are pregnant, and since your relationship wasn't exclusive there's a chance that the baby might not be his. You don't have to tell him who the other candidate is if you don't want to."

Joie hadn't considered that option. "That's true. I don't, do I?"

Brooke patted Joie's hand. "No, you don't."

"What if he gets mad and he leaves me too?"

"Given how you really feel about him—or more accurately, don't feel—would that really be the worst thing in the world?" When Joie hesitated she added, "Be honest with yourself."

She shrugged. "I guess not."

"See," Brooke said, "you have nothing to lose."

Joie chuckled.

"What's so funny?"

"Nothing, it's just that now I can see why your patients love you."

They drank in silence, as the sun beamed through the windows, warming up a crisp fall day.

"How are things with Taylor?" Joie asked between sips.

"Couldn't be better," Brooke answered as a smile spread across her face, brightening her eyes. "He's filed for divorce and has asked me to go away with him next weekend."

"That's great!" Joie perked up for the first time in days.

"Whoa. I said he asked me to go away, nothing more," she clarified. "I'm not really sure that I should."

"Are you crazy?"

"Maybe, but he is still a married man, and I'm not trying to get hurt. Been there, done that."

Joie looked at Brooke with a sad expression on her face. "You know, you'll never have to worry about getting hurt again if you don't ever open yourself up to live. And I don't know which is worse: not really living or getting hurt."

Brooke stroked her chin thoughtfully.

"Just because I'm a feather in the wind doesn't mean that I don't know which way is up."

"Coming from a bona fide free spirit, that's pretty profound. If I'm not mistaken, this pregnancy is making you pretty introspective."

Joie blushed. "It's funny that you should say that. I've been having these amazing conversations with her, and after they're over I'm really pretty clear." She hung her head. "I guess I should have asked her about Evan, huh?"

"Her?"

She smiled broadly, the flush of pregnancy lighting up her face. "It's a girl," she announced.

"You had a sonogram?" Brooke asked. She thought for sure that it was too early to tell yet.

"No. I just know."

Brooke was so happy to see joy come from within Joie. It was evident to her, even if Joie didn't know it herself yet, that she would be having the baby. They spent the rest of the day hanging out at the park, shopping for groceries, and making a fabulous meal together. Brooke couldn't help but feel that this day marked a turning point for them, both headed in directions that neither would have predicted weeks ago.

20

SEX, SUN, AND SCANDAL

Whatever reservations Brooke may have clung to about her relationship with Taylor evaporated like mist burned off by the morning sun during their weekend alone together in Jamaica. Even after her conversation with Joie, she'd still harbored some lingering doubts. Though divorce papers were filed and he would be a free man, Taylor was still another woman's husband, an unavoidable fact that had hung over Brooke's head like a dark cloud threatening an otherwise bright, sunny day. But being four hundred miles from the city distanced her from the moral realities of dating a married man.

"I could really get used to this." Brooke lay with her eyes closed under a brilliant blue sky while the sun kissed every inch of her body, except for that which was barely covered by a string bikini's bottom. She smiled to herself thinking how proud Joie would be to see her sunbathing topless on a Jamaican beach, something that just months ago she would never have even considered.

"You are so beautiful." Taylor drank in the sight of her; afraid to blink his eyes for fear she might disappear.

When she opened hers, shielding them with her hand from the sun's bright rays, Taylor was lying on his side, propped up on one arm.

So this is what it's like to be adored, she thought.

He had rented a private villa at the exclusive four-hundred-acre resort Half Moon that came with its own pool, cook, housekeeper, butler, and beach. The man sure knew how to roll.

The scrunch of shoes into sand brought their butler, who appeared carrying a tray of mojitos, Fiji bottled water, fresh fruit, and cheese and crackers. He set it down next to Brooke, careful not to stare at her seminude form.

"What time would you like dinner served, madam?" he asked in a thick, rich Jamaican accent.

Brooke looked at Taylor. "How about seven thirty?"

He nodded in agreement.

"And what would the lady like?"

She was feeling decadent. "How about lobster?" she answered, licking her lips. "Drenched in butter."

"Whatever you want," Taylor said, reaching for their mint-soaked mojitos, handing one to Brooke and taking a long swallow of the other before setting it back down on the tray.

"I'll remember you said that." She took a satisfying sip from her glass.

"I'm counting on it," he replied, reaching for the suntan oil. He squeezed a generous portion into his hand and motioned for Brooke to turn over.

It didn't get much better than this: the hot, simmering sun, ice-cold drinks, and the warm, soothing hands of a lover as he rubbed away traces of tension from the muscles that ran down her back, over her buttocks, and along her thighs and calves. Forgoing more hours of seashell hunting, sunning, and swimming, they headed back into the thatched villa to make love for the second time. The first had been the night before. It was the stuff that dreams were made of, wet or otherwise. Brooke simply had to close her eyes to recall the heat and passion from the most amazing sex she'd ever known.

After arriving at the hotel and having an in-suite dinner, she'd checked the full-length mirror in the bathroom for the fifteenth time to confirm that—yes—she looked incredible in a pair of flat mules that worked perfectly with the bloodred Japanese kimono. Her hair was swept atop her head, loose tendrils framing her face. She'd added just a hint of blush, some lip gloss, and splashed on Dolce & Gabbana cologne after showering with the complementary gel. She took a deep breath, checked her nervousness, and headed out of the bathroom door.

With Maxwell crooning seductively through the speakers, and Diptyque candles burning softly, she entered the candlelit bedroom, leaving her apprehensions behind. There was a silent understanding between them that they were crossing an important line—from exploration to intimacy, from timidity to trust—but no words were spoken. None were needed.

She reached up to lock her arms behind his neck, pulling him close to meet her lips. Their tongues spoke a language of their own as they tasted each other and danced a sexy tango to a private tune, teasing and consuming each other. When Taylor lengthened his tongue and probed it in and out of her mouth over and over again, she sucked it eagerly, each time waiting breathlessly for the next taste. He held her tighter, making love to her mouth, running his hands over the curves of her body, causing her knees to weaken and her desire to grow.

Realizing that she wanted—no, needed—more, he pulled apart with a few quick kisses and held her face in both of his hands, searching her eyes for confirmation. There he saw deep yearning, raw passion, and a simple desire that no combination of words could ever communicate. Standing back, he untied his robe, never rushing at all. Instead he savored the look of anticipation that settled on her face, watching her unconsciously lick her lips, eager to taste the man who was so boldly unveiling himself before her. It was like watching an award-winning film, while starring in it at the same time.

When he was down to his boxers, she unbelted her kimono, letting the silk garment slide down her body like water running over rapids; then she stepped away from the pile of fabric, totally nude. Reverently his eyes consumed her full, round breasts with their stiff brown nipples, and the teasing curve of her hips that seductively framed a small thatch of hair that led to her smoldering sex.

"You are so sexy," he said in a whisper-soft voice as he reached for her, this time with no intention of letting go.

She answered by inviting him onto the bed, where she welcomed the feel of his body's weight as it settled onto hers, its radiant heat warming her even though she shivered from head to toe with nervous anticipation. She felt his stiffness stirring urgently between her legs. Not conscious of thought, she let her hands roam his body, dancing past the ripples that traveled down his back, gripping his firm buttocks, edging him, guiding him, and urging him to penetrate her, to satisfy the hunger that he and the passage of too much time had created.

After he slipped on a condom, he whispered into her ear, "Are you ready?" before flicking his tongue inside, causing a delicious sensation to flow throughout her body.

Nothing could have stopped her from having her fill of him—not marriage, morals, or anything else for that matter. "Please, please . . ." was all she managed to say. Words were lost to her, but her hips moved, gyrating and repositioning themselves in her quest to capture and consume him whole.

He raised her knees in the air, opening her wider, and began licking her sex with the swollen tip of his manhood, teasing her mercilessly. She realized without a doubt that this was no nervous, stumbling college freshman, fumbling his way around; Taylor was every inch a full-grown man.

"Right . . . there—please . . . let me have it," she begged in a deep, throaty voice that she barely recognized herself. Before she could finish, he eased nine inches of hardened muscle deep into her slick wetness. She caught her breath, physically overwhelmed by the pulsating heat that radiated throughout her body. "Oh, baby . . ." she moaned. She never remembered sex feeling so good in her life. So this was what she'd been missing. A fleeting thought passed her mind: No wonder Joie is addicted.

"Oh, yes, baby." His strokes were long, strong, deep thrusts, which she met with a driving force of her own. Their blended rhythm was hot and erotic. She desperately wanted the feeling to go on forever, to lose herself in his passion and power, but instead the erotic motions, coupled with the sexy sound of his moans and her whimpers, seized her body, making her toes curl, while throes of ecstasy rolled over her body, wave after undulating wave.

Taylor held on to her tightly, allowing himself to feel the orgasmic currents that overtook her. When the crescendo began to subside, he started stroking her again, this time slow and easy, accompanied by flights of tender kisses all over her shoulders, neck, and face. The physical and emotional sensations brought tears to her eyes as she realized that she might have had sex before, but without question she'd never been made love to.

"Are you okay?" he asked between loving kisses.

"I've never been better." She smiled up at him.

"That's exactly what I wanted to hear." That was when he rolled over onto his back, guiding her on top of him without missing a stroke. Holding on to her hips, he closed his eyes and focused his mind on the intense pleasure she gave him from her deep, tight, wet massage. He felt the building tide as it began to turn, heading relentlessly for shore; he knew that his nerve endings were stoked, and he made a feeble attempt to hold back, but her body demanded everything that he had to give. Without warning he threw his head back and gripped her hips tighter; his thrusts came faster, higher, deeper. She drained him until there was nothing left. They cuddled together afterward. "Bliss" was the word that came to her mind as they both lay side by side completely satiated, having finally scratched an evasive, teasing itch, and fed a ravenous hunger.

Those memories flooded her as she showered after they left the beach. She couldn't wait to climb between the cool, smooth sheets and make hot, passionate love.

There was none of the uncertainty or racing desperation of their first time together. Instead this time was like a long, slow walk under a moonlit sky, as his kisses left a trail of heat from her neck to her nipples, finally setting a burning fire between her legs.

Away from prying eyes and bouts of conscience, Brooke wanted to stop the passage of time at that precise moment before his sucking and licking drove her completely over the edge. The pleasure he gave felt so right that she wasted no time giving it back. She reached for his erect sex and left a hot trail of her own, planting kisses up and down its thick shaft. The kisses turned to long licks, ending in a deep, sucking sensation that teased and taunted every nerve in Taylor's body, coaxing him closer to a release that only increased his desire for her. They kissed passionately, tongues searching and fingers roaming, both needing the other to solve a puzzle, scratch an itch, or quench a thirst. Once they found each other, they climbed to the peak of ecstasy, reaching the summit at the same time.

Afterward they lay together, panting happily as the sticky sweat that covered their bodies slowly evaporated, leaving a cool sheen over moist skin. The real world felt planets away, like another time and certainly another place. Brooke was happy to pretend that it didn't even exist, and instead to fully enjoy the fantasy that was now her reality. They lay in bed feeding succulent bits of lobster to each other, and licking the dripping butter from fingers and lips, meeting again later between the sheets for dessert.

21
ARRESTED DEVELOPMENT

"Kiernan, Eva's on the phone for you." LaTeesha could barely contain the excitement in her voice. She'd finally figured out just how desperate things were for Kiernan, and how badly they needed business. At first she believed Kiernan's story about a problem with the office lease, but when her boss didn't begin looking for another space, and she hadn't seen signs of Mr. Taylor in over a week, she realized that her mentor was in trouble. She wondered how her husband could leave her at such a trying time. He'd seemed like such a nice guy on the occasions when she'd seen him, but she was learning that you couldn't judge a book by its cover. She really felt bad for Kiernan and hated that there was nothing she could do to help her. But she also knew that this phone call could be the answer to Kiernan's troubles.

Kiernan scrambled frantically for the phone through the mess of files, swatches, and pictures on the cluttered desk as though it were a lifeline, and in a sense—given the situation—it was. "Hello?"

"Kiernan, it's Eva, darling. How are you?"

As usual, Eva sounded as though she didn't have a care in the world. How nice, Kiernan thought. She pulled herself together in an effort to sound like the highly cultured person she'd always presented to others. "Oh, hi, dear. I'm fine." She ignored LaTeesha's look of amazement and shooed her from the room.

"Listen, honey, I'm calling to see if you might be able to get a proposal to me as soon as possible."

Kiernan perked up like a drought-stricken flower given a taste of rainwater. "Of course, how soon do you need it?"

"By the end of next week at the latest."

It figured that the hussy would ignore her for over a month, then want action almost overnight. "Not a problem. I'll just need to stop by to take a look at the property first."

"That can be arranged. Oh, and one other thing."

"What's that?"

"I also want graphic storyboards of your proposed design."

Though that would cost extra money to produce, Kiernan didn't balk. "No problem." After they hung up the phone Kiernan was tempted to do a dance—finally something was going her way—but figured she'd hold off until she really had something to celebrate. Now she just needed a pick-me-up to help get her creative juices going.

She went looking for LaTeesha. "I need you to run an errand for me."

"Sure." She was more than ready for a break. She'd been sorting files and storing them all day long.

"I need you to meet the same woman you met before at the deli near the corner of Madison and Seventy-fifth Street."

"More jewelry?" She was surprised, since money seemed to be a problem for Kiernan.

"Yes, in fact, I'm thinking about helping her wholesale it," Kiernan lied.

This made sense to LaTeesha. Maybe Kiernan was going to try to make some extra money by helping to sell the pieces.

Kiernan handed her an envelope with cash and sent the girl on her way.

An hour later, when Kate walked through the door of Brooke's office, Brooke immediately noticed something different about her.

"So how are you?" Brooke asked, carefully observing the woman.

"Never better," Kiernan said, tossing her hair exuberantly as she delicately tucked stray ends behind her ear. She'd used some of her ill-gotten money to fund a trip to Joseph's hair salon for a touch-up and to Mario Badescu for a glycolic facial, so now at least she looked like a million dollars, even if she didn't have it. She settled onto the couch casually, as though the two women were meeting for tea and finger sandwiches, instead of to discuss her mental and emotional health.

Though Brooke was getting a handle on Kate, the woman was one patient she realized she might never completely know. Her feelings were so deeply buried that Brooke was doubtful that Kate would recognize them herself.

"That's good to hear," Brooke replied evenly. "What's happened since you were here last week?" Brooke took the chair opposite the couch, settling in for an hour of true confessions.

Kiernan dangled her leg across her knee. "Well, for one thing, I finally have some closure on my feelings toward my husband." Though this wasn't true, saying it made her feel as though she had some control of the situation. Right now all of the cards—and money—seemed to be in Taylor's hands.

The abrupt change in attitude about her husband was a red flag to Brooke, at least until she found out what had precipitated it. "I see." She nodded slowly. "Tell me about it."

"Well," Kiernan started. She scrunched her face and looked toward the ceiling, as though searching for the right words. "I'm just finally realizing that we really weren't meant to be together. Our marriage was a mistake to begin with."

From what Brooke had gathered about Kate's husband, Thomas, there didn't seem to have ever been real passion on his side either, so she was curious as to how they ended up together in the first place. "So why did you?" Sometimes a direct question was the best approach.

Kiernan bowed her head. She was silent at first, then decided that if she couldn't tell the truth to a therapist, then why bother coming? "He thought I was pregnant," she confided. "Otherwise he never would have married me." A sneer spread its way across her face, followed by a snort of contempt.

"He thought?"

"There never was a baby," she confessed. "I just told him that." She wore a blank expression that conveyed no remorse whatsoever. She knew the trick she had played on Taylor was reprehensible, but she could think of no other way to get the life that she'd envisioned for herself. Things didn't come to her the easy way. She'd had to fight tooth and nail to get anything that she'd ever gotten, and Taylor was no exception.

Brooke was appalled, but she registered no reaction. Of course, this wasn't the first time she'd heard of this ruse being played on an unsuspecting groom. "What happened when he found out the truth?"

"He wasn't exactly thrilled," she said, waving her hand dismissively. "But he got over it."

Brooke leaned back in her chair. "Kate, did you really believe that a marriage based on a lie would succeed?" The question wasn't asked sarcastically at all; she really wanted to know what Kate thought.

Kiernan's emotions switched lanes without warning. She suddenly appeared thoughtful and very sad. "All I've ever wanted was to be loved." Tears began flowing down her cheeks, and she made no attempt to stop them.

Brooke's heart broke for the pitiful emotionally underdeveloped woman who sat across from her. She was someone who'd never known true love, and therefore didn't recognize it. "Kate, love is an involuntary response. It can't be manufactured, negotiated, or demanded from other people."

"I guess not." She shrugged. "Not even from parents, huh?" At that moment she sounded like the small, scared child who'd suffered at the hands of her father.

"Do you love yourself?" Brooke asked in a soft, gentle voice.

Kiernan wiped at her tears and looked as though she'd never considered such a question before. "What's there to love?" she finally answered.

"That's exactly what you have to figure out." Brooke sat back in her chair, nibbling on the end of her pen for a few seconds. "For our next appointment, I want you to make a list of all the good things about yourself, and then I want you to make a list of things that may not be viewed as good."

"Viewed by whom?"

"By you. It's important that you know, understand, and love yourself before you can ever expect anyone else to."

"But what about other people? It's also important what they think."

Brooke could clearly imagine the heavy load of shame, guilt, and humiliation that Kate had carried around as a young child, fearing the world might somehow have seen her dirty laundry. These feelings would have been made worse by an uncaring mother who'd turned a blind eye, as if to blame the child. "Before we can worry about what other people think of you, we first have to work on your image of yourself."

"But it's other people who judge me."

"What do you think other people see when they look at you?"

Though there were no sniffles or sobs, tears again ran down her face as she explained. "Someone who is not educated enough. Didn't go to the right schools. Not tall enough. Hair not straight enough. Complexion too dark. You name it, and I fall just short enough to never make the grade."

"So how did you get where you are in life if you didn't make the grade?"

"By always cheating on the test," she said truthfully.

Brooke thought carefully about what she said. "But, Kate, if you've never really taken the test, how do you know that you would have come up short? For all you know you could have ended up with an even higher score."

Kiernan cocked her head to the side, taken by the simple logic of Brooke's comment. She thought about how bad things were for her but couldn't help but agree with the therapist. "I guess you're right."

Brooke was encouraged by this small breakthrough, but realized that acknowledgment was one thing, and that changing actual behavior was the hard part.

Kiernan sighed. The session seemed to be taking a lot out of her. "It just seems like other people have it so much easier."

Brooke leaned forward. "Kate, listen to me. You will never know the realities of another person's life unless you live it, and that's impossible to do. I'm sure on the surface there are those people who look at you and assume the same thing that you assume about others: that you have it all. The bottom line is, you don't know what other people are facing, be it a terminal illness, the death of a parent, financial ruin, or even despair."

Kiernan suddenly began to sob out loud.

"What is it?" Brooke knew that she was approaching a breakthrough with Kate and watched her closely.

"My husband's filed for divorce," she said between sobs.

So that was it. Brooke now knew the big change in Kate's life. Another abandonment would certainly throw her into a tailspin. She wanted to reach out and hold the woman and tell her that everything would be okay, but she knew that it would be unprofessional and unproductive. Besides, she wasn't so sure how things would turn out. As far as she could tell, she was just getting to know the real Kate.

Kiernan walked out onto Fifty-seventh Street after composing herself behind a pair of large, dark sunglasses. She pulled her cell phone out to check messages as she headed home. The first two were inconsequential—one was from a credit-card company threatening to sue her and the other was from her irate ex-landlord, who was screaming in Italian-accented English—but the last one stopped her in her tracks. It was from LaTeesha, who'd been arrested after giving money to Thelma for the package, which she was later surprised to discover contained cocaine.

Kiernan nearly broke out into a cold sweat as her mind ran through the repercussions of what had happened and ultimately its effect on her.

22

KISS AND TELL

That evening Brooke set aside her patients' troubles and dished it with her girl. They had just finished a Mediterranean-inspired dinner of crisp grilled sea bass, saffron risotto, and a fresh pear-walnut salad, all courtesy of Chez Parrish. Cooking was one of those simple pleasures that Brooke rarely indulged in. There was something fulfilling about combining goods from the earth—or the sea—to prepare a feast, especially for those she loved.

Joie suddenly put her glass down and looked at Brooke as though she were seeing her for the first time all day. Though physically she was the same person she was last week, there was a change in her as drastic as the one from spring to fall. A light hidden deep inside her soul had been switched from the off position to on, giving her a radiant glow that no potion known to man could create. Her steps were even lighter, more graceful and fluid.

"What aren't you telling me?" Joie finally asked.

Brooke hopped up from the table to clear away the dishes. The setting sun had reached through the west-facing window, found her, and settled across her face. "What makes you think there's something to tell?" Brooke's smile belied her denial. So did her appearance. She was always gorgeous, but today she was simply luminescent, even wearing a tangerine Juicy sweat suit and bare feet. Her movements bore a confidence that Joie had never witnessed from her before, as though her muscles, bones, and ligaments had been freed from invisible shackles. She'd never seen her friend this alive and happy, even that time when they caught a 75-percent-off sale at Gucci in Woodbury Commons.

"Brooke, you're talking to me," Joie proclaimed, giving her the eye. "So stop the bullshit and give up the goods." Frustrated, she stood up, placing a hand on her hip. "Let's get comfy so you can tell me the *real* reason for this new pep in your step."

They headed into Brooke's bedroom, where they'd sometimes spend the whole evening administering manicures, pedicures, and facials, all the tools spread out in the middle of Brooke's bed, converting her lair into a spa-inspired picnic, all while catching up on each other's lives, or more specifically Joie's, which was usually much more colorful than Brooke's. Between her patients and Joie, sometimes Brooke felt as though she spent her entire life hearing about other people's lives, rather than having one of her own; at least up until now.

"I guess it's pretty hard to fool you, huh?"

"So why even bother?"

When they'd both flopped down onto the duvet, Joie said, "Okay, so spill it." She rocked from side to side, making herself comfortable on the fluffy down.

Brook blushed; a hint of color highlighted her caramel-hued cheeks as she relived the hot, steamy nights with Taylor. She'd been hard-pressed to think of anything else. Daydreaming about it had become addictive, particularly since it was a pleasure that she could summon at will, whether during the thirty seconds spent waiting for an elevator, or the five minutes she stared at the ceiling before drifting off to sleep. Even during sessions with her clients, she sometimes found her mind adrift, making its way back to Jamaica, and into Taylor's arms. The vivid sexual imagery drew quick flashes of heat to her cheeks. Surely, she thought anyone who saw her must know that she'd recently been sexed up. In fact, the Monday after their affair in the islands, when she walked into the office, André had tilted his head, squinted his perfectly arched eyebrows, and carefully surveyed her, much the same way that Joie had done just minutes ago. Finally he proclaimed, "Either you've found the fountain of youth and took a bath in it, or you and Taylor have grown *much* closer."

"Don't keep me waiting," Joie insisted. "Give up the goods." Up till now, Brooke had simply told her that the trip had been fine, so she had assumed that Brooke had worn her chasity belt and left the key in Manhattan.

Brooke's hand covered a burgeoning smile that was spreading wider as her cheeks reddened. She looked like a young girl with a big secret that she was dying to divulge, but at the same time wanting to hold on to it, keeping it to herself just a little while longer. Finally, words burst forth like kernels turning to popped corn. "We did it! Taylor and I had sex, and it was wonderful! I mean absolutely incredible!" She grabbed one of the pillows on the bed and hugged it tightly to her body.

"Wow! I can't believe it." Joie seemed to be in shock. Though she suspected as much, it all seemed surreal for Brooke to have actually been with a man, and what was more, to be so turned out by it. She was acting like a virgin who'd lucked into an orgasm her first time out.

"What do you mean, you can't believe it? Aren't you the one who's been trying to get me laid for the last three years?"

"Yeah," Joie answered, still in a daze, "but I'd given up hope."

"Can I tell you that it was amazing?" Brooke fell backward on the bed like a limp doll, and gazed dreamily at the chandelier that hung above.

Joie took a sip. "I've been trying to tell you for years that sex is better than food, and less fattening," she announced with a quick nod of her head.

"It wasn't just the sex—which was phenomenal—but the

man himself. He's just so . . ." She gestured randomly, trying to pull the words to describe him from thin air, searching the ceiling when she still came up short.

A sudden thought hit Joie like a freight train in a darkened tunnel. "You are in love with him, aren't you?"

Brooke stopped midthought, putting a finger to her bottom lip to really consider the question. "Love" was such a big four-letter word. Though she was at a loss to describe the sheer joy she felt whenever she heard Taylor's voice, envisioned his face, or felt his touch, she wasn't sure that it qualified as love—or that it didn't. "I'm not sure," she finally said.

Joie could see the wheels turning. "Don't be so analytical about something as ethereal as love."

"That's funny," Brooke said simply.

"What? What's so funny?"

"To hear you—Ms. Noncommittal—waxing poetic about love." For as long as she had known Joie, her relationships with men had been all about sex, satisfaction, and very little else. Unlike a lot of Brooke's female patients, Joie was one woman who never confused sex with love. She was a woman with a man's libido and sensitivities. Brooke found her fascinating and had always lived her own nonexistent sex life vicariously through Joie's. Her friend certainly got enough to go around, and was never shy about sharing the details of it.

"Just because I don't happen to know Cupid personally, doesn't mean that I don't believe he exists," Joie defended herself.

Brooke glimpsed a side of Joie that was usually kept well under wraps. She wondered about the sudden unveiling. "He almost seems too perfect to be real."

"Who—Cupid or Taylor?" Joie asked.

They both laughed. "Taylor, silly," Brooke said. She twirled a strand of hair between her fingers, wearing a dreamy expression on her face. "He's just so intelligent, caring, sensitive. And he's warm, intuitive, and sexy as hell." She closed her eyes and fanned her face with one hand, whistling.

"And let's not forget married." Joie regretted saying the words the moment they left her mouth. It was stupid and cruel of her to rain on the only parade Brooke had ever had.

Brooke's eyes quickly opened. "Gee, thanks," she said, coming back down to earth.

"I'm sorry. I didn't mean to be a killjoy. Besides, if he's getting a divorce it's really no big deal," she said, trying to smooth over the fly she'd thrown into the ointment.

"I wonder," Brooke mused, not so sure. As happy as Brooke was, she couldn't help but compare her situation to Joie's. After all, life seemed to uphold the laws of motion: For every action, there was an equal and opposite reaction. While she'd always admired Joie's irreverent zest for life and the easy exploration of her sexual desires, was this pregnancy her turn to pay the piper? To pay in full for years of unadulterated, non-procreating, sheer-joy-of-the-fuck sex? If that was her price, Brooke couldn't help but wonder what her own would be for sharing blissful nights in the strong arms of another woman's husband.

"Hey, snap out of it. This is one of those times when it's not profitable or beneficial to overthink life—yours or anyone else's. Just go with it, at least for now," Joie advised.

"Now that we're on the subject, what are you going to do with your life? 'Just going with it' may not be an option." Brooke knew the deadline for a safe abortion was quickly approaching, but as far as she knew, Joie hadn't made a decision one way or another.

Joie got up from the bed, uncomfortable with the sudden shift of the spotlight. "In a way just going with it is doing something," she said, rubbing her growing stomach.

Brooke jumped up from the bed. "You're going to have her?" She was so happy that she cried tears of joy. She hadn't quite realized how hopeful she'd been that Joie would have her baby; she hadn't allowed herself that luxury. "Oh, my God, we've gotta go shopping!"

Joie laughed and cried herself, but between tears asked, "Do they even make designer baby shoes?"

"I don't know, but we'll definitely find out." They hugged each other, with the baby, whom Joie had already named, between them.

Joie grew serious. "Well, while we're at it, do you think we can find out what I should do about her father?"

"When are you telling Brent?"

"Tomorrow, so stay tuned."

"I think I need another drink." After Evan's reaction, Brooke worried about what Brent's would be. She also worried whether Evan, out of anger, might decide to kiss and tell, leaving Joie on both men's bad sides. It could be easy for him to convince Brent that Joie had initiated the relationship, and that they shouldn't let a woman—especially one like Joie—come between them.

"Why don't you have a double? One for me, and one for Olivia too."

"Olivia?" Brooke thought about the name as she said it. It felt just right to her. "I really like that."

"Now we only have to worry about her last name."

"Don't worry. Everything's going to be just fine." Unlike Kate with her situation, Brooke felt pretty sure that things would work out for Joie. The road getting there might be bumpy and winding, but she felt confident that the outcome would be worth the journey.

"From your lips to God's ears."

23

IN SINGLE FILE

After his incredible weekend away with Brooke, Taylor returned to the city on top of the world. Not only was he now a partner in his firm, but he felt sure that he'd also found a life partner. Brooke was everything he'd ever wanted in a woman: beautiful, smart, sexy, and sensitive. He felt like the luckiest man in the world.

That following Tuesday morning he left his suite at the Four Seasons walking on water. After closing the door behind him, he stooped to pick up a complimentary copy of the *New York Gazette*. Walking briskly, he casually glanced at the front page and came to a screeching halt. The headline read,

Prominent Investment Firm Mayer, Jones, and Wentworth Tied to London-based Foreign Arms Ring.

His heart started beating frantically as he stood with his mouth open in disbelief. He had to get to the office to find out what the hell was going on, so he stuffed the paper into his bag and hurried to the elevator. There had to be some mistake here. When he stepped off the elevator car, his cell phone rang.

He checked caller ID. It was his mother. "Hi, Mom."

"Taylor, what in heaven is going on?" He heard a tremor in

her voice. "Inez called me this morning and told me that your firm was on the front page of the paper. Something about money laundering." She sounded as if she were about to cry.

"Mom, I'm not sure what's going on," he said, "but I can't talk about it now."

"But what happened?"

"I can't talk now. I'll call you later." He hung up the phone. He didn't have the energy to console anyone else at the moment. He had to get to the office and find out what was going on.

Before he could duck into his car, his phone rang again. This time it was Max.

"Man, have you seen the *Gazette*?" he asked, skipping the pleasantries. "Didn't you tell me that you were working on a deal out of London?"

"Yep." By now Taylor was trying to rub the building tension from the muscles in his neck, but it wasn't working.

"Oh, shit."

" 'Oh, shit' is right."

"Listen to me carefully," Max instructed. "Until I see you this afternoon, I don't want you to discuss this with anyone. You got that?"

"What about my partners?"

"If I remember correctly, it was one of your partners who set this deal up, so I'm not so sure I'd trust any of them. In any regard, just tell them you've been advised by your attorney not to talk about it."

Taylor switched off his cell phone after they hung up to read the explosive article in peace. It raised a lot more questions than it answered about his arms-dealing, money-laundering clients.

Taylor stormed into the office demanding answers. Though he'd been advised not to discuss the matter, that was like asking Mount Saint Helens not to erupt as hot lava bubbled beneath the surface.

"Janice, get Eduard on the phone," he demanded as he marched past her desk.

"Mr. Taylor . . ." She hopped up from behind her desk, scampering behind him.

Taylor didn't hear a word she said; he was blinded by rage and confusion. When he stormed into his office there were two men seated around his private conference table with their legs crossed. Stunned, he turned around, ready to confront Janice, who nearly bumped into him as she tried in vain to warn him.

Janice whispered, "They were here first thing this morning. I couldn't get through on your cell, so Stuart spoke to Mr. Wentworth, who suggested they wait for you in here. They're with the Justice Department." She was so scared, her hands were shaking. Before Taylor could absorb another round of mortar, the two men approached him with their hands extended, and Janice scurried out of the room, anxious to be safely out of the line of fire.

"Mr. Hudson, I'm Tony Stodmire, and this is my colleague Marshal Bowling." Though the offer of a handshake seemed cordial enough, their dire expressions were anything but.

By automatic reflex Taylor extend his hand in greeting, though his brain hadn't yet caught up with the scene unfolding in front of him.

"We're here to investigate your involvement with the Beacon Hill investment group."

At the mention of the deal, which was supposed to have been his ticket to freedom, Taylor snapped out of his stupor. "I don't understand," he finally said, shaking his head. He pulled the newspaper from under his arm and waved it in front of them. "What's this all about?"

"That's exactly what we're here to find out," Tony said, raising his eyebrows. "Why don't we take a seat?" He was six feet tall, not quite Taylor's height, with thick strawberry-blond hair and a face that would best be described as nondescript.

Though it went against Taylor's grain to allow someone to play host in his office, he couldn't think of a better suggestion, so he motioned toward a nest of chairs that sat near his desk, as opposed to the more formal conference table.

Once they were seated, Tony picked up the conversation. "I'm with the Federal Bureau of Investigation, and Marshal here is with the United States National Central Bureau, which is our link to Interpol, the international criminal police organization," he explained.

Just hearing the references to the FBI and Interpol made Taylor shudder. He felt as though he'd stumbled onto the set of a spy thriller, only there was nothing entertaining about this script.

Tony rested his elbows on the armchair, forming a tepee with his fingers, carefully watching Taylor over its peak. "We've been tracking the principals at Beacon Hill for a while now. They have strong ties to a feeder organization that's attached to Middle Eastern terrorists who ultimately source, finance, and furnish arms."

Taylor had read much of this in the newspaper article. "So what does all this have to do with me?" he asked.

Marshal, who looked more like an accountant than an international spy chaser, spoke up. "Seeing as how you just helped them launder five hundred million dollars, I'd say quite a bit." He wore a sour, accusing smirk and a relentless stare.

His comment had the desired effect, causing Taylor to bristle. "Listen, I had no idea who these guys were," he insisted with outstretched hands. It was true. While normally he'd be well-advised of his clients and their connections, under the circumstances of the Beacon Hill deal—Eduard's referral, and the looming partnership—he'd let his guard down.

"Are you saying that they just wandered in off the street and dropped half a billion dollars on your desk?" Marshal asked and looked at Taylor incredulously.

Taylor was about to explain that his senior partner had instructed him to do the deal, so he had no reason to question their ethics. But he suddenly remembered Max's warning not to discuss the matter at all. After all, he knew very well that anything he said could be used against him. "Gentlemen, I've said just about enough on the subject," he said, standing. "Any further communication will have to be coordinated with my attorney."

"If that's the way you want it," Tony said. There was raw menace in his voice.

Taylor walked to the door, followed closely by the two men, who both shoved cards into his hand. "Have him give us a call, sooner rather than later. There'll be a preliminary hearing Friday for us to determine what charges to press," Marshal said.

The words "press charges" triggered a bout of nausea that was difficult for Taylor to fight off.

As they walked through the door, Marshal stopped abruptly and said, "By the way, no more trips out of the country for the time being." Then he turned and walked away.

When they were safely on the other side of the closed door, Taylor leaned back against it, realizing that they'd been following his movements over the weekend. How else would they have known that he was out of the country? He also realized that with the resources of Interpol and the FBI at their disposal they could probably tell him the calorie content of his breakfast that morning.

He gathered what was left of his composure and punched in Janice's extension. "I need to see Eduard now!" he demanded.

"I'm sorry, Mr. Hudson, but Mr. Wentworth is not in the office," she said meekly.

"Well, where the hell is he?" Taylor was close to the boiling point.

"He's out of the country, sir."

"Out of the country where?" Taylor barked, annoyed. Getting anything from her was like pulling teeth.

"Actually, sir, I don't know exactly."

"What do you mean, you don't know? I thought you said that Stuart spoke with him earlier."

"He did, but what I mean is that he's on his yacht in the Mediterranean. So I just don't know where."

Taylor was seething, ready to spit bullets. "Listen, I don't care if he's on the planet Mars: I want you to call Stuart and get him on the phone. Now!"

"Yes, sir."

The next call he made was to Brooke. "Hey, sweetie," she purred. "How's your day going?"

"Downhill fast." There was no jest in his tone, only the sound of a man in trouble, a sound that she knew all too well from some of her patients. To hear it come from Taylor, who was at all times composed, was very unsettling.

She sat up straight in her chair and her posture transformed into a knot of tension as her smile when hearing his voice faded. "What's wrong?"

"Have you seen today's paper?"

She'd snoozed through her alarm three times and had barely made it to the office in time, so she hadn't had a moment to even look at the newspaper, and had been in sessions all morning. "No. Why?"

"I can't talk about it on this phone, but I need to see you right away."

The urgency in his voice caused her even more alarm. "Why don't you meet me at my apartment for lunch?"

"I'll be there in thirty minutes."

Brooke paced the floor as she waited for Taylor. After quickly reading the newspaper article she was terrified for him. When the bell rang, she opened the door, and hugged him tightly. "Come in, babe. Are you okay?"

"Not exactly." He walked toward the den and sat on the sofa, with his hands clasped in front of him between his legs.

"What happened?" she finally asked.

He took a deep breath and turned to face her. "Do you re-member the Beacon Hill deal?"

"Of course." They'd talked about it several times, since it was the key to his partnership—and his freedom.

"There's a problem with it."

"I read the article in the *Gazette*. What does all this have to do with you?" She could feel him beating around the bush, not wanting to come straight to the point.

"The investors have been tied to a terrorist-affiliated arms group, and the money involved was dirty."

She knew it was best, for Taylor's sake, that she remain calm. "What exactly does this mean for you?"

He leveled with her. "It means that I could be charged with money laundering."

Though she heard his words, they bounced off her brain, unable to stick. "You've got to be kidding!"

"Brooke, I wish I were." Tension had etched the outline of a different man onto the face of the one she'd left with a parting kiss just two nights earlier. Every minute that had passed since this morning he'd tortured himself for not fully researching the principals in this deal. Normally—especially in the States—information on clients was always a phone call away. He either knew all of the big players, or knew someone who did, but in London he had relied almost solely on Eduard's word. Sure, he ran the equivalent of a credit check, but nothing alarming came up, so he didn't go the extra mile by checking criminal records or asking for references. He thought that Eduard's word was good enough, since his boss had been so quick to vouch for them.

Brooke thought for a moment. "Didn't you say that the man-aging partner referred this deal to you?"

Taylor rubbed the bridge of his nose, trying to stave off the assault of a nasty tension headache. "Yeah."

"How much does he know?" she asked.

"I don't really know, since I haven't been able to reach him all day. He's on a boat in the middle of the Mediterranean."

"That's awfully convenient."

"It's beginning to sound like I may have been set up."

"It definitely sounds pretty fishy."

"You're right—the sudden appearance of a lucrative deal and the even more sudden offer of partnership."

"But why would he need to make you partner to pull this off?"

"Maybe to make sure that I took the bait quickly and did the deal without too much due diligence. He probably knew there was the potential for trouble, but was prepared to take the chance as long as it wasn't his neck on the line, so he put mine there instead. I'm sure he figured that if things got messy he could throw what was left of me to the wolves, and rescind my partnership based on an ethics clause."

Brooke shook her head. "He sure sounds like a swell guy."

When Taylor returned to the office, Eduard was on the line. He'd just called in. His deep baritone rang through the phone line loud and clear, as though he were right next door, rather than a whole continent away. "Taylor, what's going on there?"

"Why don't you tell me?" he challenged.

"Seeing as how I'm thousands of miles away, it'd be pretty hard to." Taylor detected a touch of sarcasm in his tone, but then he softened it, adding, "But Stuart did give me a quick overview of what he knew, which wasn't a lot."

"Eduard, who the hell were those guys?"

"If what the papers are saying is true, it looks as though they were arms dealers," he answered evasively.

"How did you meet them?" Eduard had to know a lot more than he was saying, since he'd been the one to refer them in the first place.

"I didn't."

Taylor could tell that Eduard's answers were filtered, as if he suspected that someone could be listening in on the line—a thought that had also occurred to Taylor. After all, the FBI had

loads of toys and electronics at their disposal. "Listen, you need
to tell me everything you know," Taylor insisted. "I have the FBI
and Interpol thinking that I'm some arms-dealing money laun-
derer, and I met these clients through you."

"Don't worry. We'll straighten all of this out right away, but
I'll need the file that you took from the office. There may be
something in there that will help me to clear your name. Have
Stuart send it to me, and we'll talk right after I get it. Then we
can go to the authorities and make them understand that you
knew nothing about any of this."

Taylor began to think that maybe this was all a big misunderstanding, and even Eduard had known nothing about the
group's illegal activities. "I'll have to get it first."

"You mean it's not in the office?" He sounded alarmed.

"No, it's not. It's at the apartment." He remembered coming
home from the airport after closing the deal and having his big
fight with Kiernan. Afterward, he'd been in such a hurry to grab
some other papers for Max and get to the office that he'd mis-
takenly left that folder behind. It hadn't been a problem, since it
didn't contain the executed contract, only Eduard's original
handwritten notes.

"We'll talk after you get the file to Stuart."

"Okay." If he hurried he could make it to the apartment and
back before the last FedEx pickup.

Taylor hung up the phone, grabbed his jacket, and headed
out the door. "Janice, have my driver meet me downstairs now."

As much as he dreaded the prospect of coming face-to-face
with Kiernan, it couldn't be avoided, since that file could be the
key to clearing his name. He hopped out of the car in front of
the building, dodging throngs of pedestrians as he dashed into
the lobby.

Frank stopped him. "Mr. Hudson, I forgot to give Mrs. Malloy this FedEx when she came in. Would you mind taking it
up?" Taylor grabbed the package and headed to the elevator.
When he reached their floor he stuck his key into the lock and

turned it, but nothing happened. After several attempts it dawned on him that she'd changed the lock. Agitated, he knocked on the door, desperate to get inside. He knew she had to be there, at least according to Frank, who was very good at keeping up with residents' comings and goings.

"Kiernan, open the door." He knew she was probably on the other side watching him through the peephole.

Eventually she opened it about two inches. The chain lock was still in place. "Taylor, what do you want?" She wore a look of sheer contempt.

"I need to come in."

"Remember? You don't live here anymore." She stood with her hand planted on her hip, and a satisfied smirk on her face.

"Kiernan, open this door," he demanded.

"You didn't answer my question. What is it that you want?"

"It's a file. I have to find a file."

She appraised his demeanor, noting his anxiousness, and decided that whatever was in this file must be pretty important to him. But since she hadn't read the paper, and wasn't answering the phone to avoid bill collectors, LaTeesha, and Thelma, she had no idea why. "Sorry, but I can't help you," she said, and slammed the door shut in his face.

He'd have to figure out a way to get into that apartment. It was legally his, but he'd have to let Max work that out. In the meantime, once he returned to the office he called Eduard with the news.

"What do you mean, you don't have the file?" The calm tone from earlier was missing from Eduard's voice.

"Kiernan and I are separated. She won't let me in the apartment," Taylor confessed.

Eduard sighed and said, "Let me talk with my attorney and we'll speak later." He abruptly hung up the phone.

While Taylor sat stewing, his eye wandered to the wooden credenza with his office files that he kept locked. The wood had been slightly damaged, as though someone had tried to force it open. He immediately thought of the two agents who were there alone earlier.

"Janice, I need to see you."

The poor woman walked through the doorway as though expecting a firing squad.

"How long were those guys alone in my office?"

"Not too long, because when they entered Stuart was already here, and he left just a few minutes before you showed up."

"Stuart? What was he doing in here?"

"He said something about the server being down, and needing to check your computer."

That was when the red flags went up and began to flap. He remembered that Stuart had first been instructed by Eduard to type up the information in the file, but he'd given Taylor the original instead, which contained notations in Eduard's handwriting. He remembered thinking that it was odd, since Eduard had made a point of telling him that it would be typed, but beyond that had thought nothing else of it. Well, obviously the two of them had, and were now desperate to get their hands on it. Besides, there was no valid reason for Stuart to be in Taylor's office. He wasn't a computer technician. He must have been searching for the file, so obviously Eduard really needed it, and if it wasn't to clear Taylor of his charges, it must contain information that would incriminate Eduard himself. It all made perfect sense now—especially the reason he wouldn't take any money personally from the commission. He didn't want anything linking him to the actual transaction. Taylor had to find that file, and more important, he had to get his hands on it before his boss did.

Before he could stop reeling from the day's blows, he received another troubling call.

He prayed that this day, which had started out with him on top of the world, would soon end before he hit rock bottom.

24

LYING IN THE BED SHE MADE

Since the disastrous afternoon when Joie had told Evan that she was pregnant, he had been avoiding her as if she harbored an infectious disease, instead of an innocent child. She now realized that raw lust and real life had very little to do with each other. One was purely an involuntary physical reaction, while the other was a function of emotional maturity, a characteristic that was sorely missing from Evan's DNA. She hadn't expected him to crack open a bottle of bubbly to celebrate her unexpected news, but she was shocked by his nasty, selfish attitude.

What was even more surprising to her were her own feelings about the baby growing in her womb. She couldn't begin to articulate her change in attitude, or why she now felt so ready to bring another life into the world. For thirty-five years, her personal goals had revolved around her own freedom, her own independence, and a single-minded pursuit of her own happiness and pleasure. Perhaps she was realizing that those things weren't enough to account for a full life, or maybe her evolution was simply a function of the fabled biological clock that she hadn't heard ticking at all, until the alarm suddenly went blaring off.

In a strange way, Evan's immaturity contributed to this lesson. It taught her that life was about much more than the surface bullshit she'd reverently worshiped. Though Brent failed to leave her weak in the knees or panting in heat, he was an intelligent and compassionate person and had wonderful qualities for a father-to-be. She was going to tell him about the baby and let the chips fall where they may.

After a long shower, she smoothed on Brent's favorite perfumed lotion and pulled a silk teddy over her head, while shedding any remorse she felt for the position that she was putting him in. Right now her main concern was not for Evan or Brent, but for her child. As she faced the mirror, her hand found its way to the slight swell of her stomach, drawing strength from within. She wasn't big enough to warrant running off to Liz Lange Maternity for a shopping spree, but her stomach was definitely pronounced enough for the waistbands of her clothes to stretch taut. That growing seed of life gave her hope and an inner peace that she'd never known before; the feeling was indescribable, one that she would never have been able to imagine even a few short weeks ago.

When Brent walked through the door, he was surprised by the aroma of homemade vegetable lasagna—Joie's only homage to domesticity—flickering scented candles, soft romantic music, and a big, warm hug. For a second he felt like he'd wandered into the wrong apartment. "Wow! What did I do to deserve all this? Is it my birthday?" he asked, dropping his briefcase on the sofa.

"Who said it was for you?" Joie teased. She took his jacket and hung it in the closet, leaving him to ponder the pieces of the puzzle.

"Well, I don't see anyone else here," he said, stroking his chin thoughtfully.

"Maybe you're not looking close enough." She walked up behind him for another hug.

He turned around, perplexed by her game of cat and mouse.

She sighed deeply and took the plunge. "I'm having a baby," she finally said. Joie was careful not to say "we." Though it was only a small technicality, she did want to preserve some sense of truth.

After her words sank in, she waited breathlessly for him to respond, not knowing exactly what to expect, especially after Evan's nuclear reaction.

He turned his head to one side, as though physically aligning the foreign thought in his brain. "A baby?" The concept seemed incomprehensible to him; the thought of a child had absolutely no bearing on his current existence. He and Joie had never even discussed the idea of kids in specific terms, hadn't even talked about the prospect of a future together, let alone one that included children. He'd always intentionally treaded lightly on that sensitive subject, since Joie had made it clear from day one that wedding bells, a white picket fence, and a set of Mini Me's were nowhere in her plans. Even though he'd always hoped that one day she'd come around—most women did—he hadn't expected it quite this soon.

On the other hand, marriage and kids were in his best interest, especially for his career, even though they weren't notches he had been anxious to carve into his belt. But every year that went by without his being engaged, married, or at least a baby's daddy, was considered a personal affront to his widowed mother, who felt it was her personal right to be given grandkids before she left this world. Since he was her only child, the duty of procreation fell squarely in his lap, literally and figuratively.

So, as shocking as this was, it was also good news; at least now he wouldn't have to hear his mother's near-deathbed guilt trips about how she would never live to see her grandbabies the way her friend Ida-Mae had, forgetting the fact that Ida-Mae's grandchildren were really Bay-Bay's kids, each with a different father, and a mother—Ida-Mae's daughter—who'd rather be in the clubs every night than reading *The Cat in the Hat*.

"Brent, are you okay?" He was wearing a goofy grin on his face as all of those thoughts converged in his head. "I know this wasn't in the plans, but . . ." She shrugged her shoulders to complete the thought.

"Am I okay? I'm great," he said. "I couldn't be happier."

"Really?" His response was so different from Evan's; in fact their reactions were like night and day.

"Joie, I love you, and would want nothing more than to have a baby with you." He grabbed her and pulled her into a tight hug.

This would have been the perfect time for her to say "I love you, too," but somehow the words were stuck deep in her throat, like a wad of peanut butter. She knew she was deceiving him into thinking the child was his, but she couldn't lie about her feelings for him. A girl had to draw the line somewhere, she thought. "I'm really happy too," she finally managed to say.

"I have to admit that I am a little surprised," he confessed. "The last time we talked about kids, they were on a par with Payless shoes, something you could never see yourself suffering, or words to that effect." He laughed at the flippant way she'd summarily dismissed the notion.

She chuckled too, also remembering the analogy. "I guess one should never say never." She shrugged. "Things change."

She led him to the couch, where he held her tight, smelling the fresh scent of the Aveda shampoo in her thick, soft dreads.

The moment felt right for Joie, and for her child. Brent could give her what every mother throughout time wanted for her children: love, security, and safety.

"Well, I guess it's time to start thinking about nurseries, names, and Lamaze classes." He seemed pleased with the upcoming lifestyle change.

"I guess so," she said, smiling at the thought.

"Oh," he added, "one more thing."

"What's that?" she asked, still snuggled into the crook of his arm.

"Getting married."

"Married?" She hadn't thought about that. A baby was one thing, but getting married was quite another.

"Yeah. You know, when two people—usually a man and a woman, but not necessarily, these days—walk down the aisle and swear before God, family, friends, and foes to spend the rest of their lives together."

She didn't even like the sound of that. But she had learned one thing over the last month, and that was to keep an open mind. She turned to face him. "Brent, you don't have to marry me just 'cause I'm having a baby."

"I'm not," he insisted. "I want to marry you because I love you."

It was fortunate that he wasn't able to see the expression on her face, because it wasn't one of a blushing bride-to-be.

After Brent fell asleep that night, she slipped out of the bedroom and went to the kitchen to call Brooke. Her emotions were running rampant—probably hormones—but she just had to talk to someone, and there was no one better in an emotional crisis than Brooke.

"I told him," she whispered into the phone.

Brooke had been asleep, but woke up when she heard the urgency in Joie's voice. "So what did he say?"

"He wants to marry me."

Brooke thought for sure that she'd misheard her friend, or maybe that she was still dreaming. She and Brooke had never discussed the possibility of her marrying Brent, or anyone else, now or ever. "What did you say?"

"He wants to marry me," Joie repeated.

Brooke was speechless. The image of Joie walking down a wedding aisle with Brent at the other end of it was like a bad dream. She finally gathered her thoughts and sat up in bed. "So, again, what did you say?"

"I'm going to marry him," she stated.

"Don't sound so excited," Brooke said sarcastically.

"What's there to be excited about?"

Brooke anxiously changed the receiver from one ear to the other. "Joie, you've never even wanted to be married."

"True, but I also had never wanted to have a baby either."

Brooke used the only other argument that she could think of: "But, Joie, you don't love him."

"To quote Tina Turner, what's love got to do with it?"

Brooke let that comment slide by. "Does he know that he may not be the father?" She hated to go there, but Joie didn't seem to be thinking clearly.

There was silence, which told Brooke all that she needed to hear. "You've got to tell him the truth. Then if he still wants to get married, that's another story."

"I don't have to do anything. That's what *you'd* do, but remember you are Miss Perfect, living the perfect life, with the perfect man, and I'm Ms. Fucked-up."

Brooke wanted to tell her friend that nothing could be further from the truth, given Taylor's current predicament, but she heard Joie choking back tears. "Joie, you know that is not true. You are an amazing person, and your child will be lucky to have you for a mother."

"Yeah, right."

"Everything will be all right, and I love you."

"I love you, too."

Joie hung up the phone and crept back to lie in the bed that she'd made.

25

WHITE KNIGHT

Eduard paced the deck of his mammoth luxury yacht like a caged tiger before a delayed mealtime. Things were not going at all according to his well-hatched plan, which had been in the works for some time now. The idea was simple: It involved bringing several hundred million laundered dollars yearly into the firm, and as senior partner, Eduard would have gotten the lion's share. He'd been approached by the Beacon Hill group over a year ago, but wasn't prepared to take the personal risk associated with cleaning up their dirty money should things blow up in his face. Of course, he was given many assurances that that would not happen; after all, the group's members were mainly upstanding and well-respected businessmen much like himself. So he and a few trusted and like-minded partners hatched the plan to entice Taylor into the scheme with the promise of partnership, using the deal with Beacon Hill as their bait. It had worked beautifully, up until the newspaper article.

Eduard had been prepared in the event the scheme was discovered; there shouldn't have been any record of his complicity or involvement. But he'd underestimated the reach of stupidity. He'd specifically instructed that harebrain Stuart to copy only documents from the file that didn't have his name or handwriting on them for Taylor's benefit, and to retype the others, and of course he'd failed to follow that simple order. So now Eduard's fingerprints were on the smoking gun. It wasn't until after the feds came sniffing around and he told Stuart to destroy the documents that he realized what the numbskull had done—or more accurately, hadn't done. Now he was a sitting duck unless he could get his hands on that file.

Pacing helped him sift through the thick fog to find the light at the end of the tunnel, and right now that beacon led directly to Kiernan, Taylor's feisty soon-to-be ex-wife. He realized that he had to get to her—and the file—before Taylor did; otherwise, instead of sitting on a yacht docked in Manhattan's Hudson River, he'd be up Shit Creek without the proverbial paddle.

Kiernan sat on the floor of her living room going over the proposal for Eva's town house. The phone rang, jarring her thoughts. She checked the caller ID that had been installed after she realized she had nothing to gain by talking to or helping La-Teesha or Thelma, and therefore needed to avoid both. After all, neither of them could prove she'd had anything to do with their little drug deal gone wrong. Even if they did tell authorities that she was involved, who would they most likely believe—a thief and a drug addict, or an upstanding member of New York's society?

When she saw the name on the display she was pleasantly surprised. "Well, hello."

"Kiernan, darling, this is Eduard. How are you?"

He was the last person on Earth she would have expected a call from. "I'm just fine. How are you?"

"Very well, dear. I hope I didn't catch you at a bad time."

As far as a call from him was concerned, there was no such thing as a bad time. She ran her hands quickly through her hair, fingering it as if he could see her through the phone line. "No, not at all."

"Good. Listen, I was hoping that we could get together," he said. Being born rich, he knew Kiernan's type well: a woman who could smell cash a mile away, and fortunately for him, he reeked of it.

"I think that can be arranged." Now that her life was racing downhill faster than an avalanche, she'd been fantasizing about snagging a rich sugar daddy, and here he was. What good timing.

"Why don't you meet me at the pier in Battery Park at eight? My yacht, the *Prince of Tides,* is docked there. We can have drinks aboard and catch up."

It was already six o'clock—not exactly a lot of notice, but it wasn't as if she were Madam Social Butterfly with a full calendar these days. Besides, she was very curious about why Eduard had called. Wild horses couldn't have kept her away.

"Oh, and another thing," he said, interrupting her thoughts about what to wear, "I would appreciate it if you would not mention this to Taylor." The last thing he needed was for her to use him to make her husband jealous, meanwhile alerting Taylor to his plans.

"Fine by me. I'll see you at eight," she said, hanging up the phone. Given a choice between loyalty to Taylor, who'd betrayed her, and loyalty to Eduard, who could save her, she saw her decision as an easy one. Compared to Eduard, Taylor was a pauper, so getting next to him was definitely a step in the right direction. She bounced up from the floor, heading to her bedroom to dress for her date with Mr. Moneybags.

An hour and a half later, Kiernan hopped out of a taxi on Vesey Street, next to the World Financial Center, and headed toward the inlet of water where the rich and richer of New York City kept their water toys. She immediately saw the sleek hundred-foot boat docked in the center of the pier.

Eduard stood proudly on the boat's main deck, sporting a velvet smoking jacket, well-worn blue jeans, and Italian loafers. He was sipping a martini, looking like James Bond personified. She loved the view, and imagined herself sailing into exotic ports of call right there at his side. There was a spring in her step as she headed up the gangway. Now this man knew how to spend money, she thought.

"Come on up."

"Eduard, darling, you look fabulous, and I do love this boat," she said, gazing around in awe. Though she'd spent a lot of time in some amazing homes, many of which she'd decorated herself, this level of wealth took things to another stratosphere. She almost laughed out loud, recalling how she couldn't even convince her tightwad husband to hire a car and driver.

"No, *you* look fabulous." He gave her a kiss on the check before leading them into the grandly appointed living room.

Once they settled onto a butter-soft leather couch, a formally dressed butler appeared to take her drink order. Kiernan was beside herself. If only Eva could see her now . . . Her problems with Taylor, her bank accounts, LaTeesha, and Thelma all seemed oceans away, though in reality they were simply a cab ride back uptown.

She turned to face him, batting her eyes, giving him her most seductive look. "So to what do I owe the pleasure?"

He placed his arm around the back of the sofa. "Taylor mentioned to me that you two had separated, and I thought I'd check on you."

"He was having an affair," she offered. This was the first time she'd discussed the problems in her marriage with anyone other than her therapist. Hurt and anger bubbled briefly to the surface, but she set those emotions aside to focus on the money—ah, rather, the man—who now sat beside her.

He reached over and patted her hand, letting his linger there atop hers. "For such a smart guy, Taylor is obviously stupid about women, and my dear, you are such an incredible woman." She blushed.

When she didn't comment, he said, "Are you okay? I mean financially?" Whether she was or not, he knew that a woman like Kiernan would never pass up a stack of cold, hard cash.

Even though it was clear that he was up to something, Kiernan was still somewhat surprised that he was concerned about her financial state. She hadn't even slept with him yet. But she surmised that Eduard was not the type of guy who would let ceremony stand between himself and something that he wanted. In fact, he was a lot like her. "It's been pretty tough," she confided as she rubbed her hands together in her lap, playing the poor victim role to the hilt. Normally she wouldn't confess to dire financial straits under any circumstances, but at this point she had very little to hide where money was concerned, particularly from a man like Eduard, who could very well be her white knight.

He leaned back into the cushions of the sofa. "Maybe I can help you."

"How's that?" So far this conversation was going even better than she'd hoped. She'd thought for sure she would have to fuck him first, and then try wooing some funds out of him later. In fact, she'd worn her new La Petite Coquette undergarments just in case.

"It's really simple," he said, standing up. "There's something you have that I need, and if you get it for me, I'll make it very much worth your while." He walked over to the expansive walnut bar and accepted Kiernan's drink from the butler, returning to give it to her.

This was a curveball. "Something like what?" She was surprised that he was suggesting only a quid pro quo, rather than a relationship. So much for sailing the high seas by his side.

"A file. Taylor left it at the apartment and I need it immediately."

The smooth gentleman act was gone now, replaced by an urgency and directness that gave her a momentary chill. But Kiernan's ears also perked up. This was the second mention today of a mysterious file. First Taylor came banging on her door demanding it, and now Eduard was trying to buy it from her. Whatever was in it must be pretty important. "What kind of file?" she asked, taking a slow sip of her merlot.

"The less you know about it, the better, but for now let's just say that it's a very valuable one—for you especially. I'll pay you one hundred fifty thousand dollars for turning it over to me. Cash."

Kiernan nearly choked on her wine. Just the sound of that kind of money was music to her ears. "Are you kidding me?" She sat on the edge of the sofa, leaning closer to make sure that she heard him correctly.

"I'm dead serious," he said, not blinking an eye. He held up a finger and fixed his gaze on hers. "Oh, but there is one very important condition."

"What's that?" she asked, though she would have agreed to just about anything to get her hands on that kind of money. As far as she was concerned, this offer was a godsend, like manna from heaven.

"You can't mention this conversation to Taylor—or to any-one else, for that matter." His steely eyes held hers until she nodded in agreement.

An involuntary shudder ran through Kiernan as she realized that this benign-appearing gentleman was ready to place a knife squarely in Taylor's back. She knew that whatever he was up to had to be bad news for Taylor, but she still said, "Not a prob-lem." She had a hundred fifty thousand dollars to think about, so Taylor was on his own.

If nothing else Eduard was an excellent judge of character, and had correctly assumed that Kiernan didn't have any. He raised his glass in the air between them. "Here's to a mutually beneficial exchange."

"Cheers."

Kiernan was counting her money and he was counting his blessings as they clinked glasses like longtime partners in crime, both thinking that this little exchange had been an easy way to solve a very tough problem.

26
THREE'S COMPANY

When the doorbell rang, Brooke had been expecting Taylor, and was surprised to find Joie on her doorstep. "Come on in," she said, tossing a dish towel over her shoulder.

"I know I should have called first," Joie said, peeping over Brooke's shoulder as though she'd find Taylor in his birthday suit behind her, "but I left my cell phone at home and just had to show off Olivia's first photo shoot." She pulled out a sonogram of black, gray, and white shadows. She'd just had one of the high-tech ultrasounds. Being a photographer, she'd studied the black-and-white image closely, fully envisioning the features of her unborn child. She was elated at the idea of a daughter to hold tight, to cuddle up in soft blankets, to dress up in miniature couture, and ultimately—good or bad—to teach all that she knew. They'd be best friends for life; she could feel it. She was literally beaming with expectation. "Isn't she beautiful? My baby is even posing—look at that hand." She faked a pose with her hand held up to her neck.

Brooke dried her hands on the Eze Village apron she wore before taking the sonogram from Joie. She hoped for Joie's sake that her child was a girl, since she'd obviously grown very comfortable with that idea. "Well, of course she is." She had no idea what she was looking at, though Joie seemed to be able to make out each and every feature. "She obviously takes after her mother. By the way, if I haven't told you, you look beautiful pregnant."

"That's if you like the bloated look." Joie opened her jacket to proudly show off the growing bulge in her midsection.

Though it had been less than a week since she'd last seen Joie, Brooke would have sworn Olivia had grown by leaps and bounds. "Call it what you like, but you are the most amazing-looking pregnant woman ever." Joie did have that glow that everyone always talked about. She looked absolutely radiant.

"That's the same thing Brent said." To think that she'd been worried about how he'd take the news. As things turned out, he was as excited about the baby as she was.

They settled around the butcher-block island in the kitchen, where Brooke had all of the ingredients set out for a Greek salad to serve with the duck she had roasting in the oven. Taylor was coming over tonight, and she'd decided to impress him with her somewhat rusty culinary skills. "So are you still planning to marry him?"

"Yes, I am." Joie gave her a firm look and tossed her dreads over her shoulder.

Brooke set aside her chopping knife and asked, "Why are you doing this? You've always been an independent woman. Why do you think you need a man now?"

"It's not about me," she snapped. As far as Joie was concerned, marrying Brent was a practical matter, since she needed a father for her child. She'd grown up in a happy two-parent home and wanted the same idyllic childhood for her own daughter.

"Do you really think this is what's best for your baby?"

"Frankly, yes, I do."

"Well, it's not," Brooke insisted as she walked around to Joie's side of the island. "Believe me, witnessing a loveless marriage—or being the product of divorced parents—won't do your child any favors."

"How would you know?" she challenged. This was the

stubborn-as-nails side of Joie, the side that blindly held on to any stake she'd driven in the ground, regardless of how far the earth shifted.

Brooke put her hand on Joie's shoulder, trying to subtly break down her defensiveness. "Remember, I am a therapist, so I do know something about how a child's environment might affect her throughout life."

Joie sighed, looking up at Brooke with pleading eyes. "What I need now isn't a therapist. It's a friend."

Sometimes Brooke had trouble separating the two, especially when she saw her friend about to make a big mistake. "Joie, you know I'll always be here for you and Olivia—no matter what you decide. I'm just trying to make sure that you consider everything."

While both women were consumed by their own private thoughts, Brooke resumed mixing her salad dressing of virgin olive oil, white wine vinegar, minced garlic cloves, oregano, basil, and feta cheese to add to the other ingredients, including romaine lettuce, red onion, pitted black olives, and marinated artichoke hearts.

"Are you okay?" Joie asked. Brooke seemed more subdued than usual. Since she and Taylor had started seeing each other, she had been full of energy, the kind that went along with being newly in love. But there was no trace of it now, so something must have happened.

Brooke put her whisk down. "Not exactly," she admitted. She was hesitant to tell Joie about Taylor's problems, since she certainly had enough of her own, but what were friends for?

"What's wrong?"

"It's Taylor."

Joie had been afraid that Mr. Perfect's other shoe might fall; she only hated that it happened after both had been parked at the foot of Brooke's bed. "Don't tell me—he's decided to stay with his wife?" That was the usual ending to any story involving an affair with a married man. Joie had been there and done that too.

Brooke shook her head. "No, nothing that simple."

"What happened?"

She told Joie all about Taylor's big Beacon Hill deal and the ensuing drama that followed attaining his partnership.

"So Taylor set up this huge deal and he didn't even know the people involved?" Joie twisted her face in confusion. By all accounts, Taylor appeared to be a smart man, but this sounded pretty stupid to her.

Brooke took a deep breath. "Yes and no," she finally answered. "He didn't really know them, but with a mandate and strong character reference from his senior partner he felt comfortable doing the deal. Of course, he did some preliminary background checks, but obviously not enough. Plus, he was under pressure to close the deal quickly." Brooke felt guilty about this herself. If she hadn't insisted that he get a divorce under way, she was sure he wouldn't have been so anxious to sew up the deal and the partnership.

"Did his boss know they were crooked?"

"I don't know for sure, but given everything, I wouldn't be surprised."

"Girl, I am so sorry," Joie said. It seemed unfair that when Brooke finally found someone to open herself up to, he had to come with more trouble than he might be worth.

"So am I."

The doorbell rang, interrupting the moment.

"Is that him?" Joie asked. The excitement was back in her voice. She'd heard so much about Brooke's mystery man, she was dying to see Taylor Hudson in the flesh, money-laundering scandal or not.

"Probably," Brooke said. She removed her apron and ran her fingers through her hair. She was nervous for a couple of reasons: This was the first time she'd prepared dinner for Taylor and the first time that he'd met her best friend.

She headed down the hall with Joie hot on her heels. "Hey, baby," she said, opening the door.

He grabbed her in a tight hug. She could feel the tension in his shoulders and wanted to help ease it all away.

"I missed you," he said, never lifting his head from their embrace. He had no idea that Joie was on the other side of the door peering at the two of them.

"Ummphh." Joie stepped out into his view.

Brooke, who'd been lost in Taylor's embrace, suddenly pulled away. "I'm sorry. Taylor, this is Joie. Joie, Taylor."

Taylor looked surprised, but composed himself and extended his hand to Joie. "It's good to finally meet you." He'd heard Brooke talk about her best friend on several occasions.

She ignored his hand and gave him a hug instead. "It's good to meet you, too."

When Taylor walked through the door ahead of them, Joie turned around and gave Brooke a big thumbs-up, then proceeded to flip her wrist rapidly, as though she had touched something very hot. Brooke smiled and shook her head.

Once Joie and Taylor were settled in the living room, Brooke headed to the kitchen to get two glasses of wine and a cup of hot tea for Joie. When she returned, Joie and Taylor were kicked back chatting it up like long-lost friends.

"Now I know why you've been hiding him," she said to Brooke, winking an eye. "You're just afraid of a little competition."

"But you're getting married, remember?" Brooke thought a little reality might shock some sense into Joie.

Taylor turned to face her. "See, you've broken my heart already," he said, clutching his chest. "Congratulations anyway."

Joie, who was always quick with a comeback, seemed to not know what to say. "Listen, I should let you guys get on with your evening."

"You don't have to go," Brooke insisted.

"No, really, I do. I have an early shoot in the morning."

"Okay, let me walk you out."

"It was great meeting you," Taylor said. This time he gave her a big hug. "Oh, and congratulations on the little one, too."

"Thank you," she said, then turned to Brooke. "Don't keep him all to yourself."

Once Joie was gone, Brooke came back into the living room and sat on Taylor's lap. "How are you holding up?" she asked, rubbing the taut muscles in the back of his neck. Having Joie there had been a good diversion for both of them. He seemed a lot less stressed than he had when he'd first arrived.

"It's been rough," he admitted.

"What does your lawyer think?" Max had set him up with the best white-collar criminal-defense attorney in the country.

"He thinks any case against me would be circumstantial. It would be hard for them to prove that I knowingly laundered money, but the burden of proof to get an indictment is low enough that I could go to trail."

"What about a conviction?"

"It's hard to say. A lot depends on how zealous the prosecutor is, and with all of the corporate scandals involving Enron, ImClone, and the rest of the bunch, they're on a witch-hunt these days. But the bottom line is, I'd be a lot better off if I could turn over the file, because the main objective is to avoid an indictment to begin with. If that happens"—he shook his head— "my career is as good as over, whether I'm convicted or not."

"Well, it's a good thing that you have the file." She was hanging on to that last hope.

He hung his head low and rubbed his temples with his thumb and middle finger, trying to ease away the tension headache that had become a fixture since he had stooped to pick up that paper. "I can't count on that, since Kiernan still won't let me in the apartment, and Max doesn't think I can get a court order to get in before Friday."

Brooke racked her brain, feeling totally helpless. Every day she assisted strangers with their assorted problems, yet she couldn't think of anything that could help the man she cared so much about. "Isn't there someone who could talk to her for you?" She was grasping at straws now.

"It wouldn't do any good. Besides, to make matters worse, she's pretty strung out."

Brooke frowned. "What do you mean?"

"According to LaTeesha, a young girl she was supposed to be mentoring, she's been buying cocaine from a dealer uptown."

"You're kidding."

"I wish I were. And to make things worse, she sent LaTeesha to do the exchanges, telling her that the packages contained jewelry." He shook his head. He couldn't believe she would use a young girl who already had enough problems to do her dirty work.

Taylor's day had started out with a very unexpected message. "Sir, you have a call from the city jail," Janice said in that irritatingly timid voice of hers. Since the feds had started sniffing around she was worse than ever, as though one false move and she too could end up in jail. That was what the Martha Stewart case had done for assistants everywhere; everyone was busy covering their butts.

"The city jail?" Who on earth could be calling him from jail? But with his luck they were probably calling to confirm his reservation.

"It's a LaTeesha Ingram." This was even more confusing. What was LaTeesha doing in jail, and why was she calling him instead of Kiernan?

"Put her through." When she came on the line he said, "La-Teesha, what's going on?"

"Mr. Taylor, I've . . . been . . . arrested," she managed to get out amid a torrent of tears. He could hardly understand a word she said.

"LaTeesha, you have to calm down. Now take a deep breath and tell me what happened," he instructed.

Between sobs he heard the words "Kiernan," "drugs," and

"police," before a gruff voice in the background barked, "Your time is up."

"Don't worry. I'll be right there," he said just before the click, which was followed by a dial tone. Even though he had a mounting pile of his own problems, he didn't hesitate to call Max, whom he picked up ten minutes later. Though he didn't know LaTeesha very well, she seemed like a nice kid who deserved a break, but had gotten few in her short life.

When they arrived at the police station, Max took over as LaTeesha's lawyer and Taylor put up the funds to bail her out. An hour later, when LaTeesha was finally released, she looked as if she'd been ridden hard and hung up wet. Her face was a splotchy mess of makeup remnants and streaks of tears. She looked to Taylor like a frightened ten-year-old.

She ran into his arms. "Thank you so much. I didn't think you'd come." She was so accustomed to disappointment that she hardly ever expected anything else.

He patted her back reassuringly, as he would a scared child. "Don't worry. Max will take care of everything."

By the time the luxury Mercedes dropped her off in front of her dilapidated project in the Bronx, Taylor had gotten the full story and vowed that he'd do everything he could to help her, including paying her legal fees. He knew from what he saw of her with Kiernan that LaTeesha was a hard worker, and being poor, she was also a ready victim, not only for society, but for predators like his soon-to-be ex-wife.

27

A ZERO-SUM GAME

The next day over lunch Max said, "I have to give it to you. You never do anything small-time. When you get in trouble with the law, it's some FBI-Interpol shit." Their waitress had disappeared with their lunch orders.

"But I didn't do anything," Taylor insisted.

Max leaned back in his chair and crossed his legs in a weary manner. In typical lawyer fashion he put his own client on the hot seat to get to the bottom of things quicker. "Regardless of what you did or didn't do, your ass is in a shitload of trouble." Though his manner was jocular, it hid his grave concern. He was sure Taylor was hanging on to his composure by a thin thread, and he didn't want to be the one adding extra weight to the line.

"Tell me something I don't know," Taylor huffed. He kept wishing he could open his eyes and find that it had all been just a big misunderstanding, or one very bad nightmare, and that he could somehow pick up his life where he and Brooke had left off in Jamaica, skipping over the front-page story, the federal investigation, and his crooked partner.

"Look, man, you know I'm on your side," Max said, leaning forward to fix Taylor with a hard stare.

"That's good to know, since I feel like a cat thrown into a

packed dog pound." He leaned back, mentally exhausted. It felt as if an eternity had passed during the last few days. His bones were weary, his brain was fried, and if it weren't for Brooke, he'd be an emotional powder keg.

They'd stayed up late the night before, holding each other in the dark while she gently persuaded him to talk about everything: his life, his failed marriage, and his imploding career. Before he drifted off to sleep, he realized why Brooke was so good at her job. Surprisingly, he found that it really did help for him to talk about it. Like most black men, he thought that seeing a therapist was for rich white people to wallow in self-pity.

Taylor filled Max in on his series of conversations with Eduard, who was still MIA, and about the Beacon Hill file and the broken file cabinet.

"It sounds like you're swimming with the sharks down there on Wall Street."

"Man-eaters." The fact that Eduard had yet to surface also deeply troubled him. According to Stuart he was on his yacht for an extended vacation; Stuart wasn't sure when he would be back in the office. It all sounded a bit too pat to Taylor, and knowing his devious wife, he wouldn't put it past her to collude with Eduard against him.

Max shook his head and drew a deep breath. "Like I said yesterday, this situation is way out of my league, but your lawyer Paul Evans is the best in the business at this sort of thing." He leaned back in his chair again. "But Kiernan I can help you with."

"Speaking of her, I've got to get into that apartment to get my hands on that file."

"We shouldn't have any problem getting a judge to issue an order allowing you to enter your own home."

Taylor felt the air hissing out of his life raft. "How long will it take?" That file was his only chance he had of dodging a big bullet.

Max stroked his chin thoughtfully. "I'll file a petition this afternoon, and hopefully we can get a judge to look at it before the week's out."

Taylor slammed his fist down on the table, causing nearby patrons to turn to look. "I have to get into that apartment *now*," he insisted. "There's a preliminary hearing on Friday to decide if there's probable cause to prosecute, and if I don't have that file by then, it's all over."

"What exactly is in that file?" Max asked.

Taylor put both hands to the sides of his head, rubbing his temples as he strained to recall the details of the documents. "From what I remember, there were notes in Eduard's handwriting about the investment group. In fact"—he sat up reenergized— "one note said, 'Will instruct Taylor to contact Maurice ASAP,' and there are notes outlining his recommendations on how the deal should be structured. All of which proves I didn't have a preexisting relationship with them, and was in fact following a senior partner's orders."

"I'll see if I can get a hearing in the next twenty-four hours, but if I were you I'd hedge my bets and start pleading with the Wicked Witch."

"That may sound like a good idea, but you don't know Kiernan." He was sure she was taking a great deal of delight in his problem, and would sooner yank out her weave than help him out of it.

Max snorted. "Uhhmph. What do you mean, I don't know Kiernan? Remember, I'm the one who tried to talk you out of marrying her to begin with. And now that we are on the subject, I know even more about her." Max reached into his briefcase to pull out Taylor's next bombshell. "This is the file from the private investigator I hired."

Taylor had forgotten that Max was hiring an investigator. Since the FBI had showed up at his door, his problems with Kiernan had been placed on the back burner. He took the file and casually flipped through the pages, then returned to the first, where his eyes came to a screeching halt as he scanned one line in particular:

> Subject is currently seeing psychotherapist Brooke Parrish, using the
> alias of Kate Mathews.

Though the words were right there plain and clear, in black and white, it took several long seconds for Taylor to process their impact. He felt like a front-seat passenger in a head-on collision. He watched helplessly as his previously compartmentalized lives crashed before him. He had never been more confused; nothing made sense to him anymore.

Max looked on alarmed, but could think of nothing in the report that would be so devastating. Taylor seemed more upset by whatever it was than he had been about an impending prosecution. He actually looked physically ill. "What's wrong?" Max asked. "Are you okay?"

Taylor struggled to come to grips with this bizarre twist of fate. He closed his eyes, willing away what was right before them. "The therapist Kiernan is seeing is my girlfriend, Brooke," he said incredulously. He was still sitting in a daze, not really believing the words that had just left his very own mouth.

"What do you mean?"

"Brooke Parrish," he said, stabbing his finger at the report, "is the woman I told you about, whom I took to Jamaica."

Max's eyes glazed over in disbelief as his mind quickly calculated the repercussions. "Oh, shit! Whatever you do, you can't let Kiernan know that you're seeing Brooke. Otherwise this divorce case will get real messy, and I imagine that Brooke could have some issues with client-patient confidentiality. In fact, her career could be at stake."

" 'Oh, shit' is right." Not only was his career on the line, but now so was Brooke's.

Max shook his head, as if hoping to clear away the static. "Man, your life is better than one of those reality-TV shows."

"More dramatic, yes, but better? Not unless you like tragi-comedies." He looked around as if preparing to leave. "I've got to go warn Brooke."

Max reached over and placed his hand on Taylor's. "You may as well finish the report. It makes for some pretty interesting reading."

"I'm sure it's better than fiction, given that everything about her seems to be a big lie." Taylor wasn't sure if he could take more. "I've gotta go."

"When are you meeting with Paul?"

"In a couple of hours. He set up a meeting for us with the feds to try to get a sense of their case."

"Good. Because if you don't get this shit straightened out, you won't have to worry about Kiernan or Brooke. Instead you could be pressing license plates."

Taylor rolled his eyes. "Don't remind me."

Brooke had just gotten back to the office after a long lunch break when André gave her an urgent message to call Taylor on his cell as soon as possible. She checked her cell phone and saw that there were two other messages, but she'd never even heard the phone ring.

Given what he was going through, she was nearly breathless with anxiety while dialing the numbers. "Hi, babe, what's going on?"

"We need to talk." He sounded very stiff, as if a loaded gun were being held to his head.

Whenever someone started a conversation with those four words, the rest of it was bound to be bad. "Taylor, what's happening?"

"I need you to meet me at your place."

"I can't. I have a patient in one hour."

"Then I'll be right there." He hung up before she could protest.

Twenty-five minutes later, Taylor was in Brooke's office.

"What happened? Are you all right?" Brooke asked. While waiting for him, she had imagined one catastrophe after another, but had a hard time believing that things could get any worse for him than they already were.

"Sit down," he said, leading her to the couch where her patients usually sat. "There's something I have to tell you."

"Taylor, you're scaring me."

He took her hand and said, "I just met with my divorce attorney. He gave me a copy of a report on Kiernan from a private investigator he hired."

She looked confused. This didn't seem to have anything to do with the Beacon Hill investigation, or her, for that matter.

He couldn't think of any way to soften the blow, so he delivered it straight out: "Brooke, Kiernan is your patient."

Brooke gave him a strange, uncomprehending look. "What are you talking about? I've never even met Kiernan." She was beginning to wonder if the stress had gotten to him. What he was saying made no sense whatsoever.

He stood up, no longer able to harness his restlessness. "No, but you have met Kate. Kate Mathews."

A thick fog descended around her, clouding her ability to see things clearly. It was all surreal. How could she possibly be seeing her patient's husband? It seemed impossible that her neurotic patient Kate Mathews was Taylor's wife. "How can that be?"

Taylor watched helplessly as Brooke headed down the same one-way street he had navigated only an hour ago. There was nothing he could do to unbend the curve in the road, or cushion the impact that he knew she was feeling as her two worlds also collided. "I know it sounds unreal, but it's true."

"Oh my God, this is bad." She began shaking her head from side to side in shock as the ramifications of this news rippled through her brain. "I could lose my license for dating a patient's husband." She stood up too and began to pace nervously, as if unable to process her thoughts quickly enough sitting down.

He stopped her and held her by the shoulders. "Remember,

Brooke, you didn't know you were. Kiernan lied to you about her identity, so there's no way you could you have known."

"That doesn't matter. The fact is, I owe her my loyalty, and that trust is broken. If she ever found out, it could cause her irreparable psychological damage."

He couldn't believe that Brooke was concerned about Kiernan, but he held his tongue. Now was not the time to debate client-patient ethics. "I'm so sorry."

Brooke was still in shock when she heard André's voice come through her intercom. "Your next patient is here." She could hear the question in his voice. She always made it a point not to have anyone in her office within five minutes of her next appointment, to ensure her clients' privacy.

She snapped out of her stupor and pulled away from Taylor's embrace.

"I'd better go," he said, glancing at his watch. He had the meeting with Paul and the investigators in fifteen minutes. As it was, he'd already be late. "We'll talk later."

She headed to her desk to look over her patient log and saw the name Kate Mathews listed as her next appointment. Then it hit her that Taylor's wife was waiting on the other side of the door! Her heart nearly stopped. "Wait!" she whispered urgently. "Kiernan is in the next room."

Taylor felt as if a ton of bricks had landed on top of him, stopping him dead in his tracks with his hand still on the doorknob. Just when he thought things couldn't get any worse, he was again proven wrong. Instinctively his eyes darted around the room, looking for a means of escape, as Max's words reverberated in his mind: *Whatever you do, you can't let Kiernan know that you're seeing Brooke.*

Reading his mind, Brooke said, "There's no way out. And that's a closet," she said, watching his gaze settle on the only other door in the room.

He looked at his watch. He was due downtown in minutes, but there was no way he could come face-to-face with Kiernan in Brooke's office without having a lot of explaining to do—explanations that would not only jeopardize his divorce case and destroy any chances of his getting the file back, but worse, would jeopardize Brooke's career.

Brooke had also run through the same list of consequences, but she had others to add to it. If Kiernan saw her husband coming out of her office, it would only feed every paranoid fantasy that she had ever entertained. On the other hand, if Brooke hid him in the closet, it was a serious breach of client-patient confidentiality in the worst way. In those split seconds, she decided to deal with her breach rather than risk her patient's mental health. She didn't see any other choice.

After Taylor was hustled into the tiny closet adjacent to her office, Brooke opened the door to welcome his wife in.

With no choice but to stay tightly wedged among coats and supplies in the tiny closet, Taylor remained perfectly still, barely daring to breathe as he listened to the conversation between his wife and his lover. It suddenly occurred to him that this could work out in his favor. It could be quite a lucky break if Brooke could pry some information about the file from Kiernan. Finally he might catch a break.

Brooke held her breath as Kiernan looked around the room with a frown on her face, as if sensing something.

Observing her reaction, Brooke realized that she probably smelled a hint of the Jo Malone fragrance that Taylor always wore. She took a shallow breath and tried not to think about the closet or the skeletons that were rattling around in it. Though she realized the opportunity that this bizarre situation offered Taylor, Brooke gave Kiernan a family-emergency excuse in order to reschedule the appointment for the next day. The lie saved her from breaching all of her ethics, but also kept her from getting any information that might help Taylor.

Once again more air seeped from Taylor's sinking raft. He felt himself drowning in deep water, realizing that he was clearly on his own, unable to count on anyone to throw him a lifeline.

When Kiernan was gone, Taylor eased out of the closet. Brooke saw the look of defeat on his face, and realized that he too saw the opportunity that could have been gained.

He straightened his jacket and tie and headed to the door.

"Where are you going?" she asked.

"I've got to catch up with my lawyer. I was supposed to be at a meeting with him and the feds ten minutes ago." He was sure that not showing up was akin to waving a red flag at an irate bull. And what excuse could he give, that he was hiding in the closet? It was all too crazy for him to even begin to explain.

She held his arm. "Listen Taylor, I'm sorry. As a therapist—"

He cut her off. "Brooke, you don't have to explain anything." He honestly didn't think he could handle another blow at the moment; those he'd already sustained over the past few days were quite enough.

"But, Taylor—"

Though he admired and respected her for honoring her professional oath, he wasn't able to mask his disappointment, not when it was piled on top of so many others. He pulled away and walked out the door, not once looking back.

She collapsed onto the sofa, feeling drained. The question that she couldn't avoid was whether the possibility of losing love was worth abandoning her professional ethics. If she probed her client about her lover, Brooke realized that the conversation could help save Taylor. But the price of his freedom could most certainly be her career. What was the right thing to do? What about love? What was that worth?

She picked up the phone and dialed Taylor's cell number; the call went straight to voice mail. "Taylor, it's me, baby. Listen, I have another session with Kiernan tomorrow. We need to talk, so please call me as soon as you get the message." For the first time in her life Brooke had no idea what the right thing to do was.

The way she saw it, no matter what she did she could lose him. If she breached her professional ethics it would forever remain a wedge between them; she'd always blame him for costing her her career and her self-esteem. But if she didn't help him he could be indicted for a crime that he hadn't commited, not to mention the fact that he could be facing prison. One way she'd lose him emotionally, and the other physically. Either choice wasn't good.

28

IN THE CLOSET

A few blocks away Joie was headed down Park Avenue after a visit to her doctor's office when her cell phone rang. After digging it out of the side pocket of her backpack she answered. "Hello?" There was a note of joy in her voice and an extra skip in her step as she kept walking at a good clip. She'd been very careful to get plenty of exercise each day by forgoing a taxi ride here and there, opting to walk those extra blocks instead. Joie was determined not to be one of those women who had a baby and used it as a convenient excuse to pack on the pounds and let themselves go to pot. She saw Olivia's birth as the beginning of a life, rather than the end of her own. Besides, she had too many beautiful and expensive designer clothes to ever consider parting with any of them, and given the enormous expense of raising a child these days, they could be the last ones that she'd ever be able to afford—so come hell or high water she was getting her figure back.

"Joie. I'm so glad I caught you. It's Jimmy." He was her anal-retentive, detail-obsessed, but utterly indispensable photo assistant. He was as grounded as she was flighty, so together they were a really good team.

She reluctantly tore herself away from worries about her quickly changing figure to deal with his call. "What's up?" she asked, being sure to let her annoyance show in her voice. Though he did get on her nerves with his obsession with details, she honestly didn't know what she'd do without him.

He was breathless with worry, as usual. "I just got a call from Eric over at *Heat* magazine, and they've decided to do their fashion shoot outside, in Central Park, rather than here in the studio." He had that anxious tone that always accompanied the advent of an unplanned occurrence. Jimmy was an admitted perfectionist, and didn't like any surprises.

Joie looked at her watch. The shoot was scheduled to start at three, and it was already one thirty. "That's fine by me, as long as they understand the lighting ramifications. Oh, and another thing—do they have the permits?" Frankly, she didn't care if they did the shoot in the Bronx Zoo, as long as the lighting, makeup, and wardrobe worked. She was known as a photographer who could make gourmet lemonade out of rotten lemons, much the same way she'd done with the news of her pregnancy.

"The permit is being taken care of now," he assured her.

She shrugged. "Well, I'll see you there."

"We're all meeting at the Boat House," he continued. "I'll get there early to do a light check."

Of course he would. "Cool."

She was just about to press the end button when his voice came blaring back through the receiver. "Wait, Joie."

She stared at the phone and rolled her eyes before putting it back to her ear. "What is it now?" she moaned.

"Do you have your UV lens with you? 'Cause there aren't any here in the studio." She could see him sucking his teeth.

Leave it to Jimmy to remember such an important but easy-to-forget detail. She recalled that over the weekend she'd taken some cityscape shots for a travel publication and hadn't brought the lenses back to the office. "They're at the apartment."

"Now that we're shooting outdoors, you'll need to run home and pick them up," he ordered.

Joie sighed. She often wondered who was running the show

here: her or him. "You're right." So much for her impromptu trip to check out Oilily, a fabulous-looking upscale baby store on Madison Avenue. She'd passed it a million times on her way to the adult version, Barneys. Olivia would be born in May and might need resort wear, which was already in stores, at least for adults, and of course the diva-in-training would have to have a great summer wardrobe. She wondered what girls' baby shoes even looked like, since she'd never even considered such things. Well, she'd just have to postpone her first foray into the world of baby duds until later. Maybe, she thought, smiling, she could get Brooke to go along with her.

She was still in a great mood as she looked for a taxi headed downtown to her and Brent's apartment in the Meatpacking District to retrieve the photo lens. On the way she thought about the fact that she also needed to start shopping for another apartment. Their small one-bedroom was fine for a couple, but not nearly suitable for a family of three; after all, she did not plan on depriving herself of a nursery to decorate, either. Maybe they'd even move across the Hudson to the tristate area's best-kept secret: Hoboken, New Jersey. The charming mile-square city was only minutes away from the city by ferry, train, car, or bus, and came without the noise, smells, or hustle and bustle of Gotham. Besides, they would get much more for their money there, too.

She almost pinched herself to interrupt this string of thoughts. The next thing she knew she'd be chatting with other mothers about the consistency of baby bowel movements, diaper brands, potty training, and play dates. Who would have ever thought that Joie Blanchard would turn into a soccer mom? Or would ever be called a bride-to-be, for that matter.

Though Brent had wanted to get married right away, she'd talked him into a small civil ceremony in June, after the baby was born. She had good reason to delay. She wanted to be sure that the baby was his before taking that final step with him. She would find out his and Evan's blood types and, assuming that they weren't the same, be able to tell who was—and wasn't—the father, without making a big production of it. Assuming that Olivia was Brent's child, in deference to the big to-do that he and his mother seemed to crave, the wedding ceremony would be followed by a lavish dinner for close family and friends at Le Cirque. Though it was to be held in six months, Joie's own mother refused to acknowledge the engagement at all, so sure was she that her unpredictable daughter was apt to get cold feet and flee like a bat escaping from hell at any moment.

Brent's mother, on the other hand, called daily for progress reports on everything from the minimal wedding plans to how many ounces her grandchild had gained since the last doctor's visit. She was so excited that Joie would have thought *she* was getting married and having a child. Her enthusiasm broke Joie's heart, since there was still a fifty-fifty chance that the child she carried wasn't even Brent's.

These thoughts cut a path through her subconscious as she rode the industrial-style elevator to their fourth-floor apartment. She heard music coming from inside and figured that Brent had left the radio on when he ran out for work that morning. After opening the door, she tossed her backpack on the sofa and headed into the bedroom, where her lenses were kept in a box in the back of the closet. She walked through the door, right into the shock of her life.

She was totally unprepared for what she saw when she passed through the door's threshold, entering a world as unfamiliar to her as Pluto would have been. Her brain was in stark denial for several seconds, fiercely challenging the twisted image that her eyes clearly saw. There on her bed in front of her very eyes were Brent and Evan going at it doggy-style as though they were both off to the races. Evan was on the top and Brent was on the bottom with his face smashed into the pillow and his ass stuck high in the air. When he raised his head, his eyes were closed and he winced in pleasure or pain with every pummeling stroke that Evan delivered in his primal quest to drive the headboard of their bed right through the room's wall.

Joie shook her head slowly from side to side, trying to erase the bizarre scene that she was witnessing. While the men had always been close, Joie had had no idea just how close. One hand flew to her stomach, a protective reflex, and the other covered her mouth in abject shock. The thought that either man was bisexual was something that had never even occurred to her. And the further possibility that they were sleeping with each other was unfathomable, but she was seeing it live with her own two eyes. This wasn't secondhand gossip or idle speculation.

"Oh, my God, oh, my God." The words were barely audible as they escaped her lips. She began backing up as if she could rewind her walk through the door and somehow erase what waited for her on the other side. In her shock, she stumbled over a pile of hastily discarded clothes, bumping against the doorframe.

Brent heard the noise even though the room was full of the sound of the headboard slamming rhythmically against the wall, the music, and the lusty grunts and throaty groans of both men as they raced each other to the finish line. In just a millisecond, Brent's facial expression changed from intense pleasure—one that she'd never seen when they made love—to shocked mortification as he opened his eyes to see his worst nightmare staring him in the face. He quickly jumped up from the bed, nearly tossing Evan onto the floor, and stumbled clumsily toward her, at the last minute trying to grab the sheet, a towel, pieces of clothing, anything to cover his shame. "Joie, wait a minute. I-I-I can explain."

His movements jarred Joie out of her paralysis. She turned quickly and ran to the living room, grabbed her backpack, and rushed out the door. There was nothing to explain. The fact that another man's dick was up his back door said it all.

29

A FORK IN THE ROAD

Since the starry evening aboard Eduard's luxury yacht, when she'd given her a fantastic proposition—one in which she had nothing to lose—Kiernan had ransacked the apartment searching desperately for the file marked BEACON HILL, but so far she had found nothing. She'd diligently ripped opened every file, drawer, and cabinet, and dug around every nook and cranny in Taylor's office and their bedroom. She'd even expanded her search to include the guest bedroom and the living and dining rooms. When a hundred fifty thousand dollars was at stake, Kiernan didn't plan to leave any stone unturned. She'd even looked underneath the bed, in between the mattress and cushions, and on top of all cabinets and dressers. She was so close to the money that she could smell it, but at the same time, she was so far away that it was driving her nuts.

Racking her brain, Kiernan thought back to the day when she and LaTeesha had moved out of her downtown office, recalling the stacks of files that were scattered around, files belonging to her and Taylor. She remembered asking LaTeesha to straighten things out, but for the life of her she couldn't fathom where—other than in the cabinets and boxes that were in the office closet—the girl would have put them. And the worst part was that she couldn't very well call her, not after her arrest on drug charges. Besides, she never saw LaTeesha leave the apartment with anything, so it had to be there somewhere.

Her phone rang, interrupting her thoughts. She absently picked up the receiver. "Hello?"

"Kiernan, we need to talk." Though he would have rather given himself a root canal without painkillers, Taylor had taken Max's advice to plead with Kiernan to gain access to the apartment.

"We have nothing to talk about." Her words came out slow and lethargic, signs that he knew pointed to a trail of pills. Instead of starting her day with a cup of joe, her morning pick-me-up for a long time had been pharmaceutical. It was months into their marriage before he realized the magnitude of her problem, and when he first confronted her she had blamed her pill popping on chronic back pain. But after reading the investigator's report on her, he questioned everything that Kiernan had ever told him. It was richly ironic to him that his girlfriend probably knew his wife better than he ever had.

"Look, I know you're pissed at me, but it's critical that I get this file."

"Tell it to someone who gives a shit. I could care less about some Beacon Hill file or your mess of legal problems," she slurred. Eduard had filled her in on some of the hot water that Taylor was now in. Though she doubted that he'd be capable of money laundering, she still thought he deserved what he was getting for what he'd done to her.

"Kiernan, if I don't get those documents I could be indicted for money laundering."

"Save your breath. I know all about it, and I still don't give a shit," she huffed.

"I'm on my way there now, and I suggest you let me in. Otherwise I'll go straight to the police and name you as an accomplice in interfering with a federal investigation." Though his words were a lot of bluster, with Kiernan in a drug-induced state, he had a chance to get what he needed.

She reached for a cigarette to light, settling in to enjoy listening to him squirm. "You can go anywhere you please, but you are not getting in here."

He pulled out his remaining card. "Either you let me in, or we'll see how much your society friends like reading about Norma." He hated to go there, but right now he was desperate. Max's file had filled him in on all the details—sordid as many were—that made up Kiernan's life, including her given name.

"Unless your ass is pushin' in here with a bulldozer, you won't be settin' foot in this apartment," she spit. The phone line went dead.

The nerve of him to expect her to help save him when she was dangling in the wind herself, and all he'd ever done was to add a stiffer breeze. He'd even closed the checking account that she'd drawn against, causing checks that she wrote to bounce, only adding to the list of bill collectors hounding her. She'd just as soon see Taylor rot in jail as consider helping him, especially after that snide remark about her past. She replayed in her head the nasty sneer in his voice when he called her Norma.

She made a move to get out of the bed and felt as if she'd been hit head-on by a freight train, and in fact, she would rather have experienced that than to be hit so hard by the truth. She pulled herself up and held on to the nightstand as she began to hyperventilate. Ghosts that she'd outrun for years were catching up to her now, and it was petrifying. She sat back down on the bed and rested with her elbows on her knees, waiting for her breathing to catch up with the fast pace of her heart. How could he have found out? she wondered. She suddenly realized that it must have been Thelma. She was the only person who knew her past, and her sister's loyalty left much to be desired. "That conniving, low-life bitch," she hissed.

This was not the way she wanted to start her day, especially since she finally had an appointment tomorrow with Eva that she had to prepare for, which also meant she couldn't spend all day looking for that damn file. She pulled herself together with the help of a small plate of white powder that sat on the nightstand, and later stumbled to the shower, hoping that a blast of cold water would clear her mind.

With a fresh outlook, she called Eva to confirm tomorrow's appointment. "Good morning, Eva. It's Kiernan," she cooed into the receiver. The coke had really helped to steady her nerves. After not getting her last exchange from Thelma, Kiernan had resorted to copping drugs on the street in disguise, spending much of her remaining money in the process.

"Oh, good morning, Kiernan."

"Just calling to confirm our appointment, and find out what time's best for you."

"Four o'clock sounds good." Finally, Kiernan thought, something was going according to plan. "Pia has been singing your praises, so I'm really looking forward to seeing your boards," Eva added.

Kiernan nearly choked. With all that was going on in her life, she'd forgotten about the design boards.

"Kiernan?"

"I-I'm here."

"Anyway, I'll see you tomorrow."

Kiernan had sent painstakingly rendered illustrations to a company in Philadelphia to quickly create the laminated boards that Eva had insisted on seeing and frankly had all but forgotten about them. She remember ordering them, and they should have been delivered by now. She picked up the phone to call the company and was informed that they had been sent overnight days ago, so they must be lost. This was bad. Short of getting money from Eduard for turning over a file that she couldn't even find, getting the money from Eva was her last hope.

Kiernan reached for the plate of coke again, when suddenly a thought occurred to her: Maybe the package was down in the mailroom, and she was panicking for nothing.

She snatched up the phone. "Frank, this is Mrs. Malloy."

"Oh, hi, Mrs. Malloy. How are you?"

You don't want to know, she wanted to say. "I'm fine, but I need to ask you about a package I've been expecting."

"Who is it from?"

"A company called Philly Creations." She held her breath.

He thought for a moment. "Oh, yeah," he said.

She heard him flipping through some papers. At least he remembered it, which meant things were looking up.

"Here it is."

She finally released the breath she'd been holding. "Great. I need you to send it right up." She was about to hang up the phone.

"I already did."

"Excuse me?"

"I sent it upstairs with Mr. Hudson a couple of days ago," he said.

"You did what?" she screamed.

"I sent it up with Mr. Hudson," he repeated.

Kiernan was now mad enough to spit bullets, all aimed at Frank. "Why the fuck would you do that?" she yelled.

"Well, he is the owner of the apartment," he reminded her. A note of defensive arrogance had replaced his normal civility.

Kiernan slammed the phone down hard enough to rattle the lampshade. This had now become a bona fide disaster.

Given everything, she'd thought about canceling her rescheduled session with Brooke, but now Kiernan decided that a break, a shoulder to cry on, and another hit of coke might do her some good.

"So how are you?" Brooke asked. It was all she could do to refrain from calling her client Kiernan. The knowledge of her patient's true identity was both good and bad from a therapeutic perspective. While it gave her added insight into the woman's psyche, at the same time it made her feel as though she didn't really know her at all. One thing she did know was that Kiernan was in a very vulnerable state right now; otherwise she would have immediately tried to transfer the woman to another therapist. She realized that she couldn't continue seeing Kiernan as a patient while also seeing her husband, but she also knew that discarding her abruptly could deepen the woman's issues. This transfer had to be handled carefully; otherwise she could undo all of the progress they'd made.

"I am so stressed out," she started. "I've got a lot going on, and I'm under a ton of pressure right now." Kiernan ran her fingers through her disheveled weave, and her hand snagged in the tangle of fake hair. She simply yanked and pulled until strands were removed along with her hand, but she was barely unfazed by this bizarre spectacle. After hitting the powder so much lately, she was virtually numb.

"Is it the divorce?" The one thing that all of this proved was that Taylor hadn't lied to her about getting a divorce. Not that she didn't trust him, but as the official "other woman," she had had a tiny bit of doubt.

"Not exactly." She told Brooke that her husband had recently come banging on the door asking for something he'd left in the apartment, and that she desperately needed to find it.

Brooke knew that she had to be talking about the Beacon Hill file, but asked, "What exactly is it?"

"A file," Brooke answered.

"Why is this file so important?" Brooke asked. She had to be very careful here. This was where she could really cross the line with client-patient confidentiality, not that she hadn't already done so; after all, her patient's soon-to-be ex-husband was her lover.

"He's in some trouble at work, and this file apparently could help clear him."

"So you're looking for it in order to give it back to him?" she probed gently around this sticky situation. She prayed that Kiernan would answer yes.

Kiernan sneered at the implication that she should give a damn about Taylor. "I don't know why I should help him. He's done nothing to help me," she replied smugly. But things had shifted in the last hour; now he did have something that could help her.

"So why are you so desperate to find this file?"

"I have my reasons," she taunted, baiting Brooke to dig.

This confirmed for her that Kiernan was working with Eduard, just as Taylor suggested when they last spoke. She weighed whether to pry deeper; maybe she'd be able to persuade Kiernan to give the file back to Taylor, which, of course, would help Taylor. But ultimately it would destroy Brooke.

Even if no one else found out about her serious ethical breach, the fact that it had happened would violate everything she'd ever believed in, forcing her to question her own morality. As a therapist, she knew better than anyone just how devastating that could be. She'd never felt more torn inside than she did at this very moment. On the one hand she desperately wanted to use this opportunity to help Taylor, but on the other, she wasn't sure that she could make that sacrifice in good conscience.

30
GOING TIT FOR TAT

After Taylor left Brooke's closet, he was finally able to catch up with Paul just as the attorney was leaving the meeting with the federal investigators. "Paul, it's Taylor." He was calling from his cell phone in the backseat of the Town Car.

"Where were you?" The man was obviously annoyed at his client for standing him up in a roomful of federal agents. This was not the way to get on their good side, and based on what he'd heard, so far they'd need every advantage they could get.

"It's a long story," Taylor said, "but suffice it so say that it couldn't be helped." He could not even begin to explain how he'd ended up trapped in his lover's coat closet while his wife stood on the other side of the door. At the moment he didn't quite understand it himself.

"Well, I hope whatever kept you away was more important than a federal money-laundering investigation, though I honestly can't imagine what would be." He said this with the resigned attitude of someone who was about to witness a train wreck, but could do nothing to stop it.

"I said it couldn't be helped," Taylor snapped. He'd had enough. He was beginning to feel like a punching bag in Mike Tyson's personal gym.

"Listen, Taylor, I'm not trying to beat up on you, but you know these boys aren't playing," he warned.

No shit, Taylor thought. Tell me something that I don't know.

"Have you spoken to Eduard?" Paul asked.

"I did, and his tune has definitely changed. Now it's a solo. He's insisting—for the benefit of a taped call, I'm sure—that he had no knowledge whatsoever of the deal. And with no witnesses or corroborating documents, it's my word against his."

And given a choice, Taylor had no doubt whose version a panel of WASP judicial system regulators would choose to believe.

"Just what I expected."

"Unfortunately, I can't say I'm surprised either. So what happened at the meeting?" Taylor asked.

"We can go over it this evening—I have another appointment that I'm running to now—but the bottom line is, if we don't walk in there Friday with a smoking gun with someone else's fingerprints on it, they will indict."

All night Taylor reflected on those words. After another failed plea to Kiernan, he decided the next day to torture himself and try again. He'd grovel, beg, or bribe—basically do whatever was necessary—to get into that apartment to get that file. Whatever Eduard was offering to give her, he'd pay more, though his pocket was nowhere near as deep as the old man's.

After replaying his last conversation with Kiernan he was convinced that she and Eduard were plotting together. He remembered her using the name Beacon Hill. He hadn't mentioned it in his previous conversations with her, nor was it ever mentioned in the newspapers. How else would she have known it? Now he was simply gambling that she hadn't handed the file over to his boss yet. Knowing her—as he was just beginning to—she would relish rubbing his nose in it right after the fact.

He was about to dial the number when he noticed that he had two messages. One was from Brooke, which he saved, and the other one, oddly enough, was from Kiernan. He called the apartment wondering if this was the call for her to rub his nose in the mess that she'd made by handing the file over to Eduard. He resigned himself and placed the call.

"Kiernan, it's Taylor." He held his breath, waiting for the guillotine to slide down onto his neck.

"Oh, hi, Taylor." She made sure to sound as if things between them were hunky-dory, since she'd already braced herself to eat a large dose of crow.

For a minute he thought he'd dialed the wrong number. "I'm returning your call," he said, playing it cool.

"Oh, yeah," she said, feigning a casualness that she certainly didn't feel. "When you were here the other day, did Frank send a delivery up with you?"

He thought for a minute before realizing that the doorman had given him a FedEx package, but when she hadn't let him in the apartment, he'd taken it back to his office, and with all the other drama that was unfolding at the time, he'd quickly forgotten about it. "I do seem to remember that. Why?" His antenna was now up and searching for a strong signal, one that would hopefully mean he might escape the death sentence—at least for now.

"I need that box." He heard the urgency—no, desperation—in her voice.

"How ironic." He chuckled. "If you'd been civil and let me into the apartment to begin with you'd have it." He couldn't resist saying that.

"Taylor," she pleaded, "it's crucial that I get that box."

"That plea sounds awfully familiar to me." Though he was being petty, considering all that he was going through, he couldn't help but gloat a little.

"You don't understand. I have no money. I have to get that box, or I'll lose a very lucrative contract."

He decided to stop beating around the bush. "Look, Kiernan, it's real simple. You let me in the apartment to get my file, and you can have your box."

She weighed her options carefully. She could either let him come get the file and lose the opportunity to sell it to Eduard, or she could deny him the file and lose her chance at a lucrative design job. After considering her diminished chances of actually finding the file, she decided to take the option that offered her the better odds. "Come on over," she said.

This was the best news he'd had all week long. "I'll be right there." He quickly headed to the office to pick up the long-forgotten FedEx box and raced over to the apartment as fast as New York traffic would allow.

31

MISERY'S COMPANY

Joie was waiting on Brooke's apartment stoop when she arrived home from work. The angst she'd carried since Taylor had walked out of her closet dejected was reflected in her friend's face. It mirrored how bad she felt herself. She dropped her briefcase and knelt beside Joie, who sat in a state of shock.

"What's wrong?" Brooke asked the question even though she wasn't altogether sure she wanted to hear the answer; she didn't know if she could take another shocking development. For years she'd borne the heavy burden of her patients' troubles without signs of fatigue, but now that her own burdens were so heavy, she felt mentally overwhelmed.

Joie's eyes were swollen and red. "Everything."

"Come on, let's go inside," Brooke said, helping Joie up from the stairs. Whatever the problem was, the front stoop wasn't the place to sort it out. Her first fear was that something might be wrong with the baby. She couldn't imagine anything else reducing Joie to tears.

Joie settled into her second-favorite place in Brooke's apartment—the kitchen's window seat—and curled up on the ledge in a sitting fetal position with both knees tucked under her chin, something she used to do with ease, but not now.

Pregnancy definitely caused a lot of changes in life, she thought. Some were physical, but up to now the most significant ones had been mental.

"What happened? Is it the baby?"

Joie closed her eyes tight to dim the harsh vision of her fiancé and ex-lover having sex. "It's Brent and Evan," she finally said. She had trouble forming the other words needed to describe what she had seen.

Of course, Brooke had no idea what she was talking about and wouldn't have guessed in a million years. "What happened? Did Brent find out about Evan?" That was about the worst scandal she could have imagined involving Joie's two lovers. She'd always thought that someday there was bound to be a confrontation between them.

Joie took a deep breath and faced Brooke. "They were fucking each other," she said flatly. There was simply no other way to put it.

Brooke squinted her eyes and twisted her face, then shook her head from side to side, trying, but failing, to make sense out of the latest absurd development of the day. "What are you talking about?"

Joie pulled a Kleenex from her pocket and blew her nose. "Try this," she said, composing herself. "They have been booty buddies all along. So while I was worrying about fucking both of them, they were busy fucking each other." If it weren't for the implications to her unborn child, she would have laughed at the incredible irony of it.

Brooke, who thought she'd heard it all over the years, was clearly flabbergasted. "No!" Her eyes were the size of saucers, and her brain seemed incapable of processing what her ears had heard. It would have been easier to believe the two were CIA operatives than to imagine them having sex with each other. It just did not compute.

Joie saw the look of disbelief on her friend's face and

couldn't blame her. If she hadn't seen it with her own eyes, she was not sure she would believe it either. "Brooke, I caught them in the act," Joie said firmly.

To say that Brooke was shocked was an understatement. The only thing she could do to keep from standing there with her mouth wide-open was to make tea. She wasn't up for the nitty-gritty specifics, but knew that wouldn't stop Joie from going into graphic detail as she delivered a blow-by-blow account of the entire X-rated saga.

"So what did you do?" By now Brooke was sitting on one of the stools surrounding the small island, nursing her tea while the story unfolded.

"I ran out as fast as I could." She spread both hands out questioningly. "What was I supposed to do? I guess if it were up to them I would have joined in for a cozy ménage à trois."

That brought up an interesting question in Brooke's mind. "Do you think Brent and Evan knew all along that you were sleeping with them both?" It always seemed odd to her that Joie could have gotten away with such a blatant affair for so long.

Joie hadn't thought of that. She sighed deeply. "I don't really know, but it's definitely possible. They were obviously much closer than I thought."

"So what are you going to do now?"

"For starters, I think it's safe to say that the wedding is off." When Brooke didn't comment she continued. "I know you didn't condone it anyway."

"I just thought you were doing it for the wrong reasons, that's all." Brooke realized that Joie still had her head buried in the sand. The canceled wedding was the least of the issues that she needed to come to grips with. The most important one was the decision of whether or not to forge a relationship with her baby's father, be it Brent or Evan.

"So did you go to the photo shoot?" Brooke asked to change the subject. She was not one who gloated over I-told-you-so's.

"No, I didn't. I called another photographer and had him fill in for me, though I'm sure the magazine isn't happy about it."

"They'll get over it," Brooke said, trying to provide some comfort to her distraught friend.

"You know, somehow I seem to get myself in the most bizarre and fucked-up situations."

"As strange as this sounds, just like your pregnancy, this could be a blessing in disguise for you." Brooke really meant that. If this was what it took to derail Joie's misguided trip down the aisle, then so be it.

"If it is a blessing, it's definitively well disguised, because I don't see a thing." Joie shook her head.

Brooke put her cup down on the kitchen counter. "Think about it, Joie. If this hadn't happened you might have gone ahead with the wedding, or at the very least misled Brent about the baby's paternity for the next five months, and we both know you are not in love with him. No matter what, he deserves to know the truth. It's unfair to let him think for months that he's the father, and then later say, 'Oops, my bad.' "

Joie couldn't argue with her, because—as usual—she was right. Her and Brent's relationship was borne of necessity and convenience: They had both needed a roommate, she was mildly attracted to him, and he had the hots for her, and from there the relationship just sort of fell into place, along with their furniture and household accessories.

Evan had been another story altogether. Since the first time they'd met, she'd been like a bitch in heat. Not that she confused that with love, but it was certainly a whole lot better than the lukewarm excuse for sex that Brent gave her. In either case, she had to admit, she hadn't exactly selected perfectly suited breeding material from the gene pool, but between the two evils, Brent appeared to be the lesser.

When she didn't say anything Brooke pushed her. "So it's not the end of the world, right?"

"I guess not," she finally admitted, though she still looked crestfallen.

"What's the big deal, then?"

"Try that Brent was cheating on me with another man." Her bruised ego, she realized, was her biggest problem. She had heard about men who were in relationships with women and weren't classified as gay or bisexual, but just liked to have sex with other men. She had just never thought that *her* man could be one of them.

"Well, so were you. And with the same man." They looked at each other and both fell over laughing.

Aside from her sore ego, Joie realized that her hurt feelings were the result of the betrayal that the two men were going behind her back. Then again, she'd done the same thing. Joie sighed. "You know, it's just that I had no idea that either of them was gay. And you know that my gaydar is usually right on target."

"Who said anything about either of them being gay?"

"I don't know about you, but that's what I call it when two guys have sex together."

"Haven't you ever heard of the term 'bisexual'? Or"—she held up a finger—"I have another one for you—guys on the down-low. They don't consider themselves gay or bi. They just like having sex with other men from time to time."

"I know. I got the J. L. King memo, and read his book *On the Down Low*. You can call it what you want, but one man having another man's dick up his ass is still gay to me."

"You know, for such a liberal, you are being awfully narrow-minded. What do you call female models who have sex with each other for kicks?"

"They're bi and are usually doing it for titillation, or to fulfill some guy's threesome fantasy."

"So are they gay?"

"I get your point," Joie finally admitted. "It's just that I don't like it when it involves my own boyfriend or, excuse me, fiancé."

"Speaking of Brent, what are you going to do?"

"I'm moving out as soon as possible. I can't spend another night in that apartment, especially in that bed." She shivered at the thought.

"Where're you going?"

"I really don't know. I had been thinking about us moving to Hoboken earlier, so maybe I'll still check it out."

"Until you find a place, you are welcome to stay here," Brooke offered.

"Are you sure?"

"Of course I'm sure."

"What about Taylor? I'm assuming you guys want your privacy."

The drama of her afternoon came rushing back. Joie's colorful tale had temporarily given her a much-needed diversion. "That's a long story," she said solemnly.

"It can't be longer than mine," Joie said, shifting to get comfortable.

"Let's put it this way: We'll have to move to the bedroom for this one." Which, of course, was where they had most of their serious conversations.

"Oh, boy. I don't know if Olivia and I can stand any more surprises today."

"Well, in that case you'd better stay put, 'cause this one will blow your socks off."

Joie was up from the window seat in two seconds. "Let's go." She could be in the throes of labor and still listen to a good juicy story, especially one from Brooke, who usually never had any scandalous fodder.

Once they were settled on the bed with mugs of jasmine tea, Brooke gave Joie the complete rundown, starting with Taylor's desperation to get his hands on the file and his wife's refusal to let him enter the apartment, followed by his urgent phone call to her and his quick trip to her office. When she got to the part where he told her that her patient Kate Mathews was his wife, Kiernan Malloy, Joie's eyes nearly bulged out of her head.

"Oh, my God. That's crazy!"

"It gets crazier," Brooke assured her.

"I can't imagine."

"Well, try this. While he's still in my office, my next patient arrives in the waiting room—and remember there's no way out of my private office—and guess who it is." Brooke raised her brows in a challenge.

Joie's hands flew to her mouth as the realization hit her. "Oh, no!"

Brooke nodded her head. "Yes, Kiernan."

"Wow! This is better than *Days of Our Lives*."

"Well, I wish at the moment that it were someone else's life. You know, I'm not accustomed to all this drama. I'm much more comfortable as an outside observer."

By now Joie had placed her mug on Brooke's nightstand and was lying on her side, settling in for the rest of the dramatic tale. "So what happened when they saw each other?"

"They didn't."

"But there's no other way out."

"But there is a closet."

"Damn," Joie said, sitting up. "So let me get this straight, okay? Today your man went running into the closet hiding from his wife, while mine came out of it in the arms of another man? Boy, misery does love company." Joie rolled over, laughing at the sheer absurdity of it all.

Okay, Brooke thought, I can see that the old Joie is back. Maybe finding Brent and Evan together had jolted some sense into her—kind of like electric shock treatment. But still, Brooke found no humor in it.

When her friend failed to laugh, Joie grew serious again. "I'm sorry. I'm sure that had to be very traumatic for you."

"That's not all of it."

"Please don't tell me there's more," she said, anxiously waiting for it.

"The worst part of all of it was that I had the opportunity to probe and get information that could have helped him, or maybe even encouraged her to turn the file over, but even though it could have been Taylor's best chance yet, I didn't do it."

"I would've sold her out quicker than a New York minute."

"Yeah, but you're not her therapist."

"Even if I were, I would have," Joie argued. "Based on what you've said, she's an evil liar who's content to send an innocent man—yours, by the way—to jail for a crime that he didn't commit."

"Have you ever heard the term 'client-patient confidentiality'?"

"Oh."

"It's like I lose either way. If I help him, I could lose my license to practice, and definitely my morality, but if I don't, he could be indicted."

"What are you gonna do?"

"I have another appointment with Kate—I mean Kiernan—so I could still do it. But after that, I'll begin the process of reassigning her to another therapist."

"If you're not planning to help him, why not get rid of her right away?"

"I'm afraid if I handled it abruptly that it could be detrimental to her mental state."

"What about yours? And Taylor's?"

Brooke shrugged her shoulders. "She's my patient. I have a moral and ethical duty to look after her best interests."

"I'd still work her over first."

"As a therapist it's *not* my role to use her problems to solve my own."

"But as a woman, what *is* your role?"

"In this situation, I can't say that I have the answer."

"Well, take some advice from me: If you don't figure it out soon, you might not have a man, either."

32
END OF THE LINE

"Kiernan, this is Eduard." The usual joviality was absent from his voice. Instead he sounded like a hungry shark circling a school of minnows; they weren't quite the meal he had in mind, but would do for a light snack.

"Oh, hi, Eduard. How are you?" She hadn't bothered to return any of his calls over the last couple of days, since she hadn't had any luck finding the file. She'd hoped that he'd simply give up and go away.

"I'd be much better if I had that file." There was a bite of menace in his tone.

"So would I, because then I'd also have the money," she said, trying for a light touch.

But Eduard was all business, so he cut to the chase. "Kiernan, where is my file?" He'd lost all patience when he realized that a net had been cast in his waters, and he'd be damned if he planned to get caught in it. Stuart called earlier, informing him that he'd received a formal request for an interview with federal investigators, and it wasn't engraved. This development shook Eduard up. Sure, there was a good chance they only wanted to talk to him about Taylor, but he'd feel a lot more confident if he had the file in his hand, or at least knew for sure that Taylor didn't. And the way Kiernan was avoiding him gave him pause for thought: Maybe she'd double-crossed him and handed the file over to Taylor.

"Eduard, I've searched this apartment high and low, and I haven't found this file of yours." She failed to tell him that at that very moment Taylor was on the way over to do some searching of his own.

"Do I need to remind you who I am?"

Now his tone had grown threatening; Kiernan could feel the tiny hairs on the back of her neck rise. "Excuse me?"

He took his white gloves off. "You'll be excused when I'm damned well ready for you to be excused. In the meantime I suggest you stop fucking with me and give me that goddamned file."

"Eduard, I've been totally straight with you, so w-w-why would I do that?" she stammered. She was taken completely off guard by his language. What happened to the dignified and refined gentleman he'd been before?

"Maybe you decided to give it back to Taylor in exchange for a good fuck, you pathetic, lyin' bitch."

Now he'd gone street on her. She had no idea he had it in him. His words shook her as hard as if he'd landed an unsuspected uppercut, but she sucked it up and decided to meet him in the alley; surely she had more experience there than he did. "I did no such thing," she said. "And how do you know the file was ever here to begin with? Did it ever occur to you that Taylor was fucking with you?" she asked snidely.

"Don't play games with me, you sour cunt. I'll run you out of New York and back to that seedy ghetto you crawled here from."

That was a body blow. Did he know something about her background? She was so completely stunned now that her brain was unable to tell her mouth what to say, but before it mattered anymore, she heard a loud crack, followed by the steady hum of a dial tone.

Fuck him, she thought, staring at the piece of plastic. With any luck he'd be sharing a jail cell with Taylor. Now she needed a nice hit of coke to help steady her nerves after going this nasty round with Eduard.

Five minutes later Kiernan's husband was standing at the door holding the key to her future: the design boards for her presentation with Eva.

"Let me have it," she demanded, sticking out her hand.

Taylor brushed past her to enter the apartment, dropping the package on the table in the foyer along the way.

She grabbed it as though the box might sprout legs and run back out the door. "Don't take too long," she said to Taylor's back. "I have a meeting to go to."

Taylor ignored her and headed straight for the desk in his old office. That was where he seemed to last remember laying the file, but his heart sank when he saw it wasn't there. He felt a glimmer of hope when he realized that the office had been totally rearranged, as if Kiernan were now working from here instead of her SoHo office. Maybe it was just misplaced. He removed his jacket and tie and systematically went though every drawer, file, and box in the room, but to no avail. He again wondered if Kiernan had already given the file to Eduard. Just then he looked up and saw her standing in the doorway, watching as if waiting to see if he had found it, so maybe she hadn't. "Kiernan, have you seen the file marked 'Beacon Hill'?"

"No, I haven't," she answered evenly.

She didn't appear to be lying, but with her, he never knew. He left the office and decided to search the master bedroom, leaving her standing in the office doorway.

The bedroom was the only other place he'd spent any time that day, so he scoured it as well. He ended up leaving the apartment empty-handed, but still carrying a very heavy burden. The big meeting was tomorrow morning and he had nothing to defend himself with.

After he left, Kiernan dressed to the nines in a fabulous-fitting Dolce & Gabbana pin-striped pantsuit, a crisp white blouse, and a pair of kick-ass pointy-toed Fendi boots. It was critical that she make just the right impression at this appointment. She needed to look stylish, yet efficient and powerful. She stood back and admired herself in front of her full-length mirror. Her weave was tight, her presentation was rock-solid, and she was ready to take on the world.

She was marching out the door armed for battle, with her spirits as high as Everest, when the phone rang. She started not to answer, but thought better of it.

Kiernan picked up the line in the foyer. "Hello?"

"Hi, Kiernan. It's Eva."

She put a song in her voice. "Hi, Eva. I was just on my way over," she said, smiling her best fake smile, even though the woman couldn't see her through the phone line. It didn't matter; she was in a great mood. She had her design boards, her coke high was still going, and she was on her way to sign a lucrative contract. *That* she was sure of. Only yesterday Pia had phoned to tell her who the competition for the job was, and they'd mutually agreed none of them could hold a scented candle to Kiernan. So the gospel according to Pia read that the job was hers for the taking. Finally she could breathe a little easier; something was going her way.

"I'm glad I caught you. My dear friend Eduard just called—you do know Eduard Wentworth, don't you?"

Kiernan's high deflated upon hearing the evil man's name.

"We ran into each other last week at the Met and I mentioned to him that I was thinking of using you on my project. Anyway, he just phoned a moment ago with a recommendation for someone he thinks I should use instead. I really feel badly, but he said that you would understand. And of course, I feel compelled to take any recommendation of his. You see, he manages my personal estate, as well as some of my charities, and you know how those things work. Anyway, I wanted to let you know not to bother coming over, since I'd hate to waste your time."

Kiernan stared at the phone in shocked disbelief. There she was standing in the doorway fully dressed, hand on the doorknob, carrying a portfolio of design boards that she'd traded for the promise of one hundred fifty thousand dollars, and the psychotic bitch said she didn't want to waste her time! A boiling rage filled her so completely that she could taste its bitter residue on the tip of her tongue. "You fucking bitch!" she spit into the phone.

"Why, Kiernan!" Eva was shocked and appalled at her response. Civilized people didn't show such raw, unchecked emotion. Ever. Eva had no idea why Eduard had called out of the blue so concerned about her interior designer, and furthermore had no idea why Kiernan was jumping into the gutter as a result of it. At least according to everything she'd heard, the woman had plenty of clients—just look at that fabulous apartment she lived in—so she couldn't need the business that badly. Eva couldn't wait to get off the phone so that she could immediately get back on it to call Pia and tell her. It never failed to amaze her, the kind of people who were passing themselves off as civilized these days.

In Keirnan's fury she'd lost her ingrained ability to censor herself, so her anger spewed forth like ash from a volcano. "Just because you're rich, you think you can shit all over people like me? Well, I oughta come over there and kick your skinny, anorexic little ass," she screamed. She went on and on, cursing, screaming, and screeching long after another dial tone began blaring between the pauses in her rants and raves.

Kiernan felt like a drowned corpse anchored to the bottom of a deep, dark, foggy swamp. It seemed to her as if all the planets, the moon, and every star in the galaxy were suddenly aligned against her. The harder she tried to reach for happiness, the more elusive it proved to be, floating whimsically through the universe liberally sprinkling happy dust on everyone but her.

She remembered what Brooke once said about the importance of loving herself first. She stumbled over to the mirror at her vanity table, trying to find someone in there worth loving. All she saw, beyond the mascara-streaked, red-rimmed eyes, was the ghost of the homeless woman she'd seen cowering on the corner the night of the Guggenheim event, and the shadows of her drunken mother and drug-addicted sister. She realized then that she could run from them, but no matter where she lived or what she wore, she couldn't hide from her past or from herself. She picked up a perfume bottle and smashed her own image into splintered pieces. Though the glass shattered it never fell apart. It reminded her of herself: broken, but somehow miraculously still standing.

She stood up and went to find her drug stash, looking for something, anything, to help ease the pain. Instead of pills or powder, she found a note. It read:

Dear Kiernan,
While searching for the file I found your stash of drugs.
Though things didn't work out between us, I hope one
day you will find happiness, and it's not in a pile of pills
or a stash of cocaine. I flushed them all down the toilet,
and pray that you'll get the help that you need instead of
another supply.

Taylor

She tore the note into tiny pieces, which fluttered like spent confetti to the carpeted floor. Tears streamed down her face as she screamed, "I hate you!" over and over again at the top of her lungs. The odd thing was that she didn't know whether her words were directed at Taylor, Eduard, Eva, or herself. After her sessions with Brooke she now realized that much of the hatred that she spewed out into the world was the result of it first ricocheting off herself.

She crumpled to the floor, badly wrinkling her two-thousand-dollar suit, but she didn't care. She sat there crying for nearly an hour, mourning her lost childhood and her fabricated adulthood. And as the tears washed away her carefully applied makeup, they revealed the person behind the facade, someone Kiernan needed to get to know. She took a deep, cleansing breath that brought with it some answers that she'd never bothered to even seek before, and they came to her effortlessly.

33

THE OTHER MAN

The morning after Joie caught Brent and Evan together, she woke up disoriented on the sofa bed in Brooke's living room. It was five o'clock in the morning. She sat up rubbing her eyes, slowly remembering where she was and why. What a difference a day made. The day before, there was no way she would have believed she'd be sleeping on her friend's sofa because her fiancé was sharing their bed with another man.

She got up and slowly stretched her muscles before grabbing her clothes off the coffee table and heading into the bathroom to shower, carefully closing the door behind her, not daring to wake Brooke, who hated the early morning hours.

In twenty minutes she was closing Brooke's front door behind her, heading downtown to finish opening a can of worms. A cab ride later she walked into her apartment, deliberately blocking out the lurid images from the last time she'd passed through the very same doorway. Her plan was simply to quickly pack as many of her things as she could fit into a set of luggage and head back uptown to Brooke's. Fortunately she didn't have a photo shoot scheduled today.

"Joie, I'm so glad you came back." There in the bedroom doorway stood Brent in his bathrobe.

"I didn't," she said, tossing her backpack onto the sofa. "I'm only here to pick up a few things. I'll get the rest later."

"You really don't have to go. We can work this out," he pleaded. He realized that what she witnessed must have been shocking to her. He just needed to explain it and everything would be okay.

"What do you mean, work this out?" she demanded. "There's nothing to work out. I'm leaving, so you and your booty buddy can keep getting it on."

"It's not like that. I want you."

"Oh, so you're one of those who want it both ways—to give it and to get it. Do you suck his dick, too?" she spit. She regretted saying the words the second they left her mouth. The situation was what it was, and there was no need for her to be ugly about it; after all, she hadn't exactly been a saint herself.

Fury lit his eyes. "Shut the fuck up," he shouted. Brent didn't want to hear it. As far as he was concerned, he was not gay or bi. What he and Brent did together was just another form of physical stimulation. He didn't know why people made such a big deal over two men having sex every now and then, but since they did he was always forced to play the role of the heterosexual male. When in fact an orgasm was a purely physical reaction from stimulation, it didn't really matter whether that stimulation came from a man, a woman, a vibrator, or his own hands—it was all the same thing. It just so happened that only another man had the equipment to stimulate him anally, stroking his prostate in just the right way. Heck, if she could do it for him, that could be the end of his dalliances with Evan, or any of the others, for that matter. But the simple truth was that she couldn't.

"I'm outta here." She pushed past him into the bedroom, headed to the closet to retrieve her luggage.

"You can't just walk out," he insisted. He followed her into the bedroom.

"You can't tell me what I can or can't do."

"I can when you're carrying my child." Having played his trump card, he folded his arms across his chest.

She spun around to confront him. "Who said it was your child?" she asked.

He looked momentarily confused. "You did."

"No. I said that *I* was having a child. And *you* automatically assumed it meant you were too." She hadn't planned to be so blunt in addressing the issue of her child's paternity, but her anger and his arrogance drove the words right out of her mouth.

He looked stunned, as though the notion that her child could be anyone's but his had never even crossed his mind. That was when she realized that even though he and Evan were lovers, her and Evan's affair had remained a big secret between them. So Evan had fucked Brent in more ways than one.

"What are you saying?"

"It's simple, really. You could be the father just as easily as you could not be."

She gave him a nonchalant look that ripped his heart right out of his chest. Even though he'd been cheating on her, it was different to him; it was with a man who gave him something that she couldn't. What could another man possibly give her that he wasn't able to?

"You slut" escaped his mouth.

"Faggot," she spit back. Again she regretted what she said. It was such a nasty word, leaving a foul taste in her mouth that wasn't easily rinsed away. But "slut" wasn't such a high compliment either.

Brent closed his eyes to absorb the insult in private. Her pregnancy had seemed like such a blessing to him. Or better put, the prospect of becoming a father had really been the great blessing. For him it erased any question in other people's minds about whether he was gay, validating his manhood to his mother, his colleagues, and everyone else. And now Joie was yanking that cushy rug straight out from under him, leaving him sprawled awkwardly on the floor for all to see. How would he explain to his mother that not only wasn't he getting married now, but that the baby Joie carried might not even be his? He could only hope that Joie hadn't told the world that he was a closeted homosexual to boot. He realized that was the conclusion that she and everyone else would come to. Those thoughts added fuel to his anger. "Get out!"

"Gladly," she replied, as she began pulling clothes from the closet.

He turned to leave the room a broken man, but stopped when the next obvious question occurred to him. "So who's behind door number two?"

"Excuse me?"

"Who else were you fucking, Joie?"

"The same person you were," she said, and resumed packing.

34

COUCH CONFESSIONS

Everything Joie brought from her and Brent's apartment was stored neatly in Brooke's hall closet and part of the one in her bedroom. Joie wondered how neatly things would work out for Brent, Evan, and herself once the baby was born and the true paternity was determined. Whether Joie wanted to or not, for her daughter's sake she'd have to deal with her baby's father, one way or another.

Today Brooke faced her own heavy issues, beginning with whether to try getting information from her patient that might help Taylor in time for his eleven-o'clock hearing, not to mention starting the process of transferring her to another therapist.

To make matters worse, Taylor still hadn't returned her phone calls. She couldn't help but feel she'd let him down at a time when he needed her most. But what about her needs? And her patients'? It was times like this that she wished she still had her own therapist.

She dressed and headed to the office, unsure what she would do once she got there. When she walked in, André gave her a puzzled look and asked, "What exactly happened here the other day?" He'd seen Taylor go in and not come out before Kate Mathews did. He couldn't imagine what connection Taylor could possibly have with the patient, or why Brooke would have allowed him to stay.

"That explanation would take more time than I have right now. My first appointment—which, by the way, is with Kiernan—I mean Kate—is due in a few minutes." For professional reasons she did owe him an explanation, which she planned to give him. Just not right now. She felt like a one-armed juggler managing her own problems, and Joie's, Taylor's, and Kiernan's, not to mention those of her other patients.

"I'll buzz you as soon as she arrives."

Brooke sat behind her desk and took in the plaques and diplomas that lined her office wall. She questioned whether a personal relationship was ever worth risking all that they signified. Before an answer revealed itself, André was on the intercom announcing Kiernan's arrival.

"Send her in," Brooke said as she stood to welcome Taylor's wife.

Kiernan looked like she'd seen much better days too. Her hair was disheveled, and she looked as though she hadn't slept in days. "How are you?" Brooke asked. She was alarmed by her patient's appearance.

"I've been better," Kiernan quietly replied. She seemed to be on the verge of tears, but even so, there was a calmness about her that Brooke hadn't seen before.

They both took their seats, Kiernan on the couch and Brooke on her chair opposite it. "What happened?"

"It's over." Kiernan's voice quavered in her effort to hold on to her emotions.

"What's over?"

"Everything," she said, burying her head in her hands. "I have no husband, no money, and now no reputation. I'm all finished. I have nothing." Since her cat fight with Eva, it had been put out all over town that she'd cursed the socialite out like a common street whore and was desperate for clients because her husband, who was under suspicion for money laundering, had left her. The woman must have gotten on the radio and broadcast the news on the airways, because in no time Kiernan had gotten more than a dozen calls from nosy biddies up and down Manhattan trying to get extra details about her demise to add to the growing scandal. And her dear friend Pia hadn't returned any of her calls.

"It's not true that you don't have anything," Brooke said.

Kiernan lifted her head solemnly. "What do I have?" she implored. Tears streamed down her face. "I don't have the file or the contract, all thanks to my husband."

"Do you really think your current situation is his fault?"

Kiernan wiped tears away with the back of her hand, though she wouldn't answer the question.

Brooke stood up, headed to her desk drawer, and pulled out a handheld mirror. "Kate, look in this mirror and tell me whose actions are really the cause of the situation you are in right now."

At first Kiernan wouldn't even take the mirror, but Brooke kept it in her outstretched hand. "Take it," she insisted.

As tears poured, Kiernan really looked at her image without the benefits of makeup or wardrobe, and saw herself clearly for the first time in many years.

"Who is *really* responsible for your life today? Not when you were a child, but today, as a woman?"

"I am," she said in a barely audible voice. Again she cried for the little girl who'd been so abused, for the young woman who'd run away from everything—including herself—and for the grown woman who was now faced with the daunting prospect of putting all of those shattered pieces back together. But she also felt something different, something she'd never experienced fully before. For the first time, as miserable as she was, Kiernan felt free. Free from the shackles of her own web of lies and ghosts from the past.

When she'd calmed down, Brooke said, "You will be okay, but you have to start by being honest with yourself, *and* with other people. Now we've spent enough time in the past. Let's talk about your future."

Kiernan slowly nodded her head. "You know, I've been thinking about leaving town," she suddenly announced.

"Where would you go?"

"I've got some relatives in Atlanta who'll let me stay with them until I get back on my feet." She'd even thought of talking Thelma into coming with her to make a clean start. Now that she saw her life more clearly, she felt bad about how things were between them, and even worse for leaving her sister behind to be the next victim of their father's abuse and their mother's neglect. Maybe they would both be stronger today had they stayed together all those years ago, and as the older sister, Kiernan thought, that responsibility had been hers.

"That sounds like a good plan," Brooke said, nodding her head approvingly. It was best for Kiernan to start fresh somewhere else, rather than trying to climb out of depression carrying baggage from her past in New York. Brooke didn't think she was strong enough to handle it and heal herself at the same time.

The plan was a good one for Brooke too. Now she didn't have to worry about canceling Kiernan as one of her patients. She'd fretted for two days over what explanation she could possibly give that wouldn't be a lie or a true confession. The other dilemma was how to go on dating Taylor—that was if he even wanted to—without eventually being seen around town by Kiernan. Though over eight million people lived on the island of Manhattan, Brooke had learned that socially it was a *very* small town.

Kiernan had solved both of those problems for her and taken a dramatic turn in her treatment at the same time. With her current patient's problems solved for the time being, maybe Brooke should tackle another set: Taylor's. Since Kiernan was so open and forthcoming, maybe she would also be open to discussing Taylor's boss and the missing file. . . .

35
THE TROPHY CASE

It was Friday morning, and though Taylor looked cool as an ice cube in his dark blue pin-striped suit, pale blue shirt, and thickly knotted burgundy tie, he was a bundle of tangled nerves while he waited for Paul in his office. The lawyer had instructed Taylor to continue coming to work each day, since failing to do so might imply he had something to hide.

The two men were due in the FBI's New York field office at eleven o'clock sharp. Taylor just prayed he'd somehow walk out of there without an indictment. Though it wouldn't be the same as a conviction, it would certainly be the beginning of an expensive and exhausting nightmare from which it would be difficult to ever recover completely. He'd always be the black Wall Street financier who was indicted for money laundering, as well as aiding arms trafficking. If only he could have found the file, then he'd be able to put the brakes on this runaway freight train, but without it the locomotive was building up steam as it barreled down the tracks.

Unable to sleep the night before, he'd tossed and turned until finally giving up minutes before the alarm went off. He'd gone over every likely place in the apartment the file could have been, mentally and physically retracing his steps after arriving from

London, trying his best to remember where he'd placed it. But that day was mostly a fast-moving blur that he couldn't bring into sharp enough focus. He remembered being excited to have gotten the Beacon Hill deal closed in record time—of course, now he knew why—then the nasty fight with Kiernan in the bedroom. After that he remembered wanting desperately to get out of the apartment as quickly as possible.

Again he wondered if Kiernan had beaten him to it and already given it to Eduard, but somehow he doubted that. Knowing her, if she'd already bartered it away he'd have seen parts of her victory dance for having outmaneuvered him. As manipulative and deceitful as she was, he still couldn't help feeling sorry for her, especially after he found her hidden stash of drugs.

The other reason he doubted that she'd found it was because so far Eduard had failed to show his face in the office. The company line was that the crafty old man was sailing the Mediterranean, but Taylor highly suspected that he was simply lying low to see how things shook out with the feds before showing his face. Of course, his expensive lawyer had served as his perfunctory mouthpiece, and issued a statement about his "shock and dismay at Mr. Hudson's alleged involvement in such an unscrupulous incident," saying that "the firm was not in any way associated—except through Mr. Hudson—with the criminals involved." And, of course, those criminals had all slipped out of England and disappeared into the wind, leaving Taylor the Lone Ranger without a cavalry: a solo target.

His private line rang and he picked it up himself. "Taylor here."

"How are we doing, buddy?" It was Max.

"I've been better, but I have to also remember that things can always get worse, so call me this afternoon to see how much." He looked out the window of his office; rain was coming down in buckets. It was a dreadful gray day, befitting his mood. He felt like a death row inmate on the morning of his scheduled execution.

"Don't think like that. Have some faith. You know Paul is the best."

"Unless he's also a magician, my faith is waning like a budget surplus. Not finding that file is a major blow. My only defense is that my boss told me to do it, and I have nothing to back it up." Just talking about it was giving him a pounding headache. He rubbed his temples, fearing that that too would only get worse.

"Hang in there, man."

"I'll call you later."

When Taylor hung up the phone, his other line rang almost immediately. This time it was Janice informing him that Paul had arrived.

After she ushered him in, the lawyer walked over and shook Taylor's hand. "Are you ready?"

"About as ready as I'll ever be."

"Well, let's do it."

Taylor grabbed his trench coat and headed toward the door as if he were being led to a public execution. As they rode the elevator down, Taylor asked, "So what are my chances?"

Paul took a deep breath. "It's going to be tough. The assistant director for the New York field office is very ambitious. In fact, he's shooting for a top spot, and unfortunately your scalp would be a great trophy for his case. You know, tough on terrorism and Wall Street white-collar crime at the same time. Two birds for the price of one stone."

"I thought you were supposed to make me feel better." Taylor had never felt worse in his life.

"I told you last week that I'll always level with you."

Taylor only groaned. On top of everything else, now he found out that he had an FBI federal director gunning for his head, to stuff and hang like a prize catch. He'd never felt more alone in the world.

But when the door opened on the street level, there was a familiar face waiting on the elevator to take it back up. LaTeesha was soaked from the rain, and out of breath.

"LaTeesha?"

Her eyes lit up when she saw him. "I'm so glad I caught you." She could barely get the words out, as she tried to catch her breath at the same time.

"What are you doing here?" Taylor asked, puzzled.

"I'm just glad I got here in time," she said, still breathing hard. "I found this in some boxes this morning." She pulled a familiar file out of her bag and proudly handed it over to him.

Early that morning a clash of thunder had awakened her. Unable to get back to sleep she'd lain in bed thinking about everything and nothing when a thought struck her like a bolt of lightning. She remembered hearing Taylor and Max talk in grave tones on the morning they bailed her out of jail about Kiernan not letting Taylor in the apartment to find the Beacon Hill file and about an important meeting Friday at eleven o'clock. Not until that second did she recall carrying a bunch of files to the apartment building's storage room the day Kiernan had asked her to straighten up the office. She wasn't sure that his would be there, but felt she had to find out, so she had jumped straight up out of bed, dressed in a flash, and headed into the city. Fortunately Frank allowed her into the storage room, thinking she still worked for Kiernan. An hour later she hit pay dirt and ran out of the building, headed to the address printed on the business card Taylor had given her after getting her out of jail.

He stared at the folder in disbelief. Gratitude consumed him; he could barely believe that he was finally holding the elusive file. Finding it was like locating the Holy Grail.

Still excited and breathless from the rush, LaTeesha barely slowed down to tell her story. "I suddenly remembered that I'd boxed up some stuff that was in your old office after we moved. I took a bunch of it down to the building's storage room. I'd totally forgotten until this morning," she said apologetically. "But as soon as I remembered I ran over to see, and fortunately Frank let me in."

He grabbed her in a big bear hug and swung her around. "I

can never thank you enough." He couldn't believe it; he'd given up any hope of a last-minute reprieve.

After he and LaTeesha settled down, he opened the file and, with Paul looking over his shoulder, scanned the documents. They both realized immediately that everything would be okay. A profound relief swept over Taylor, washing away the immense fear that had consumed him.

When the three of them headed out of the building, dashing through the rain toward Taylor's car, they all stopped when they heard someone call out. "Taylor!" It was Brooke.

"I—" she started to say.

Taylor put his finger to her lips. "You don't have to say anything." He raised the file to show her. "I have all that I need right here, thanks to LaTeesha." He gestured over to the blushing girl. She'd never been the subject of so much positive attention before in her life. She was just happy that she was able to pay Taylor back for bailing her out of jail. She'd called him that day out of desperation. Besides Kiernan, he was the only other person she knew who might have the money to do it. Fortunately she had remembered the name of his company from the letterhead that she'd seen when clearing his office.

Brooke closed her eyes and smiled in relief.

"Ahem." Paul cleared his throat to get Taylor's attention. "I think we'd better get going. We have an investigation to stop."

"I wouldn't want to keep them waiting," Taylor said, helping LaTeesha into the car.

Brooke touched his arm to get his attention. "So you don't hate me?"

He looked at her as though she'd spoken another language. "Hate you? Why would I hate you?"

"For not getting the information from Kiernan."

"Brooke, I love you," he said, looking her in the eyes to make sure she heard his words clearly. "I would never ask you to do anything that would hurt you or your career."

"But you didn't call me back."

"I know. The reason I didn't was so you wouldn't feel pressured or guilted into doing something you'd later regret. I thought the best way I could help you was to stay away until I got past today."

She couldn't believe his selflessness. At a time when he would have been forgiven for thinking only of himself, he'd put his own troubles aside and thought of her instead. "I love you too," she said. They held each other on the sidewalk, both thankful for so many things as they stood together in the cold, pelting rain.

Suddenly she knew the answer to the question that Joie had asked her: What is love? She decided it was the ultimate desire to sacrifice for the good of another.

"Come on," he said. "Let's go get 'em." He helped Brooke into the car and they all headed to the Federal Building.

Two hours later they walked out of the hearing with Taylor a vindicated man. As if on cue the rain had moved on, replaced by a bright, sunny sky. It was true, Brooke thought; you really did have to go through the rain in order to enjoy the sunshine, and they'd definitely been through, and weathered, the storm.

EPILOGUE

"These are too adorable!" Joie squealed as she dangled a pair of lacy pink baby shoes with aqua silk ribbons. By now her stomach was so big she could barely fit through the aisles of miniature clothing in the baby department upstairs at Barneys.

"Check this out. It's the matching jumper—and oh, the hat! She's gotta have the hat," Brooke insisted. Thankfully, the doctor had confirmed Joie's suspicions: She was having a baby girl.

"Who knew shopping for infant clothes could be so much fun?" Joie said, fingering the delicate stitching. She was glowing with happiness and anticipation. She'd bought a town house in Hoboken and was having a great time getting it ready for Olivia's arrival. She'd also come to terms with Brent. Though they were strictly platonic friends, he insisted on being there for her, whether Olivia was his child or not; in fact, he was her Lamaze coach. The more she saw of him as a friend, the more convinced she was that he would make a fabulous father—regardless of his sexual orientation. She just hoped that the blood tests agreed. As far as Evan was concerned, he had disappeared from both their lives like mist at daybreak.

"I never thought I'd see the day when Joie Blanchard walked out of Barneys with a slew of shopping bags, and nothing for herself. Not even one pair of shoes," Brooke joked as they headed up Madison Avenue carrying armloads of bags.

"Girl, my feet are so swollen, I don't know if they'll ever see the inside of a stiletto again, and you know what? I don't even care."

Kiernan reached over and put the back of her hand to Joie's forehead as if checking for fever. They both laughed.

"I know. The next thing you know, I'll be taking group Pilates classes and speaking in strings of indecipherable nonwords."

Brooke shook her head. "It's only a matter of time." Though she had seen her share of people change right before her eyes, Joie's metamorphosis had to be the most radical and complete she'd ever seen. She had transformed from an independent, career-focused, me-oriented person to a warm, caring mother-to-be. Wonders never ceased.

"Speaking of time, I'm starving, and you know I get evil when I don't eat. I am eating for two, you know."

"Why don't we have dinner at Il Cantinori?"

"That sounds good to me. I could really go for some of their calf's liver."

Brooke frowned at the thought. "I'll call and get us a reservation."

"Maybe Taylor would want to join us," Joie suggested. She really liked him, and thought he and Brooke were the best couple ever.

"Great idea." She dialed his office. "Hi, LaTeesha, it's Brooke. Is Taylor available?"

"I'll put you right through." Taylor had left Mayer, Jones, and Wentworth and started his own investment firm. His first executive decision was to hire LaTeesha. Even better than that, Max had the drug charges against her dropped, as well as having the shoplifting sentence overturned, since there was no proof she'd taken anything to begin with. Not only was her record completely expunged, but she was also taking night classes toward a college degree. Though Kiernan had her issues—as did everyone—

LaTeesha was thankful to her for introducing her to a whole different world.

"Hey, baby, what's up?" Taylor said when he came on the line.

"Joie and I are headed over to Il Cantinori for dinner. You wanna join us?"

"Sure, but I was meeting Max for a drink after work. Mind if he comes along?"

Brooke looked over at Joie. "Sure," she said. Joie needed to meet a nice guy, and aside from Taylor, Max was the nicest one she had ever met. He was a loyal friend to Taylor and had all but taken LaTeesha under his wing. Though he still harbored a dislike for Kiernan, he'd followed Taylor's wishes and given her a very generous divorce settlement, enough for her to open and establish an interior design company in Atlanta. By all accounts, she and Thelma were both doing well.

When Brooke hung up the phone she turned to Joie. "Max is joining us too," she said.

"Max?"

"Yeah. You know, he's a really nice guy."

"Brooke, in case you haven't noticed, I'm over eight months pregnant. Not exactly dating material."

"Who said anything about dating? Just get to know him, that's all."

Joie dropped her packages in the middle of Madison Avenue and held her stomach as she laughed out loud.

Brooke dropped hers too and stared at Joie, wondering if hysteria was a precursor to labor. Maybe she should call Brent. "What's wrong?"

"Nothing," she said, catching her breath. "It's just that I know things have really changed when *you* are encouraging *me* to get to know a guy."

"Yeah, I guess they have."

They picked up their bags and continued up Madison Avenue side by side.

ABOUT THE AUTHOR

Tracie Howard is the former director of sales for American Express. A graduate of Georgia State University with a degree in marketing, she also worked for the Atlanta Committee for the Olympic Games, Xerox Corporation, and Johnson & Johnson, and was the lifestyle correspondent for *Savoy* magazine. Visit her Web site at www.traciehoward.com.

Tracie Howard

NEVER KISS
AND TELL

A CONVERSATION WITH TRACIE HOWARD

Q. You tend to write a lot about upscale, glitzy, glamorous African-Americans. Is this to make a social statement?

A. Though my work is written foremost to entertain, I have always been excited about the ability to portray an under-represented segment of African-American life, one different from the hip-hop/rap, ghetto-fabulous, or drug-dealing lifestyle that permeates the mainstream media in America. If you didn't know any better (and those living in the Midwest or London might not), you'd think we all wore baggy pants and belly rings, and this is so untrue. There are African-Americans who are sophisticated, smart, and doing quite well. Does this represent all of us? No, but neither do the negative images that consume media in all forms, from publishing to film and TV. I want our kids and the world to see—and read about—affluence in our community, so that it doesn't continue to feel foreign.

Q. Do you think that by doing so you may encourage African-American youths to worship "things" as opposed to achievement?

A. I think it's crucial that our youth look beyond the glitz and bling-bling and realize that while those things may be attractive—and that's a matter of personal opinion—it's sexier *and* more attractive to have your act together, which is why I create characters who are accomplished in diverse fields. They have worked hard to become successful and achieve the financial ability to afford the things they have. Imagine Saxton in *Why Sleeping Dogs Lie*, who, through scholarship and academic achievement, earned his degrees and ultimately his success, after starting out in a poor family in North Carolina; or Dakota, in *Revenge Is Best Served Cold*, who toiled every day on Wall Street to get to where she did; or Mallory (*WSDL*), who is a writer; or Joie, a photographer, and Brooke, a psychotherapist, in this novel. The point is to show successful African-Americans who didn't get their Benzes because of athletic prowess with a ball, or because of musical ability. I want our kids to move beyond those ingrained preconceptions about our physical and mental ability and to conquer other fields as well.

Q. What are the biggest differences between writing with a coauthor and as a solo author?

A. There are definite advantages to both. For example, the best thing about writing with a coauthor is the brainstorming process. If you have good creative energy with your partner, it can result in a situation in which the sum is greater than the parts. On the other hand, one of the greatest things about writing solo is the ability to have a very pure representation of your ideas and vision—collaboration, by definition, results in a series of compromises.

Q. How does real life play a part in your characters or story?

A. It has been proven again and again that life is indeed stranger than fiction! Add to that the fact that I live in one of the most colorful metropolitan areas in the world—New York City—so life becomes great fodder for fiction, but usually only provides the kernel for ideas or characters. The planting, watering, weeding, and feeding is always the result of a fertile imagination.

Q. *How do you categorize* Never Kiss and Tell?

A. *Never Kiss and Tell* is a steamy story that explores the depths to which we are willing to go for the sake of love. It's the ultimate look at compromising positions, questioning that delicate balance between social ethics and personal desires. The characters are very real in the sense that they are like all of us: explicably flawed and in an unconscious search for that which makes us whole—though the answers are often not at all what we consciously seek.

Q. *What made you decide to write in the Chick Lit genre?*

A. My first novel, *Revenge Is Best Served Cold*, was written *before* there was the trend called Chick Lit, so in a sense Danita Carter and I are pioneers of this genre, particularly in the realm of African-American literature. I write this type of book for two reasons. First, it's the life that I know and live in New York, and second (and more important), I believe it's important that African-Americans are shown in mainstream situations, as lawyers, executives, movers in finance, and key players *off* the basketball court and the stage. We come in diverse forms, but too often are only depicted in and of the ghetto. Writing is my contribution to changing these perceptions that are offered to the rest of the world. I just sold a film option for *Why Sleeping Dogs Lie* and it pleases me to offer an alternative film image from those shown in the film *Soul Plane* and others of that genre.

Q. How have readers responded to your work?

A. It has been very interesting. Most readers love my work and are thrilled to read about upscale African-Americans, but there is a small contingent of readers who seem to resent the affluence that's described as a part of this lifestyle. Perhaps they don't believe it's "keepin' it real," not realizing that what's "real" for one person isn't to another. Sometimes I believe that we'd rather buy in to and perpetuate the stereotypes than embrace diversity.

QUESTIONS FOR DISCUSSION

1. Should Brooke have continued seeing Kiernan at all after learning that she was Taylor's wife?

2. Do you think that Brooke would have betrayed her client to save her lover? Is it ever okay for a professional to exploit client-patient confidentiality? What if it's for the broader good of humanity?

3. Was Joie's sexual behavior reprehensible? Though she hadn't made a commitment to Brent, did she still owe him fidelity? Is it ever okay for a woman to have the kind of sexual freedom that Joie experienced?

4. Do you feel that Joie got what she deserved when Brent and Evan ultimately betrayed her? Was their betrayal more or less hurtful because of her behavior?

5. Why is it more acceptable for men to be promiscuous than women? Is that right?